ALSO BY NIGEL BARLEY

monso

SNOW OVER SURABAYA

Nigel Barley was born south of London in 1947. After taking a
d   e in modern languages at Cambridge, he gained a doctorate
i   thropology at Oxford. Barley originally trained as an
    opologist and worked in West Africa, spending time with
    owayo people of North Cameroon. He survived to move to
    hnography Department of the British Museum and it was
    connection that he first travelled to Southeast Asia. After
    s into Thailand, Malaysia, Singapore, Japan and Burma,
    y settled on Indonesia as his principal research interest and
    worked on both the history and contemporary culture of
    rea.

    fter escaping from the museum, he is now a writer and
    dcaster and divides his time between London and Indonesia.

SNOW OVER SURABAYA

NIGEL BARLEY

monsoon

monsoonbooks

First published in 2017
by Monsoon Books Ltd
www.monsoonbooks.co.uk

No.1 Duke of Windsor Suite, Burrough Court,
Burrough on the Hill, Leicestershire LE14 2QS, UK

First edition.

ISBN (paperback): 978-1-912049-00-4
ISBN (ebook): 978-1-912049-01-1

Cover design by CoverKitchen.

A Cataloguing-in-Publication data record is available from the British
Library.

Printed in Great Britain by Clays Ltd, St Ives plc
20 19 18 17   1 2 3 4 5

Kepada Malcolm McLeod, teman yang setia.

Introduction

Although it deals with real events, this is largely a work of fantasy but provoked by another work of fantasy that it may well bring closer to the truth. All one can be really sure of – we have the pieces of paper – is that a girl to be named Muriel Stuart Walker was born in Glasgow in the year 1898, where she first embarked on that circuitous perambulation that we term a life. The nature of that life is subject to conflicting accounts, deliberate manipulations, forgettings, subjectivities and the myriad uncertainties that post-modernists and theoretical historians wallow in so luxuriously. Muriel would grow up to be a deliberate chamaeleon, wandering from continent to continent – Europe, America, Asia – frequently changing name, profession, identity, in short completely reinventing herself in various tongues and accents so that it is legitimate to wonder whether, at the end, anything at all remained of the larrikin original. In the course of it she moved, most improbably, from being a Scottish schoolgirl to a heroine of the Indonesian Revolution and took the name K'tut Tantri.

Many of her romantic tales are obvious inventions, the work of a proxy Baroness Munchhausen, yet some have a ring of truth about them and are firmly rooted in reality. She gathered her biographical tales all together in a book published as *Revolt in Paradise* published in 1960 both as an account of her past within the Indonesian Revolution after WWII and a blueprint for what she wanted to become, since there can be no doubt that – like all good fantasists – she came to believe many of her own fabulations.

Needless to say, she has been 'rediscovered' several times by the West, by the East, by the sceptical and by the credulous. Special thanks are due to Tim Hannigan whose original suggestion this book was and, more generally, it is truly a child of *Biku*, that unique Balinese mixture of tearoom, restaurant and literary salon, presided over by the inimitable Jero Asri Kerthyasa.

We are also fortunate to have another excellent work about Muriel Walker, Timothy Lindsey's *The Romance of K'tut Tantri and Indonesia* (1997) where her imaginings and psyche are forensically dissected and held up to the light. As Lindsey points out, the reason for the neglect of K'tut Tantri's rôle in Indonesia's independence struggle lies not so much in the relation between her story and truth as in the manner of its telling – falling between the genres of war story, biography, romance and travel book. As his title indicates, it is perhaps closest to what was once termed 'romance' (less politely 'shopgirl fiction' or more modernly 'chicklit') and he argues that the whole purpose of her life was to construct, defend and live that romance.

A further work sheds light on Muriel's later life and character, when she had decided to give her story to the world both as a book and a film script: Michael Campbell's, *The Princess In England* (1964), based on his experience of the difficulties of working with her as a (soon to be betrayed and discarded) ghostwriter.

But frankly, K'tut Tantri's fantasies are not very good fantasies, being limited by the conventions of the oversyrupy romance genre as it developed after WWII. At times she reads like a Barbara Cartland impersonator to whose bizarre and stilted sense of sexual propriety she is eager to conform and in her prose, as in her visual art, she is chocolate-boxy even in an imagination that is firmly rooted in conventional, Western notions of the Orient as an exotic paradise. The result is an account of stirring times that impoverishes rather than enriches them. Previous discussions of K'tut Tantri have sought to free her from her fantasies. This book is an attempt rather to free the fantasies from the limitations of the chocolate box – a sort of 'K'tut unchained'.

For those who know little of the postwar events that led to the birth of a free Indonesia, almost nothing here is pure invention though links have been deliberately made and liberties taken that historians would consider outrageous. The Hollywood film of her life that Muriel dreamed of making never quite happened. She insisted that it should feature neither sex nor smoking and – at that time – a film without smoking was unthinkable.

Chapter One

'Muriel Walker, come and get yer piece ye wee bastard!' The voice of love. In Glaswegian. The voice of my mother, Ma, calling from an upstairs window, echoing around the close, summoning me to what I have now learned to call 'lunch'. And, for those who do not know, a 'piece' is more technically a 'jeely piece', a doorstep-thick slice of bread, smeared with butter or margarine and then spread dripping with tinned jam. It is the original and authentic fast food of the Glasgow poor, the preferred dessert course, the explanation for their rotted teeth and one of the ancient wisdoms of my people. Except, of course, they are *not* my people. Everything denies it, even Ma's use of that word 'bastard'.

It is 1910 and my eleven-year-old allegedly 'female' brain already feels alienation and revulsion from the surrounding grey depression of a Glasgow tenement with its weed-sprouting, flagged yard and leaky, brick privy. My flaming red hair, so different from my mother's mousy mop, cries out a secret ancestry, as do the almond eyes that earn me the nickname of 'Chinky' at school and the short stature that stands in contrast to the lankiness of all my so-called kin – to say nothing of their ghastly taste in soft furnishings. To anticipate the song, I am a lonely, little petunia in an onion patch.

On a scholarship to the local girls' grammar school my English is being starched, pleated and pressed, while I am acquiring the practical skills that will help me to survive in the modern world – such as being able to talk to the Ancient Romans and calculate the volume of a pyramid – but the Bible is already being drummed into my pliant mind by the busy agents of the Wee Free Kirk, greedy for my soul, and it has absorbed the tale of Moses in the bulrushes as my own secret biography – only reversed. I am an exotic princess found by slaves, stripped of my birthright, and raised to hardship and poverty and mean thoughts. In the pocket atlas of Great Britain that forms the rest of our library up on the third floor, the object of constant, dreamy study, I am drawn to islands, islands off islands, islands in the middle of lakes in islands off islands. The Isle of Man is my first discovery, a distant foreign land, a fortress surrounded by sea, home of Vikings and elfin seers and monstrous creatures with three legs but no bodies – as far as my baby brain can reach. As an only child, I live in my own imagination. And from the top floor I imagine I can almost see it through winter mists. It is the first of many candidates to be considered my real home in a search that will consume my life.

'For the last time of telling, come and get yer piece, or yer da will give ye a belt!'

Concern for well-being is equated with the threat of physical violence, just part of the crazy logic that governs the link of parents to children. The single privy that is shared by all the families – what I would now term a 'non-suite bathroom' – echoes to the sound of gasps and groans, the simultaneous, tearing evacuation of gas from both ends, to be followed by the ripping of newspaper and the Christmassy jangle of the cistern chain like a dog rising reluctantly to its feet. I get myself up off the sandstone step, its dished centre the perfect shape to cup young buttocks – product not so much of feet as of a thousand sharpenings of Sunday carving knives – and go in the back door and back to the prison of my 'family' home. I steel myself against the grinding sense of them watching me and intuitively know it is essential I do not betray my secret knowledge of who I really am – especially to the man there in the privy who calls himself my 'da' and whose boots I can hear clattering on the stairs behind me and cutting off all retreat.

Mr. Walker is a boilermaker in the shipyards – a dangerous and demanding occupation that is often solitary and leaves him ingrown and moody and turns his hands into shaking, scarred crab's pincers incapable of gentle touch. It is a Saturday so there is no sit-down midday meal or mother's godfearing – they are for tomorrow – but later he will be off to football and rambling trade union talk in the pub afterwards. Mr. Walker is strong on the union. It's workers this and workers that and behind it all the evil conspiracy of the English employers who are somehow the same thing as the Jews of his rarer but longer anti-Semitic rants. He is not a very warm father to me – though perhaps that has something to do with the fact that I call him very determinedly 'Mr. Walker' to his face. Perhaps I am being unfair to him. After trying all methods known to civilised man to bring a child to gentle reason and light – shaking, smacks, punches, strappings, starvation, doses of castor oil, half-drownings, incarceration in a light and airless coalhole that swarms with cockroaches – he has given up and contemplates with blank resignation the presence of this exotic cuckoo in his nest.

* * *

1915 brought us the continuing distraction of the First World War that few in Glasgow felt to concern them. It was an English war that was of interest only to the employers and their men with the soft hands in Edinburgh and the buzz of propaganda blurred into the background of fuzzy, patriotic noise coming from the south that was a constant of empire and simply ignored. Far more important to us that year was the attempt by our landlords to hike the rents of the poor and evict vulnerable war widows whose noble sacrifice was being trumpeted elsewhere. Mary Barbour, the leader of the resulting rent strike, was a friend of my mother and helped her organise a general refusal to pay the increase demanded. All the women banded together to pay only the old rate. Attempted evictions followed but we all had a grand time pelting the sheriff's men with flour bombs and then posing as wee, starving bairns thrown out into the snow for the newspapermen, many of whom were elbow-patched sympathisers. There are few walls more formidable than a row of self-righteous Glasgow mothers with their arms folded, closing off the street. Hadrian could have saved himself a lot of trouble and expense. When the owners moved to the courts, only munitions workers that the government needed desperately to fill shells turned up to be jailed and I was proud to be one of the 10,000 that marched on the assizes and terrified the government into freezing rents by law. A great victory for the workers – except that the men were unsettled to see their women taking on the High Hiedyins, the big cheeses, and beating them – which they never had. A rash of itchy strikes broke out all over Scotland.

But it was not so much raw, socialist zeal as the attractions of the tram itself that drove me to the strikebound shipyards on that balmy autumn evening when golden sunshine coaxed poignant beauty even from the skeletons of the derricks and the rags on the washing lines. Trams were still new enough to have a wonder of their own, the novelty of horseless carriagery, the modernist rumble and thunk of steel on bare steel. As a young woman in ungainful employment – I now worked in a city office with evening classes in the fiendish new technology of the typewriter – I was part of the modern age and acquired a new, more English, accent appropriate to my new position. For some education is heaven, for others hell. For me it was at that moment the only route of escape on offer.

But it was not the beauties of Nature that had charmed my girlish heart. It was the young conductor. I had seen him before on this run as he danced between the benches or twirled his hips up the spiral staircase. Our eyes had met over the dispensing of tickets and a whole encyclopaedia of forbidden knowledge had flashed between us in one bat of his long eyelashes and the almost accidental passage of silken heat from his hand into mine as he counted out change. He was simply the most beautiful thing I had ever seen. To look at him made me want to cry and Muriel Walker is not a girl much given to crying. Now, he came down the stairs in one glamorous slide, supporting his weight on the handrails, crutch thrust out, converting an act of labour into how I imagine a ballet to be and stood in the stairwell with his eyes boldly blazing into mine. And what eyes! Dark, smouldering, with a curious lilt to them like a grace note in a melody. I stared back entranced, breathing heavily as he shifted his moneybag deliberately from side to front and seemed to undergo a sudden, significant rise in the size of his takings.

The tram juddered round a corner with bacon-slicer noises of resistance between rail and wheel and there came the din of another kind of resistance screamed from a thousand angry mouths as the pickets – pinned between dockyard gates and a line of police – greeted our arrival as if we were a blockade-busting battleship and surged forward. A banner made from an old sheet on broom handles wavered towards us, Mr. Walker grim-faced beneath it like a coffin-bearer. 'Fair Wages for Free Men.' My conductor stood firm, a captain on the bridge of his orange ship in the full glamour of his uniform as the driver pushed on slowly through the tide of confused bodies, waving and shouting to clear the tracks. The police were bemused, unsure whether freedom of passage was one of the things they are supposed to be protecting here or whether this was simply a vehicle bringing reinforcements for the enemy. And then the matter was sharply resolved. With one leap, my conductor grabbed the door rail and swung outside with waving fist.

'Down with the Keystone Cops!'

With cheering laughter, the strikers rushed forward again, the whole thing now become carnival – knocking off helmets like coconuts at the fair – and a fat sergeant went down, notebook and truncheon trampled pitilessly underfoot. Others stumbled, tripped over the greasy tramlines. Law-enforcing backsides were roundly kicked with stout, steel-tipped dockyard boots. Placards and banners rained from above on the police like the eagles of Roman legions and suddenly I am there at the door too, body pressed hard against my hero, eyes shining, as the structures of capitalism tumble around us in the heady screech of police whistles.

Breaking glass, blood, broken heads, screaming and bellowing, a maelstrom of anger and despair, revenge and terror! There is a wonderful excitement and creativity in the smashing of things. Every shattered window draws a line through time. That night, we presented ourselves at home, myself and Mr. Walker, he clutching the trophy of a police helmet like a taken head – bound in unwilling comradeship, both stained with the blood of martyrs – and surrendered ourselves to dabbing rags dipped in disinfectant for our wounds. There was something horribly akin to paternal pride in his face. I shuddered as he said, 'She's a braw wee lass, mother. Ye should ha' seen the way she heaved a brick at yon black Maria.'

Except the blood all over me isn't just martyr blood. This

is the day of my fulfilment as a woman – behind a blackberry hedge that is heavy with the symbolism of late-ripened fruit in the midst of thorns and with the strident shout of battle in our ears. It comes through the good offices of a derailed and flyly unbuttoned employee of the Glasgow Tramway and Omnibus Company with beautiful, dark eyes.

* * *

Sin was to be found everywhere in Glasgow, almost without looking, and especially on a Sunday, for it had been drummed into me that there was nothing on earth more wicked than sinning on Sunday – a proposition I have spent my life disproving. It hung in the air and dripped down the walls like condensation on wash day. It was in the breath of the horses and the scent that ladies dabbed behind their ears. It was in the drinking in the pubs around Sauchiehall Street and the painted women of easy virtue who lurked there. Sometimes it was visible only to the godly for it festered in the churches of any denomination but your own and the damned, hell-bound devil-worshippers that frequented them and their smoking altars. For the very pure, it was even to be found in the swings in the parks that must be chained up on a Sunday to prevent the evil of children's laughter on the Lord's Day. It is the last of these that I am about – not swings but roundabout pleasure – in the comely form of Hamish Friend, 17-year-old incarnation of the sins of the flesh and the primal fall of Eve and part-time tram conductor. Ironically, it was the strictures of the godly that made all this possible. Ham knew how to tickle open the lock of a nearby sports pavilion secure in the knowledge that God would strike down anyone else using it on the Sabbath. So it was here amongst the decayed smell of sweaty armpits and unwashed feet that we made the beast with two backs on a splintery pine floor, with undarned socks abandoned in corners like forlorn hopes. This association of lust and male dirt, once established, is very convenient to a young girl in a world where women make love while men merely grab grubby sex. I chased away the thought that Ham might have been here before and done more than unlace and dubbin his football boots in all-male company.

Not being a visitor of the art galleries, I had never seen a completely naked, male body before. In those prudish days, many men had probably never seen one either and the finally revealed secret of what human beings really look like was astonishing to me. I explored and probed his body deliciously and shamelessly as he blushed coyly – the unexpected pubic hair, the outrageousness of the old man's scrotum between smooth, young thighs all challenged me like the three-legged monsters of the Isle of Man. I had missed out on a lot by avoiding art galleries and this was the moment when I decided to take up painting. I told him my true origins, that my father was a Manxman by birth, an African archaeologist, dead to a tropical fever – no – eaten by cannibals after the discovery of a lost city in the jungles of the Sahara. Most people found this astonishing. But there was more to Ham than met the eye. His skin had a beautiful olive softness unlike the uncooked pastry appearance of most Glaswegians. That on the shaft of his penis was definitely brown. Perhaps he is one of the 'Sons of Ham' that the Wee Free thunder against. My fair, dark Ham tells me a romantic story to explain it away in a voice with the soft accents of the far west, a voice that breathes of peat and malt whisky.

'Once upon a time there was a great laird in India. He ran the whole country for John Company. One day, the King of Bally, a beautiful island in the South Seas, sent him two fine boy slaves as a present. Their fathers were also great men of the country but the wicked King of Bally had killed them and taken their lands and now wanted to be rid of their sons by sending them far, far away. So they entered the service of the great laird of India and he, not knowing what else to do with them and being a godly man, had them sent to school there and baptised them Edmund Friend and Francis Mann to remind himself that – though once slaves – they were his friends and fellow men. And they lived in a great palace with fountains and peacocks and a harem of lovely ladies. But the laird's enemies were plotting against him at home and he was recalled to Scotland and the boys they came too as just part of his luggage, along with the silk umbrellas and the gold robes and the feathered hats. The peacocks came too but they lost their voices when they left India and became mute for the rest of their days. But the great laird died on the way home and so the lads were left to run wild in the family castle in the north of Scotland. There they learned Scots and hunted and fished and finally married local women – though these were far beneath them – and raised families of which I am the latest, fairest fruit. The two families have always kept in touch. My father was a Friend. My mother a Mann.'

The last line made me giggle, being so unlike my own life, but I found it hard to believe a word of all this. People make up such silly tales. A fairy story, then. But why tell the ugly truth when something else can be so much more lovely? I looked at him again. I would definitely take up painting.

* * *

1919 and the Great War is over. Too late for me. Poor Ham lies broken and buried somewhere in Northern France, conscripted on his eighteenth birthday as a fresh sacrifice to the profits of the international arms industry and dead on his third day at the front. It is a year before I know – the news broken casually by a fellow tram conductor as he reshuffles his ticket rack – with me screaming and wailing in the tram's rattling stairwell and comforted by patting women who have seen it all before as some perky, young telegraph boy skips whistling up to their door bearing news from the War Office of their father, brother, husband or son.

There were strikes everywhere, docks, railways, shipyards, a heaving underswell of turbulence and disaffection was passing through the nation as a swallowed goat passes down a snake, stretching the seams. The streets were dotted with broken windows. The Battle of George Square led Winston Churchill to order the army into the city and there were tanks and soldiers billeted in all the parks with Lewis guns mounted on street corners and nervous, wall-eyed Englishmen in khaki clutching them as though for comfort. Glaswegian troops were shipped south and safely out of the city. The High Hiedyins were terrified of a Bolshevik uprising like the one they were having in Russia, but this is still Britain and the sheriff's bumbling attempts to read the Riot Act are prevented by the simple expedient of Mr. Walker and other members of the Workers' Councils hitting him on the head with it and tearing it up. This is Mr. Walker's moment of glory but shortlived like himself, for, as the court officers turn, hitch up their robes and flee womanishly up the town hall steps, he clutches at his heart and goes down. An unsuccessful life crowned by a successful death. But then the last thing he sees is the words, 'unlawfully, riotously and tumultuously remain' blowing on a paper fragment of the Riot Act and plastered to his face by the wind, to be followed by a triumphant 'God Save the King'.

I will never know what led my mother, a most unadventurous

person, to up sticks at her time of life and move to America. Certainly, it could be nothing that I had said or done. America was very far from my dreams. Yet, there hung around us all, a sense of things coming to an inevitable end, something that was no more to be resisted and the passing of Mr. Walker seemed to draw a line under a whole section of her life. So there she sat after the extravagant trade union funeral with its clenched fist salutes, with all her worldly goods tied up in the curtains as though for a moonlight flit from a pressing landlord. Only when we were well down the road on the back of a fish truck – we were travelling in style, really poor people went by horse and cart – did I even discover that we were indeed leaving without bothering to pay the rent or the gas. Perhaps that was Ma's way of having the last word. It taught me the lesson that not everything in life has to be faced. It's not a form of weakness to simply walk away. It takes real moxie.

Chapter Two

Joseph Kennedy was a big beanpole of a man with one of those Boston Irish cabbage faces and finally starting to slap on some weight around the belly. He leaned back in his chair and drew fragrant breath through his cigar, said, 'Of all my female employees, Manxi, I guess you're about the only one I've never tried to screw.' He scratched his crotch thoughtfully as though I was ruining his collection. You had to admit that fancy education and Harvard fraternities had not quite rubbed off all of his rough corners. Joe was a serial fornicator who brought his business methods to his love life. I once heard him explaining to someone on the phone, 'Never settle for a workaday fuck before four in the afternoon. You might still get a better offer later before close of business and come up short before you can restore liquidity.' Rose, his poor wife dumped back in Boston, was about the only other woman in the States not to be on the receiving end of his attentions – but somehow maintained a mysterious state of constant pregnancy. Perhaps Joe could fornicate even over the phone.

I asked, 'Is that meant as a compliment or an insult, Joe?' I had asked Gloria Swanson the same question once when she had remarked that, in bed, Joe was a total animal.

He laughed and flicked ash, waggled his blazing red tip at me. 'Maybe a little of both, honey. After all, I like 'em dumb, scrawny and obliging.'

New York had been a terrible place, an ugly, cruel city – even worse than Glasgow since Ma was scared of the black men – never having seen one before – and no one could understand a word she said. I, of course, had long acclimatised to American and assumed its modalities just as I borrowed Auntie BBC's English back in Glasgow for office use. Joe sometimes joked that mine was an accent I had picked up from the silent screen. California was better – much better – though I thought at the start I was getting the fuzzy end of the lollipop again. I took an office job with a small motion pictures outfit, Film Booking Offices of America, a shoestring operation that churned out cheapie movies, mostly Westerns. The horses cost more than the actors who were just cheap camera fodder and often a little too quick on the draw with the office help. Then it seemed that FBO was going AOT and I had already started scanning the wanted ads. At the last minute, Joe turned up, bought out the operation, brought in his boys, refloated, refinanced, flipped some companies, did some shouting down the telephones, cut some deals and suddenly the money was pouring in. Joe's real business, of course, was knowing people. His father was in the saloons trade which exposed him to a wide range of contacts. The result was that Joe ended up married to the mayor's daughter while being well-connected with the absolute cream of organised crime – bootlegging across the Canadian border being his most profitable activity. At the same time, he had enough contacts in the trading rooms to be the first to get inside information or be able to fix the markets so that no investment ever turned bad for him. I suppose he should have set my socialist principles on edge but he was less a stodgy financier than an outlaw, bringing ever nearer Mr. Walker's inevitable destruction of late capitalism. I ran the local office and answered the telephone to Rose, always having a new story to hand to explain Joe's non-availability. Mostly, his non-availability was owing to his close-ups with Gloria Swanson. Gloria, at that time, was at the height of her fame but spreading her legs for a studio director was a good way for a girl to make sure she kept all her options open. She was spending $12,000 on a dress, $6,000 a year on perfume but the real extravagance must be the $10,000 a year she splashed out on knickers that she hardly ever had on. To be blunt, one way or another she was working her arse off so I invented a whole network of secret government projects to take Joe out of town to unknown, undisclosable locations – especially around five in the afternoon. You would often see Gloria's Lancia – upholstered in fabulous leopard skin – outside the same addresses. Joe called me his 'head scriptwriter'. That was all before they fell out, of course – him and Gloria – when she discovered she was the golden goose being systematically plucked as well as … I also wrote for the scandal rags under another name but I never blabbed on Joe, he had too many friends who could make you fall off the end of a pier.

'I've got a little job for you, Manxi. Right up your alley.' We were in his private office, sour LA sunshine leaking through the Venetian blinds and he had both feet up on the desk, clad in great Irish boots and the thick navvy's socks that made him feel secure. All Kennedy boys had flat feet and big noses to grab as much free earth and air as possible. He sipped coffee from an army mug and looked at me hard. I chugged illegal Scotch, poured from the office bottle, one part of my cultural heritage that I still embraced. Joe saw the Irish whiskey-swilling thing as a cliché and refused to go to hell on a cliché, so he seldom drank. Movies people! 'The key to making money in the movies business is to control both the film production and the movie theatres that show them. Then you can load the dice against the competition and crowd them out with your own cut-price films. There's a business I've had my eye on, Pantages Pictures, with a holding of 84 houses up and down the West coast and Canada – all making money. I've offered that little Greek shit Alex Pantages 8 million bucks and he's turned me down flat. I've cut off our films to him. Since we control talkie copyrights through RKO, we're squeezing his balls from all sides but still he won't budge. That's undemocratic, unAmerican. I reckon it's time for him to suffer a little misfortune with one of his dancers. It seems Alex is going to attack poor, innocent, little, Eunice Pringle – great little mover – in a broom cupboard at the theatre and make her do a jolly jig against the wall. Being, as she is, an untouched virgin from convent school this will lead her to run out into the street, screaming, blind with distress and her clothes all torn.' He chuckled. 'Reporters will happen to be there. The Hirst newspapers have been fixed to be sympathetic to our – poor Eunice's – cause but she'll need coaching so she can tell a good tale at the trial and give the journalists what they want. Pretty little twat she is, a brain she ain't. Do you reckon you could do that for me, head scriptwriter? Needless to say, I'll show myself very, very grateful.'

I meet 17-year-old Eunice in a hotel down on the Strip and explain to the management that we're rehearsing scenes from a movie – not exactly a lie. I'm a method perjurer. Eunice was a beauty all right with lots of thick, dark hair and lips like a boiled clam. We act out her violation, fix times, responses, escape routes, what drawers she was wearing, decide which questions she will answer in shocking detail, which she will demur at with maidenly modesty, when she will cry and at what signal she will finally break down and swoon, making sure she shows her legs. We rehearse her screams and pleadings and discuss the advisability of a failed suicide attempt before the hearing – finally deciding against it. On the whole it's hard work but a hoot. And then, when they put her on the stand, beautifully prepared, and ask her to tell, in her own words, what happened, she just says, 'Aw gee, he schtupped me but good, honey, with this fat Greek schlong.'

Never mind. The judge clearly thought she was too dumb to lie. After his first conviction, Partages is ruined and has to sell up to RKO for a knock-down $3.5 million. Sure he gets off on a retrial having learned his lesson and hired a lawyer who can read and write. Needless to say, I'm not the one who gets the missing $5 million but then neither is dear Eunice.

* * *

Mine was what you might term a 'marriage of inconvenience'. I had suffered a mismarriage. Karl Pearson was not the world's greatest catch – tall, skinny, the trout-like suspicion of a wall-eye – but Ma liked him, which got her off my back. He lived in the same building and Ma dragged him home one day with a leg of lamb and the rest of the shopping but more like a cat would a rat and dumped him on the doormat. Sure, he was irritating but it was not all bad – like all men who work with wood, he was good with his hands. He also had a cute smile and an American passport and I had a use for the latter. Karl made a nice, steady living refinishing old furniture that he sold around the new developments shooting up all over LA. I am not a beautiful woman but I know how to be exotic and exotic gets men every time. I cooked him a few traditional Manx dishes as learned from my Viking forefathers and he was hooked like a Manx herring so that, in a few short months, I had him wed, pussy-whipped and sleeping in separate beds with the wedding photos safely stowed on the secondhand piano. Let him find relief in French-polishing his big chests and rubbing up his tallboys. A husband who smelled of fish glue and sawdust was not what I was used to in the movie business.

Karl began to hit the bottle like Mr. Walker before him. I didn't mind that until it started, in turn, hitting the finances. Booze was illegal and expensive and Joe Kennedy didn't give discounts to his workers. Then Ma took up the habit and I would come home to the pair of them passed out with stupid grins pasted on their faces and something that looked and smelled like a speakeasy at daybreak and with enough empty bottles up and down the hallway to set up a bowling alley. Something had to give. I sat down and started to write a movie script about a woman who plans to murder her dypso husband in a faked car crash and frame her own mother. It came easily and flowed from my pen. If I say so myself, it was brilliant.

* * *

Unlike Randolph Hearst's yacht, Louella Parsons, queen of Hollywood gossip, was totally unsinkable. Not that their fates were not firmly entwined. The *Oneida* had once been the German Kaiser's gin palace until newspaper magnate Hearst bought it and had the final, lingering marks of good taste expensively removed to please his starlet mistress, Marion Davies. And Louella happened to be on that yacht off Catalina, with her busy, little pencil, when the cowboy star, Tom Mix, mysteriously died of acute indigestion following a shot to the head that somehow escaped notice in the medical examiner's report. What followed immediately was a fat syndication deal for her Hollywood gossip column with Hearst Newspapers and the rest was silence. Not that, at parties, she didn't do a brilliant and vicious impersonation of Marion in her silent movie days when she was afflicted with a terrible stammer. Hearst claimed to have cured her through some Italian speech guru who put marbles in her mouth. Louella always said it was Charlie Chaplin who popped in something much more challenging and t-t-t-tasty. And there she sat over the other side of the room, prune-faced and wearing a silly hat like a strawberry pavlova on her head and a cross round her scrawny, hypocritical neck big enough to nail a bishop to.

The Depression had hit Hollywood hard. People without enough to eat didn't think about popcorn. The studios had cut back on the falling stars, many were teetering on the edge of bankruptcy and at parties both diamonds and caviar had been replaced by different kinds of cheap paste of fishy origin. Worse still, the moral strictures of the Hays Code had made the films boring and actors were now following in their footsteps and losing the wild eccentricity that had once made them such fun. All over town the gilt was peeling off the cherubs and official Hollywood henceforth only existed above the waist.

Louella – Lolly – had written the odd movie script and was a fellow journalist so we were old friends. I carried over one of her favourite triple martinis and joined her on the sofa.

'Hi, Manxi. What's cooking?'

I settled in snugly. Louella was kind of touchy. With her it was never love at first slight. But she and I had an old sparring-partner relationship. 'Well, Lolly, I can give you an exclusive. Joe Kennedy and I are planning to marry as soon as his divorce from Rose on the grounds of her adultery with the Pope is final. We have to act fast because I'm due in two months with twins. If they turn out to be white, we'll keep them and tell everyone they're Joe's rather than name them after the whole basketball team that fathered them.'

She made a sour puss. 'Don't joke about tragedy, honey. You should never joke about your bread and butter. The Good Lord doesn't like it and neither do I. If any of that was true you could name your own price for the story and you know it.' She gulped and her eyes became moist at the thought of losing so much money that never was.

'Lolly, you're so right to remind me that we live beneath the sway of a benevolent deity. Why! Only this morning I had a terrible pain in the arse and the Lord, in his infinite mercy, gave me a greater pain in the neck to help me get my mind off it.'

I looked around. It was another of those endless Hollywood cocktail parties that are all surface gloss and peanut brittle bitchiness – like walking on broken glass – and I was, I guess, a little overtired and sad. I had made an effort to look my best lest my enemies carry away the news of my total collapse into frumphood. But there were somehow always too many competing bodies in Tinseltown. No one had looked up when I came in and, as dear Gloria used to say, every girl appreciates a big, warm hand on her entrance. I didn't do too well at glitzy places with all these heavy-breasted showgirls fluttering their eyelashes and gasping at the fascinating chatup lines of fat moguls. Some silly blonde girl was throwing herself into appreciating George Cukor's jokes, leaning backwards and giving him a faceful of hot cleavage at every guffaw. She must be new not to know George was a 'Twilight Gentleman' and as gay as a naval parade. A nice young waiter bent and replaced his empty glass with a full one, a twist of lemon and a twisted smile as George slipped a patting, fatherly hand on his pert backside and squeezed – one of Hollywood's less unpleasant forms of feeling the pinch. George enjoyed a certain immunity from Louella, being on her kiss-and-tell informants' list following an indiscretion with a sailor at the YMCA that went heavily unreported in all the newspapers some time before. Both their backs were well-scratched.

Louella scowled at the impiety, then her thoughts turned back to business. 'Of course, Manxi dear, if I could ever persuade you to open those tight, little lips of yours about your employer and name some of the names of his toasty teatime treats, it might be worth some folding money from me. But then maybe you're on that list too.' She appraised sharply over the infinity pool of her martini glass. Louella had a whole economy of scandal going – what a story was worth to the papers, what it was worth to a star *not* to publish it, what a small favour to a studio now might be worth in future returns when some erring lamb made it big. Her little, black book held the number of every studio exec. and bent cop in LA. Come to think of it, it was a *very big*, black book.

'Actually, Lolly, I'm writing a film script and I wondered …'

Her whole face collapsed and she turned away in disgust. 'Oh, darling, who isn't?'

Outside by the fish-shaped pool, the new hottie, Mae West, had been poured into some tight, shiny sheath dress like a performing seal and excessorized with the sort of jewellery you might hang on a horse. She was in characteristic, narcissistic pose, patting her hair, other hand on hip, leg thrust out, surrounded by lapping gigolos and ogling some dark hunk of chuck steak in tight trunks, an English boy called Archie Leach, who had made a bit of a name in a bit part in a film called, oddly, *Singapore Sue*. They both looked overblown in every possible sense. Not surprisingly she snapped him up for her big hit *She Done Him Wrong*. From what I saw that night, omit the last word and you've got it right.

* * *

I didn't often go down Hollywood Boulevard, a place of flaking stucco and ravaged hookers even in broad daylight. Another prime feature was those medical practices where the doctor slipped you something that accidentally got rid of unscripted babies or where he was known to be usefully quick with the needle for those patients of a nervous disposition. Louella's own husband was a studio doctor specialising in much the same line with a little bit of celebrity clap on the side. I always wondered how that squared with a wife who dealt in celebrity claptrap professionally. They must have a 'no-talking-in-bed' rule. It was mid-1932 and I was feeling, as usual, a little depressed and hung over and a rare chill rain was blowing down from the hills, stirring up muddy dust and memories. Down on Hollywood is a friendly hair salon where a lot of the struggling actresses go to get a cheap makeover. In fact plenty of the girls who go there have given up struggling altogether and decided to just lie back and accept the inevitable but they do you a good Marcel wave which I always find lifts me like a Hollywood happy pill. And then, as I am passing an obscure film theatre on the way home, I see a poster for one of those odd, little movies that never make the main circuit, *Bali, The Last Paradise*. In RKO I am a pro in that off-piste area of the cinematographic art and I am intrigued. I buy a ticket and go in.

I suppose it's a silly film really – all love under the palm trees – but to those of us who have known real love under the palm trees and the jolly dancing of ripe coconuts, it's the only love there is. But the sheer beauty of the place and the people – both men and women wandering bare-chested and innocent as Adam and Eve – blow me away in that sleazy fleapit, full of coughing cigarette-smokers and saliva-slurping afternoon adulterers. The music, the dancing, the cascading streams carry me away to the place of my dreams. And then the penny drops. Bali. Bally! The ancient island home of poor, dear Ham and his ghost looms up again in the full, barbarous splendour of the Glasgow Tramway and Omnibus Company uniform of so many years ago and tears spring to my eyes. It is a long time since Muriel Walker had a good cry, having transformed herself from a raw doughgirl into a hard-baked cookie, but I sit in that tacky dump and cry all the tears I have held back for years, a seismic eruption of grief and guilty regret. I cry for plucked blackberries and football pavilions and dark, bottomless eyes, for dead hopes and ambitions and accepted compromises and the sheer ugliness of the life I am trapped in. Then, as I sit on the sticky, mock moquette, I feel myself rise, phoenix-like from the ashes of Mrs. Muriel Pearson and a new me is born that soars on gossamer wings and leaves all this dross behind. In the lobby is a telephone booth. I dial Louella's number and we have a long, meaningful chat. I will go to Bali and realise that new self. I will start to paint again. I have neglected it too long. Painting is a window onto my soul and it is time to fling it wide and let the sunshine back in. I walk straight out of there and find only grimy LA rain. I try to look up at the sky and see, across the way, an unfortunate, rooftop billboard that blocks the view where a big-boobed, breastbound bimbo – maybe George Cukor's friend from the other night – urges me – shoulders back – to 'Stand out with the new, "cutting-edge" bra from Babelle.' Ouch! A blatant image of everything I want to get off my chest. I get an attack of the giggles at the sheer, irrecoverable idiocy of the world, take a happy, rainstreaked, yellow streetcar to the nearest shipping line – the other passengers glaring at me as I sit and openly laugh through tears like a mad woman – and book myself on the next ship east. Sod Ma and Karl Pearson. They will be happy together – or maybe not.

Chapter Three

Batavia! Capital of the Dutch East Indies. A modern city of civic monuments and clean streets punctuated by sparkling canals where the wind smelt of spice and frangipani and fresh-scrubbed natives. Little streetcars nicknamed 'coffeepots' rumbled between the deft pony carts and an incredible blend of people of all shapes and sizes bustled through the thoroughfares under the shade trees. I played the part of a good tourist but after a few days I realised that this Indies of spanking white buildings and grovelling servants was not the Indies that I had come to see. I still had a little money left over from Lolly's stringent bounty and I sewed it into my canvas belt, packed my traps and hired a car to drive across Java. As the hotel boys were strapping on my luggage, my easel and my paints, a tiny, native child came up to the side of the car. His appealing eyes and ragged clothes spoke of his need for love as poignantly as his skinny outstretched hand spoke of an innocence without words. He seemed to me to embody the whole desperation of the Javanese poor yearning and calling me beyond the confines of the city.

'My name Pito.'

'Hallo, Pito. What can I do for you?'

'You want jig-a-jig?' he enquired with the smile of an angel. 'Okay. I fix.'

The hotel boys chased him away.

I made good progress on the excellent and mostly empty Dutch colonial roads, staying in the *pasangrahan* rest houses that served both colonial officials and tourists. I had never felt safer or freer and was enchanted by the politeness of everybody after the constant crude pushing and shoving of America as hustlers bellied up to the Hollywood trough. I have always appreciated politeness, the virtue that immediately makes you smile and say sorry when someone treads on your foot in a tram. Javanese had it in spades. Every night, I teased my palate with delicious, local delicacies, spiked with chilli and felt my soul expand as the moneybelt shrank. Even my taste buds were being spanked into new life. As in that movie back in LA, I once more gazed in wonder at the beauty of the jungles and mountains, the streams and valleys and the incredible comeliness of the natives, feeling myself bloated and clumsy in comparison. Wherever I felt the urge, I could just stop and paint. A large crowd always gathered round and I swiftly made friends with them as they stared in wonder at the vast, layered images I coaxed out onto a small, flat canvas. My imagination was fired. Yet here it was all for real and I had less a sense of novelty than one of finally coming home and my whole body tingled with excitement as I approached Banyuwangi and the narrow, storm-lashed straight that divided Java from Bali.

I pulled up at the harbour front, a ramshackle dockside of picturesque rocks, warehouses and a couple of leggy cranes. The thrum of the engine still echoed in my ears and warred with the gusting wind and the chatter of excited natives but soon I was haggling and bargaining over the sea crossing and found the street drama refreshing as I shamelessly simulated astonishment, outrage, womanly fear, attraction and disdain with a melodramatic range that would have cowed Clara Bow. The adoption of an actor's role seemed like a preparation for my new self, the first trying on of a new hat. The sailors laughed back at me but we agreed on a price that struck me as impossibly low. Perhaps I was being carried off by pirates into the white slave trade. But no. After a storm-tossed night, I and the car arrived in Gilimanuk and one of the crew helped me from the boat with the charming civility of an 18th-century marquis taking my hand for a minuet. As agreed, I crossed the palm of that hand with gold that it clutched to its heart. I would have to learn that, in the Indies, blue collars did not necessarily produce red necks. As Ma would say, I felt like Lady Muck from Turd Hill.

My drive across the island was another enchanted journey beneath the whispering palms but the magic faded as I approach Denpasar with its cheap Arab and Chinese shops, its crowds of overdressed Dutch and Eurasians and white walls stained with blood-red betel juice, damp and urine. It was as if the famous massacre of the Dutch invasion had just happened and the reddened walls cried out its lingering shame to the world. I shall *not* speak droolingly – yet again – about the bare breasts of the Balinese women. This will distinguish me from every other writer who has ever visited the island – mostly men, of course. Let me comment instead on the beautifully sculpted, bare chests of the local men who certainly had more to offer than Karl Pearson even after a few drinks on Thanksgiving.

I have only been staying at the Bali Hotel for a few days when the Dutch leeches begin circling. Can leeches circle? All right then, the sharks, in the form of the Assistant Controleur – all blue eyes and blond hair of which he is so enamoured that he constantly touches it with wonder just like Mae West. In his white ducks and gold epaulettes, he must be as catnip to the bored, local wives. First, he blusters, there are taxes and permits to be paid. I tell him I have already dealt with that in Batavia. Well then I must register as a foreigner. I must visit the office in person within three days or face deportation. What is it I am after in Bali? It is a common ploy of those who have no real work to do to go round demanding that others justify their existence. I learned that one from Joe Kennedy. I tell him I am an artist which enables him to pigeonhole me and soothes his frustrated administrative zeal. My proposal to go and live in a village is greeted with hilarity and condescension, which tells me it is something really worth doing.

Bali encourages a mystical frame of mind. The Balinese do not live in a random, statistical universe. Everything happens for a reason and fate governs all. I had seen those famous Balinese photographs from before the First World War, published to wide acclaim by the German doctor, Krause, of the innocently naked fauns and nymphs of the villages but then again I had also been to the New York nightclub called *The Sins of Bali* where it seemed these were pretty much the same as the sins of old New York. Now, I know photographers are simply morons who open a hole in a box and point it at someone yet they claim to be artists so I decided to simply drive out into the countryside to see reality for myself. Dr. Krause had worked for the Dutch in Bangli and that would be a good place to start.

I drive and the enchantment of the countryside enfolds me in a gossamer web spun from silver and gold. Time slows so that chickens seem to flash past in the honeyed air. I follow the signs to Bangli but it never seems to get any closer and I begin to fixate on the fuel gauge that shows empty. Finally, when I begin to think that I have a magic car that runs on air, the engine coughs and dies and I coast to a stop. A magnificent split gateway with spread wings beckons me up some steps. From within comes the gentle wail and tinkle of Balinese music. I set off towards it. A child encounters me at the top, screams and takes to his heels. A slightly older lad appears and gives a look, howls something and runs too. I pause and cough politely, clap my hands to attract attention.

Perhaps this is a forbidden place. Then a bent, old man peers round the corner, looking worried, gasps and takes off swiftly on knobbly legs. Finally, a beautiful young man with a fine, bold face and long, wavy hair, gloriously dressed in an iridescent, green and gold sarong – colours of a dragonfly – and a headdress teased up into a nodding flame, comes to the top of the steps and ... laughs at me.

'Do you know what they were saying? No? They said a demon was coming. Our demons all have red hair like yours. Proper human beings all have black hair. Please come in, lady demon.' He has a smile that lights up the whole courtyard with its ancient, mossy statues and fragrant flowers – the courtyard has them, I mean, not the smile. My first real encounter with Bali and it goes far better than I could ever have dreamed. This is Anak Agung Nura, handsome son of the Rajah of Bangli, a sweet and refined man who is to become the brother I never had. Educated in Holland and well travelled, he speaks English and will be my bridge into Balinese culture. I tell him my tale of running out of petrol, of being sent by fate, the gods, anything but that I had read Krause and come quite deliberately. To make it short – he introduces me to his father, a simply wonderful, gentle old man – an old gentleman. His father accepts my coming as a present from on high and I'm invited to join the court as a divinely bestowed gift. There is general rejoicing. I have a family. I am a princess, living in a glittering palace that looks down over the river where the locals come and bathe every evening in fairyland enchantment just as in Krause's photos. The next morning, after the servants have organised my bath and served my breakfast while crawling on their knees, I set up my easel and start to paint again! The Balinese are angels and make simply heavenly hosts.

That's my version and I'm sticking to it. Of course, I could tell a different story. I could say, I was put up in a guest house a bit like a garage, with cockroaches, and they charged me rent. I could say that I paid the rent in kind – or kindness. That's what the Dutch say. But then a Dutch woman would have been obliged to put down her riverside binoculars and start screeching in outrage about the naked bathers. All women will understand the delicious torment of sweaty, tossing sleeplessness, of wondering whether the Rudolph Valentino of their compulsive thoughts was coming or not, the hope that he would and yet the fear that he might. Then the faint, erotic whisper of bare feet and the rustled dropping of a sarong. Perhaps he came, we saw, I concurred. Perhaps.

I dyed my hair black, I learned Balinese and Malay and took to the Balinese sarong. I became a proper human being. In return I was comprehensively shunned by the Dutch who circled their wagons against me and spoke of race treachery. This troubled me not one iota. I spent my time with the Balinese and travelled all over the island with my new family, took part in all kinds of ceremonies straight out of a Hollywood movie and gained a deep knowledge and respect for Balinese ways. Finally, I am given my Balinese name in a special ceremony by a Brahman priest and become K'tut Tantri. K'tut means fourth-born, the rajah accepting me as his latest daughter and Tantri, the heroine of an ancient Balinese tale. I feel the whole of Bali has embraced me and I sink down gratefully into that warm embrace.

* * *

Much of my time in Bali was spent with Nura and his friends. Open-minded and politically advanced, they let me join in their discussions of the best route to a free Indonesia. The only Westerners that I was friends with were my fellow artists for

Bali hosted a community of progressive thinkers and brilliant intellectuals with whom I could feel at ease and who were as much the object of colonial disapproval as myself. There was Le Mayeur, a member of the Belgian royal family who married a beautiful, young Balinese dancer and painted her obsessively like Degas his tiny ballerinas. There was Theo Meier, a Swiss who became Balinese to the point of marrying two Balinese and having a child by each. And there were others, who just passed through, having drunk and refreshed themselves at the unpolluted well of Balinese nature. But above all there was Walter Spies, a German who had escaped from an oppressive Europe and installed himself in a fairyland setting by the river surrounded by his animals and admirers – surprisingly many of them female. I guess Walter was what would be called, in later times, a 'hag fag' since he adored adoring women. With his blonde hair, blue eyes and dancer's body he would have made a fitting model for one of the Führer's Aryan god statues but had declined that honour by just running away – a kindred spirit then. Walter and I were firm friends and met frequently, spending hours discussing together painting technique and art and enjoying the free play of our bubbling ideas as we stared down into the crystal water that flowed from the mountains and past his doorstep.

'It has always seemed to me, Walter, that painting and music are one. What was it Kandinsky said? "Colour is the keyboard, the eyes are the hammers, the soul is the piano with many strings. The artist is the hand which plays, touching one key or another, to cause vibrations in the soul."'

He made a soft farting noise, 'Pfui! Manxi. I had to listen to so much of that stuff back in Germany. Our eyes and our ears are stuffed up with big thoughts till we cannot see and hear and feel any more. That is what we come to Bali to unlearn. We must stop putting ourselves at the centre of everything and be what we were meant to be, just part of the enduring whole. Does this drink taste right to you?' We were sitting in the swimming pool that Barbara Hutton, the original 'poor, little rich girl' who owned Woolworth's, had excavated for him, and drinking his house cocktail, the Baboon's Arse, named from its glowing red colour that derived from a shot of grenadine to liven up the mix of whisky, tea and grapefruit.

'But surely, Walter, you as a musician must agree …?'

'You know. I think the boys must have got the bottles muddled up again. They do that. Usually it's not dangerous as they stick to the bottles on the sideboard but once I put down a bottle of Collis-Browne's compound – you know the thing for diarrhoea with morphine in – and it got stirred in. It tasted simply heavenly and the immediate effect was terribly liberating but none of us went to the shithouse for a fortnight. We were as constipated as bicycle tubes.'

'But the notion of harmony in music surely must carry over …'

'There was a bottle of paraffin by the back door this morning but it doesn't smell like that. It's sort of heady and perfumed.' He sniffed and frowned. 'I could ask them, I suppose, but it always gets so complicated when you have to explain this and that and the other … and they are having so much fun in the water that it seems a shame to bother them.'

Two young men of Walter's staff were taking turns to leap off a high rock into a deep spot in the river below, turning somersaults in midair, screaming in delicious anticipation and disappearing into the water for what seemed an age before they burst back through the surface in a splashy explosion of joy. Domestic staff turns into pure geometry. They were simply lovely, coltish creatures of nature, slim, muscular, long, black, wavy hair and perfect teeth and so completely, almost tragically, happy and able to live wholly in the moment. Surely they were the way God intended Man to look and feel. I shut up about art.

Another figure slipped into the water beside us, blonde, body well-maintained, in the latest style of swimsuit, and bobbed up, smoothing back her hair. I never put my head under water. Ma convinced me that water leaks in through your ears and rots your brain. 'Hello, darlings.' It was Vicki Baum, Austrian author of *Grand Hotel*, the international bestseller, that had gone on to grace the stage around the world before becoming the movie that carried off the Academy Best Film Award of that year. She stared down at her arm and flexed it the way Westerners do when they suddenly discover they have bodies in a tropical climate. She had arms and shoulders like a basketball player and I remembered that she had practised boxing at the same Berlin gym as Garbo. That would have made a match you could sell tickets to. 'I hope you don't want to be alooone,' she cooed huskily, as if reading my mind.

'Was that line in the original book, Vicki? Or did the scriptwriter just stick it in?'

'Stick it in? In Garbo you mean? What? Oh, I see. Sorry darling I have a dirty mind. Oh, to tell you the truth, I couldn't tell you any more what's mine and what isn't. As you know, in the Hollywood writers' buildings a hundred other guys are borrowing your toothbrush and every sheet of toilet paper has been used at least twice over before by someone else. Anyway, it was poor, old Garbo that got stuck with the line. It saved her thinking one up for herself, I suppose.'

Walter grinned across. 'Actually, I remember her saying it was a running gag from her early silent pictures between her and a cameraman and then the studio decided to use it and play it up to make her into a woman of mystery rather than someone just tired of talking to fools. They say she has given up the movies and is collecting art. Is that true? She hasn't asked for one of mine.' He pouted and sulked.

'She's got some movie coming out soon – I forget what. You know she loves to work with George Cukor. They just adore each other – real soul sisters. But it's true she's gone big on art and bought a load of Renoirs and Bonnards and Kandinsky's and nailed them up all over the walls of her place. She said decorators were so expensive that it was cheaper in New York than having the walls repainted. Don't worry darling I'm sure she'll want something from you even if she has to build more walls.'

'Talking of Kandinsky and art ...' I said.

'Oh and you too, Manxi. Hey! Can I ask you, Walter? I've lost a great, big bottle of eau de cologne somewhere. I thought I left it on the sideboard last night after dabbing my fevered temples after dinner. Any idea where it could have gone?'

Walter lay back in the sunlight filtering through the tall bamboo and smiled lazily. 'Aha! Don't worry about it. It'll turn up. In time all mysteries sort themselves out. Unless of course the monkeys have got it, in which case it's gone for good. Why not have a drink? A great, big Baboon's Arse for you, darling? The boys have given its tail a new tweak.'

* * *

I sometimes accompanied visitors who wished to get to know my own Bali, quite different from the version they received from the Dutch hotels. From me they got dances, weaving, rituals – all in the actual villages. And it is on these travels around the island that I discover the fabulous beach of Kuta, a swathe of brilliant sand untouched even by fishermen and I know with the certainty of a Muslim hearing the call to Mecca that this is to be *my* place. The Dutch did not allow foreigners to buy land but the poor villagers were happy to lease it to me at a price I could not believe. It was just enough to pay the taxes that the Dutch squeezed out of them so I was happily able to free them of that burden. Of course, I realised that in opposing the Dutch I was still fighting the English shipyard owners of my Scottish childhood, Mr. Walker's exploitative curse of foreign capital turned on its head. There on that beach, one day, I planned to build my own hotel for discriminating guests of all races and religions and be free of my own. Artists would stay free of charge.

This happened sooner than I imagined. One day, I was showing the beach to a visiting Frenchman, a man of great exploitative foreign capital and telling him of my dream. 'Let us do it, Tantri,' he says simply. 'Let us do it together.' And so my hotel is born, the Bali Beach Hotel, with nothing but the finest craftsmanship, an Arabian Nights fantasy. I know all the greatest Balinese carvers and painters and hire them to construct a shimmering jewel that calls like a lighthouse to kindred spirits from afar. It has ancient doors of gold carving, is enbosomed in banana and palm groves and has a rough white, coral wall with inset statues and lamps that separate it from the beach of everybody's dreams. Inside, the staff are all accomplished dancers and weavers and artists. I quote, of course, from my own brochure.

But, while building a hotel may be a matter of taste and artistic flair, running one calls for other, meaner skills and the sort of low, commercial grind I have always abhorred. It is at this point that I fall foul of Bob Koke and his wife, Louise. My French patron has faded away as patrons always do and I am desperately short of money. Bob insinuates himself into my affections and finances by playing the Hollywood card. He claims to have worked on *Mutiny on the Bounty* on Catalina Island and be a friend of my old chum, Clark Gable, he surfs, he is a tennis coach, a master of all the gigolo arts. Before I know it, the Kokes have declared themselves my partners and – like cuckoos in my own nest – they start to elbow me out.

* * *

'Godammit Manxi you can't go on fighting with the Dutch like this!' Bob Koke, red in the face, slamming his fist into his hand, shaking with rage. Louise nodding over his shoulder with an I-told-you-so smirk on her fat face. I have just sent some Dutch packing, off to the rival Bali Hotel, for being rude to the staff who had laid out their clothes without putting on white gloves first. Balinese are the cleanest people on earth, like cats they are always washing. The gloves had nothing to do with actual dirt. They had everything to do with insulting the locals. This had been coming for a long time. The Kokes and I had argued over everything, the potato peelings in the kitchen, the amount of salt in the food – Asians like it salty and the chef dumped it in by the handful – Louise's taste in lampshades …

'Why shouldn't I fight with them? It is a matter of pride to me that I am banned from the Bali Hotel. Have you heard the stories they tell about me? They say I'm running a knocking shop for the Dutch airforce just up the beach. They accuse me of sleeping with any Balinese man they see me out with whereas I live the life of a nun. The closest I get to physical excitement is cutting my own toenails.'

'Yeah, well. Whatever … Frankly, Manxi, I don't care if

you're easier to make than a peanut butter sandwich. But that reminds me.' Bob looking at his wife's face for support. 'We seem to be having some problems with the accounts. These claims for mileage. Private shopping trips are not strictly deductible. And fees for tours should be paid to the hotel, not into your private account. You can't keep all the income and shuffle off all the expenses onto us.' Louise smirking over his shoulder again. God how I'd love to smack her in the kisser.

'The hotel is mine. The land is mine. The original idea was mine. You can scarcely expect to be regarded as my equals in the business.' Harsh words lead to more harsh words. Louise, the witch, pitches in. She has one of those droning, nagging voices that make you want to do anything just to stop her talking – marry her, kill her – anything. Things that should never be said are shouted out in front of astonished guests and staff.

I withdraw to my bungalow and weep to see the hotel, my lovechild, debauched and debased with Louise's bad taste and Bob's money-grubbing. The staff desert and come to live with me, providently bringing much of the linen and china, though I warn them that I have no money to pay their wages. I have no means left, no prospects, no hope.

Then, one morning, they are there, gathered together on my veranda and, laughing, they gently push towards me a cloth knotted at the top. 'For you, *nyonya*.' It is full of ancient, silver dollars, shining in the sun!

'But how ...? Why ...?'

They are in tears. I am in tears. 'We are simple farmers who have little and live by the rhythms of nature. We have mortgaged our ricefields with the Chinese. Now you have the money to build your dream without a partner. Everybody in Bali loves you, *nyonya*. Everyone has given. You are our mother and we your children. Everyone would lay down their lives for you, *nyonya*.'

And so it goes. We rebuild over the other side of the road in the staggered bungalow style of Walter Spies's hotel up in Campuan and my establishment slowly begins to flourish again with the crème de la crème of world society patronising our ballroom and dining rooms. Every night, they glow with fine silks and sparkling jewels but always in the heat of Dutch jealousy and hatred. We replant the garden thickly with banana and papaya and coax enchantment from the soil so that, after dark, little lamps wink among the greenery. But I'm damned if I'm giving up the name of my hotel to Bob and Louise, so now there are two Bali Beach Hotels side by side and not talking to each other, which I hope causes Bob and his bookkeepers a little more of that administrative difficulty.

Our greatest triumph is the visit of Lord and Lady Duff Cooper, the British plenipotentiary and his wife, the society beauty Lady Manners, on a tour of British installations in the East. They have booked to come to us but the Dutch will not have it. First the authorities try to hijack them at the airport in a fleet of limousines – all shiny and black like scrabbling cockroaches – to carry them off to the Residence. As they stand outside, bowing and grimly beard-wagging at the couple, their speeches of welcome grasped in their hands like undertakers presenting their bill, we draw up honking and laughing. We have decked out our old convertible with garlands of flowers and the prettiest girls and boys all waving and smiling. The Duff Coopers take one look and throw their luggage at us and we flee, giggling like naughty schoolchildren. The Bali Hotel, the 'official' Dutch hotel, pulls strings to try to stop the best Balinese musicians and dancers from coming to our establishment to entertain them, threatening to blacklist any who do. They laugh and come anyway. 'You, nyonya,' they say, 'are one of us.'

After the stuffiness of officialdom, the Duff Coopers were delighted with the elegant simplicity of our hotel, the beach, the bamboo bar, the fresh seafood lavishly served on a shell. We drank cocktails from half coconuts and listened to the crash of the surf on the flawless beach. Only the conversation was gloomy.

'The East is about to blow up, K'tut. Singapore is impregnable, of course, and the Japanese will not dare bypass it to get here but they will try and in their attempt some very bad things will happen.'

In thanks for the success of their visit, the Dutch Controleur then tries to deport me but I appeal over his head to the Governor General via the American consul, who is an art lover and a friend of mine. The order is rescinded. The local Dutch hate me still more.

Steadily and unstoppably, the war clouds gather and clot. Pearl Harbour. The Japanese invasion of Malaya. The fall of impregnable Singapore. Japanese forces spread like a great bloodstain over the map and pour down towards the Indies. Allied navies clash and gore at the Japanese advance and Western imperial pride goes down in a great gurgle of lost tonnage. The Dutch are a little less arrogant nowadays. Prince Nura is frantic with fear for me. He offers me marriage, as do many of the very highest aristocrats, anxious to make me safe. I tell them, 'I shall never marry except for love. I hold an American passport, an ally of Holland, the more outside enemies cluster around the safer I am. What could possibly happen to me here?' More to the point, there is always the problem of husband Karl, still in LA but still doggedly alive and dog-in-the–manger married to me.

Then, one morning, Bob Koke is there, banging on my door in his absurd, California leisure wear, pineapples swarming all over his back in garish colours, the first time he has ever set foot in my Bali Beach Hotel. 'I just got a message from the American Consul. All Americans should get the hell out and I guess you qualify. The Japs will be here in days.' He turns and strides away, crunching purposefully across the sand. The war will be good for people like Bob, lending them an importance they lack in everyday life. From over the road I can hear Louise wailing like an air raid siren. She always loved drama.

Chapter Four

The Japanese officer behind the Dutch desk looked down at my pass, back up at me and blew smoke. He gave me one of those male glances so rampant and appraising that you feel it tugging at the elastic of your knickers. 'So you are adopted Balinese,' he purred. He shook his head at the nonsense of it, would have liked to make more of it but was intimidated by the signature of the commander of Surabaya who was an art lover and inevitably admired my work. 'What is your final destination?'

'Denpasar.' He looked at the hot Surabaya sun outside the office and was reluctant to step out of the draught of the office fan. The window had a neat, little lace curtain stretched over it as if a maiden aunt had crotcheted it and sent it to him from Kyoto. 'It says you are transporting books. Is there such a need of books in Bali?' He picked up his hat with a sigh of duty. 'Come, let us look at these needful books.'

Japanese were everywhere. Their steel ships sliced through the waves offshore. Their patrols scoured the countryside for white refugees and pulled people out of cars and buses at roadblocks to drag them off with kicks and blows, yanking the rings and earrings from the women and the wristwatches from the men. The skies were dark with their paratroops. I could pass for a half-caste Indo, in native dress with skin scorched from my days at the beach. My red hair was dyed black and I had that God-given oriental cast to the eyes. Nothing could change their piercing blue colour, however, so I hid them behind sunglasses. Prince Nura had taken me down to the Dutch Controleur's old office in Denpasar and registered me as an adopted member of his family. I got a life-saving pass and a rising sun armband that kept me out of the prison camps, where most of the Dutch were to be penned up, and allowed me to move about. Many of the most arrogant members of Denpasar's white community had been at the office too, humbly queuing in the corridors and suddenly vaunting some obscure touch of the tarbrush that they would have fought tooth and nail to deny a week ago so they could be classed as Eurasian. We were all learning to be someone else in order to survive and we all bowed low – really low – to any passing Japanese soldier to show we accepted our new, lowly place in the order of things.

Nura and the other locals – soon to be Indonesians – are confused by the Japanese battlecry of 'Asia for the Asians!' Can the announced Greater East Asia Co-prosperity Sphere really mean the end of the hated Dutch occupation of their islands after hundreds of years? Are the Dutch East Indies really to become the single, free state so long dreamed about by a few scruffy intellectuals and religious madmen in Java? The ancient prophecies of the 12th century seer Joyoboyo are dusted off – that the Europeans would be driven out by a race of yellow dwarves from the north whose own rule would last for the time of just one maize crop before the day of the Ratu Adil – the Just Ruler – would finally dawn.

At first the Japanese were like kind, old uncles and sweet-faced nephews. They arrived more like policemen than an army. No rapes. No looting. In Bali not one shot was fired. They were all smiles and tousled the hair of blond children. Here they were smart navy men, anyway, not soldiers hardened by jungle combat. Then they began to turn the screw, turn after turn after turn, until the Indonesians realised that the Japanese were even more brutal than the Dutch in their exactions. They seized food, manufactures and demanded women for their brothels. Any resistance was met with death. Nura and his friends were disillusioned. They had long supported the principle of being free of the Dutch but never really agreed how this was to be brought about in those long and rambling conversations where we took the ideas of the day and discussed them far into the night. That I was privileged to listen in and offer my advice shows how far they had come towards accepting me as one of them and, as a Scot, my whole being resonated to our shared experience of being colonised persons. Yet there were bitter arguments even among the leaders of the independence struggle. On posters everywhere, Soekarno's sunlit face beamed down and urged the people to support the Japanese to win the fight against the Dutch and thousands of ardent, young volunteers, *romusha*, were shipped off to work for them in the forests and swamps of Burma, building railways and such. We see their happy faces and pumping fists in the newsreels as they leave but none ever come back.

In the newspapers, Hatta, the intellectual of the group, carried his ventriloquist-dummy grin and sweaty brow from rally to rally and meeting to meeting while Sutan Sjahrir went underground and joined the anti-Japanese resistance. It is he who becomes our inspiration and makes us realise that soft words are all very well but we need arms to make sure the Just Ruler doesn't turn up to find us empty-handed. Which is why I am in Java, flaunting my pass and my armband in a borrowed Buick and trying to get travel permits. The idea was to establish a travelling group of Balinese dancers that would freely tour Java to entertain the Japanese and also transport arms and information behind their backs while making a little money on the side. People in Bali were starving with the exactions of the occupying forces. I had to force myself to play the part of a good-time girl, mixing and flirting with Japanese in all the smartest clubs though secretly I hated them for what they were doing to Bali. Even my beautiful hotel had been levelled to the ground.

The officer came out to the car and clicked his fingers to a soldier, dressed in the usual flour-sack uniform, to open the trunk. There was the box – books on top all right but the real stuff – grenades, small arms, dynamite – underneath. He flicked disdainfully through the titles. Books on Japanese art, history, culture, the photo of the weedy emperor on horseback – an amulet lovingly propped upright with a flower at its feet and not lightly to be just grabbed and displaced. He pouted approvingly, saluted, nodded to the flour-sack who slammed the trunk shut and stalked away. I started to breathe again. I slid behind the wheel, shaking, barely able to see, the whole world spinning and was a hundred yards down the road towards far Banyuwangi and the wild sea-crossing back to Bali before I realised where I was and what I was doing and my own unruly feelings overwhelmed me. I pulled in by the roadside and burst into quivering tears.

* * *

I made other trips. It all became routine. The guards at the roadblocks came to know me, waved me through, even smiled and I slipped into sloppy habits. One night, as I was preparing for bed in Surabaya, there came a hammering at the door. It was of course the Kempeitai, the feared Japanese secret police that even their own people were scared of, checking up on guest houses. The sloppy habit I am in at that late hour is a thin nightgown. At first, their visit seemed fairly routine. They went in for the usual business of slaps and insults and upending suitcases on the floor and trampling the precious contents, laughing, under their boots – the silly, schoolboy stuff you expect from all armies of occupation. And then one of them sneeringly lifted up my nightie in gratuitous humiliation and they all froze. At first I took it as a compliment, then grabbed the hem back and pushed it back down but it was all too late. Carroty pubic hair is an undyed, red flag to them. Sloppy, as I said. The dark glasses were knocked from my nose to reveal even more incriminating blue eyes. My cover as an Indo-Balinese was blown. A more thorough search revealed the concealed American passport afforded by my marriage to Karl Pearson, stupidly tucked inside the pillowcase. Even out here, Karl is still giving me grief. I was beaten to the ground, dragged outside to a car and whisked off to headquarters as an American spy. Kempeitai headquarters was a terrifying, blank-faced building that people didn't even pass without crossing over the other side of the street. I never saw anyone walk into that place. I never saw anyone simply riding there in a car. More to the point, no one ever walked out either. They always had to be, in some sense, just an unconscious body being dragged. As a fancy, foreign spy they clapped me up for two days in a deluxe cell like an oven with bare concrete walls and an iron door before they moved me to an economy semi-detached of rusty bars with a woman who screamed all night at the demons in her own mind.

From that day on, I woke every morning with the wish for death. This is no melodramatic exaggeration. The return of consciousness brought me nothing but despair. I lay naked on a scrap of filthy matting and felt vermin crawling over my body in the dark. At dawn, inasmuch as we ever saw dawn, a dollop of foul slop was thrown at me on a banana leaf and then I cowered and waited for the inevitable sound of approaching feet and the jangle of keys. Yet, every day, I still hoped that today at least they would not come. If I was on the floor they kicked me to my feet. If I was on my feet they beat me to the ground. Then I was dragged to the interrogation room and it was always the same questions. 'Who are you? What is your mission? Who are your contacts?' Questions I could not answer so each one was followed by a punch, first to one side of the face, then to the other. I found it oddly upsetting when my torturer lost the rhythm and got the order wrong. The world made that much less sense. When I finally blacked out, they threw water over me and then they started again. 'Who are you? What is your mission? Who are your contacts?'

With their rifle butts, they drove me naked across the town square, paraded me in front of jeering troops, hoping to break my spirit but my body no longer belonged to me. It was outside me, a separate thing, something out there. They could do anything with it that they wished. On one wonderful day, they told me I was to be shot and I was hauled to a yard with big, high walls topped with barbed wire and tied to a bullet-chewed post and blindfolded. There followed the sound of troops being shuffled into a line in the dust and the purposeful click of shells being loaded into rifles. 'Take aim! Fire!' There came the crash of gunfire and an enormous force thudded into my chest and then I was floating, floating, finally free. So there is life after death! Joy, liberation. The Wee Free Kirk was right! Who on earth would have thought it? In that moment I understood that fear of death is simply fear of losing the story in our heads that is ourselves, it is fear of losing the end of that story. And then the grinning officer was there, tearing off the blindfold, holding the rock he had just hurled into my chest and they were all leaning on their rifles and laughing. And I felt no relief to be still alive, just the greatest possible disappointment. I wept as they dragged me back to the interrogation room and 'Who are you? What is your mission?

Who are your contacts?' And then, one day, they turned me loose.

* * *

My reprieve was short-lived. Perhaps it was a deliberate, vicious tactic to make me think the agony was over just so they could renew it. There is nothing crueller than hope. After two days, the Kempeitai returned in their costume of trench coats and felt hats. I was bundled into the back of a car with two agents suffering from a fishy halitosis of such monumental pungency that it momentarily dispelled my fear. This time, it is the Ambarawa concentration camp in Central Java where some 24,000 white women are kept. But, oddly, they didn't put me in with the others. Instead, I was kept in a cell completely on my own, totally bare except for a sleeping mat, and with bars high up to allow in a little light and air. So not a single person knew I was there. At first, it was horribly lonely but, quite frankly, I could do without the kind of human company I had been enjoying recently and it offered me a wonderful sense of peace to try to knit together my shattered body and spirit. A trustie brought me rice and gruel and water once a day. I tried desperately to engage her in conversation, anything that would confirm our common humanity. She opened her mouth to show a gaping, scarred hole and the absence of a tongue. She was mute. The Japanese had ripped it out. There would be no small talk.

I entered a world of silence. There were no visitors, no interrogations. I felt like a file that had been misplaced and forgotten. I watched the *cicak* lizards hunting bluebottles. One night, the cell was invaded by fireflies that danced and turned like wayward fireworks. The next night they were replaced by squadrons of mosquitoes that dive-bombed throughout the hours of darkness. In daylight, there was a little square of blue sky that could just be seen from high in one corner, like the sea view of a cheap boarding house. Prisoners are always supposed to be obsessed with recording the passage of time. I surrendered to it blindly. I have no idea how long they kept me there. Waking and sleeping blended into one as when, back in Glasgow, mothers would quieten fractious children by slipping the gas ring under their blankets and turning it on for a couple of minutes. After a while, the silence, the lack of food and stimulation, released me from my own body. I felt myself begin to float once more. I knew that one day soon I would float away like a helium balloon and never return.

My salvation is a pack of cards. Their creation is a work of absolute genius. I unpick some bands of dried leaf from my sleeping mat and snap them into squares, make paint of ground red tile from the floor and white plaster from the wall, create black from a scrap of charcoal and paint my own playing cards. I play patience, recreate games of bridge from the past and rejoin the rich and elegant people with whom I played in the long, velvet evenings of Bali. I hear again the crash of the swirling surf on Kuta beach and the tinkle of civilised laughter over drinks. I read my own future in the cards, the interplay of fate and design, purpose and randomness, whirling me away. I laugh when they tell me I should prepare for possible bad changes in my circumstances.

And then the Kempeitai came back. It was the usual routine of beatings, insults but, by now, I was inured to pain. I stared at my feet and refused to speak or even cry out in agony. Sometimes, as their most famous prisoner, they dressed me up and painted my face and made me pose with Japanese officers, forcing me to smile in some ghastly caricature of social life. I knew they would use the pictures to try to convince my friends that I was collaborating and so persuade them to confess in turn. What could I do? I tried to look as unhappy and unattractive as possible but they knew what I was doing. More clever than the rest, one of them drove me one night to a pretty little villa with a beautiful bathroom and locked me in with a wonderful bath filled with scented oils and the sound of Rachmaninov pulsing through the wall. I knew that if I refused, they would throw me in and scrub me against my will. Food, I could reject but the thought of immersing my tired and tortured body in clean, healing water was more than I could withstand. As I lay cossetted by silky warmth, the aches, the pain, flowed out of me and I dissolved in tears in the bathtub, silently asking the forgiveness of my comrades. I became one of Charles Kingsley's water babies. I dried myself in a cool, fluffy towel as soft moonlight streamed through the window and I thought of all the scenes in art and music – Anthony and Cleopatra, Romeo and Juliet, Rosalka – where parted lovers gazed at the moon and thought of how it was the same moon that their loved ones were staring at – and so they were brought together.

The thought and recalled sensation of that bath might have strengthened me through the weeks that followed but it had done something terrible to my brain and also restored to me the sense of having a body at all so that the kickings and beatings suddenly had a renewed power I thought had gone for ever.

And then something changes. It is like the first stirrings of the spring thaw in the new year, a strange sensation in the air, a surreptitious crackling spreading through the ice underfoot, an awareness of motion and unfreezing. Suddenly the endlessly trumpeted series of Japanese victories is no more. The faces of the officers register unusual emotions – doubt, worry, fear – and they are less harsh, less ready with the boot and the fist. The food improves. I am allowed exercise. One day, as I walk in the dusty yard outside my cell, I hear the sound of a prisoner in the neighbouring compound softly singing some old, Dutch song, carried away in it, gently humming those bits where she has forgotten the words. Normally, any such sign of simple, human joy would be a provocation that the guards would slash to the ground with bamboo clubs. Now one of them taps his fingers against the wall in time to the song and looks the other way. The hair on my neck stands on end. And there are conversations with other prisoners exchanged in rasping whispers. We have all heard crazy rumours before and had our hopes dashed and cannot believe what we are hearing now. This is surely the craziest of all. The war is already over! There is a magical, new weapon that turns people to dust and the Japanese have surrendered to it. Their army is just waiting to be shovelled away by the victorious Allies. Can it possibly be true? What of their threat that in defeat they will kill all prisoners and then themselves?

One cold, stiff morning, I awake to a strange howling on the wind and gunfire. My first thought is that the feared massacre of prisoners has started and I sit quietly in one corner with my hands in my lap and wait with calm resolve for the end. There is a crashing of iron on iron at the far end of the corridor as the door is flung open, the sound of my approaching executioners' boots coming to take me. And then the key turns in the lock and it is not a pinched Japanese face that looks in at me but a beautiful Indonesian one with wide, brown eyes, all smiles.

'Si K'tut? I have been sent for you. *Merdeka*! Freedom!' Other young men crowd in, shouldering guns, laughing, waving fists in the air. I am carried on their joyous, strong shoulders out to liberty and into the sunshine, dazzled like a pit pony brought up from the mines. The war is over. My life has begun again!

Chapter Five

The kaleidoscope has been given another twist, rearranging the same, familiar pieces into strange and unfamiliar patterns. The Surabaya docks swarm with Japanese, but no longer proud conquerors. Japanese arrogance has collapsed like a badly made soufflé and been blown away by an atom bomb. Now they are reduced to being Asian coolies, crouched shivering in the rain, stripped to ragged *fundoshi* loincloths and odd, squelching, rubber boots that have a separate big toe, hissing like polite geese and hauling the luggage of white faces off and on the ships that are coming in from Singapore and the wider world. To someone, somewhere, they must be a fetishist's wet dream. Surabaya is one great waiting room. Westerners with fresh uniforms and plump, pink faces, are waiting to get in, other Westerners from the camps – mere yellow-skinned bags of bones – are waiting to get out, and everyone is waiting for some clear pattern to emerge from the dust and rain and heat haze. Drooling, toothless mouths to feed, bemerded backsides to wipe and clean, the world is reduced to its Marxist fundamentals. And everywhere is the rubble of the war, gutted factories, once-trim villas with tarpaulins for roofs and walls daubed with a red hand, gripping a wavy dagger dripping with blood and that single word *Merdeka*, 'freedom,' that is to be the solution to everything. And the sign is everywhere.

The new Republic of Indonesia is independent – in name at least. Soekarno, the collaborator with the Japs, the hero, the heretic, the apostate, the betrayer and defender of the people has been forced by enthusiastic students to hop off the fence and read the fatal words of the Freedom Proclamation and now that he has been acclaimed President there is no stuffing the genie back in the bottle. The date 17th August 1945 will never be the same again. In the British Consul-General's former villa in far Batavia – renamed Jakarta – as Rear Admiral Tadashi snores in cherry blossom, Japanese dreams upstairs, downstairs they haggle over who is to sign the Proclamation of Independence and what it should actually say. Other Japanese are against the act and so it has to be done in public – but secretly – like something carried out in a public lavatory. After all, just two days before, in Tokyo, the army attempted a coup to stop another radio broadcast from the Emperor, so that his surrender had to be smuggled out of the palace on a gramophone record in a laundry basket like a royal bastard child. The solution to the conundrum is obvious. An outside broadcast. The nimble technicians from the Batavia – sorry now Jakarta – *Hoso Kyoko* radio station have set up the microphone. The new flag of the nation – the old flag of the Javanese Majapahit empire – proud red and white – is unfurled. The passage from Netherlands to Indonesian rule can now be neatly and economically marked all over the archipelago by simply ripping off the third blue strip of the Dutch flag – a most parsimonious proceeding that one might have otherwise expected to find favour in provident, Dutch eyes. The intellectual Hatta stands beside wavering Soekarno. And behind stands sharp-eyed Adam Malik, ever watchful lest the other, slippery pair slide away again leaving the fateful deed still undone.

In Surabaya, the Pemuda young bloods are thrilled. Only in the young does hope ever really completely triumph over fear. 'K'tut, this has to go out to the world or they will try to hush it up. Can you translate the Proclamation into American and read it out over the radio? We need you, K'tut. You must be our voice to the world.'

I shrug. I am staying in an exploded Dutch house with a bunch of students, surrounded by jettisoned Japanese military hardware and only gradually getting used again to human kindness. Like real food to a starving body, it can overwhelm you, make you worse, I think you can even be killed with sudden kindness. I am walking in a dream as if permanently stunned. Boxes of grenades are stacked against one wall, rifles against another but all good Javanese boys dream of tanks. Someone, at some stage, has fired a mortar through the roof. Dutch? Japanese? British? No one knows. Violence is random. Poignant reminders of gentility haunt the building – shattered paintings, a headless cherub and the vast garden is a tangle of roses run wild. The students and freedom fighters who inhabit the building have planted yams among them and stocked the weed-filled pond with strictly practical fish, the garden become a battleground between native, economic necessity and foreign self-indulgence. My white face is now a military asset again, a passport that allows me access to places that my local friends cannot visit. I carry messages, count ships, pick up gossip in the bars and pass it on to my contacts in the Pemuda. On the other hand, I can no longer wander at will and alone in the outer suburbs. Something has changed. There, my white face would lead me to be spat upon, even attacked. It is all out in the open now.

The British are here. Since the Dutch are in no position to take back their eastern empire, they have tricked the British into doing it for them. Officially, they are simply here to maintain social order and free the internees and arrange for their safe transport back to so-called civilisation but their relations with the Pemuda are just short of open hostility since both sides know they are merely keeping a place warm for the Dutch to slip their fat backsides into again. Apparently the British Commander in Chief told the head of the operation, 'We don't have the forces for anything but a gentle occupation. It's pussyfooting, old man, and you're the pussy.' Their position isn't helped by the fact that they are being boycotted by the local Dutch who reproach them for not launching an open attack on the rebels. Yet the Dutch burghers are clear which side their bread is buttered on. Wits among them have replaced their 'Beware of the Dog' signs with 'Beware of the Ghurka.' As for the Brits, the poor ninnies were told to expect their foremost problem to be the damping down of the wild enthusiasm of the Indonesians at having the Dutch back, that they would snuggle under the Dutch flag as a tricolore treat – but then the Brits also always blindly insisted that – deep down – the Indians *really* loved them too. No one seemed to realise that, with the sudden, official outbreak of peace, the real war would not end but be displaced, have to go somewhere else and be internalised.

Meanwhile the young freedom fighters rage in frustration against a cautious, older generation who fight with pieces of paper and votes in unrecognised forums but a lot of their own conflict is carried out in slogans and flags. The Japanese refuse to haul theirs down, the Indonesians rip down that of the Dutch, the Brits modestly fly theirs in miniature form, on the front of their trucks as if to pretend that is all the territory they claim for themselves and every night heroes from all sides switch the flags around on the public buildings and trip over each other in nasty, little firefights. In technologically sophisticated Jakarta, the students boobytrap the flagpoles by electrifying them but it is my country boys who overrun the fancy Hotel Yamato and join in a pitched battle with Dutchmen and the Japanese guards who are trying to change the sign back to 'Hotel Oranje' under a flagpole where the hated symbol of oppression has been raised once more. In the scrap that follows, any kind of weapon will serve. One man does great damage with a well-used bicycle, spontaneously dismantling it and converting each part into an implement of offence. One of the lither boys climbs up, gripping the pole with his hands and shreds the blue strip from the Dutch flag with his teeth – a fine image of patriotic hatred. Some describe the Dutchmen as wearing dinner jackets and being well-oiled on Bols which makes attacking them an act of worker solidarity as well. According to others they are just a bunch of hysterical Dutch kids fresh back from the camps, an experience that has understandably shortened their tempers. Of course, many thousands of the Dutch were never in the camps at all, being members of the pro-Nazi NSB but after the war, they and all official mention of them evaporate into thin air and everyone becomes a free-Dutch patriot who spent the war singing the popular song, 'We are not afraid'. In revenge for the hotel incident, shortly afterwards, pro-Dutch Eurasians hideously murder a harmless Chinese hairdresser in silk pyjamas for flaunting a politically ambiguous red and white barber's pole outside his shophouse.

Lanky Lukman walks around the garden in his Japanese-style uniform, shaking, puffing cigarettes, still high on Oranje adrenalin, with blood left proudly on his face – actually his own – someone has accidentally elbowed him in the nose. He usually spends most of his time fighting the good fight with a screwdriver, unblocking wireless sets that the Japanese had fixed so they could only pick up their own stations. 'The old men in Jakarta just talk and give away everything we have gained by fighting. They want the Dutch to still be their friends and tell us to sit on our hands. Well we won't. You can never have too many enemies, K'tut. They help you know who you are. Love may lie. Enmity never does.'

Gentle Reza disagrees, pouting like one of the practical fish. 'The future of the revolution is to bring people together. For example, there is no conflict between Islam ...' He plucks a white rose. 'And socialism.' He plucks a red, holds them together and offers them to me blushingly like the corsage a boy gives to a girl before her first prom. There is great tenderness in the way he touches the flowers. He is the principal planter of yams. 'The imams have declared this a holy war. Most of the boys here are from Islamic schools. I was at an agricultural school.' Red and white roses. Hadn't I done all this in my own education? Part of English history? The Wars of the Roses. Had that ended well? I couldn't remember but I rather doubted it. But it was all very Indonesian. The arrival of a new belief – Hinduism, Buddhism, Islam, Christianity, Socialism – did not entail the jettisoning of the old that it conflicted with. You just added another layer and ignored the contradictions as part of the rich tapestry of life.

Then little Uki with the soft brown eyes that would melt any heart speaks up. 'We need you, K'tut. You must be our voice to the world. Tell them in English about our Proclamation of Independence. On the radio.'

I look at those shining, happy faces and feel a greater love than I have ever known, maternal, self-sacrificing but tinged with a sad awareness of its own, inevitable evanescence. In my life I have often had to fight against my better instincts. I tell myself that experience of the world will soon snuff out that wonderful innocence of theirs in a few short weeks, but for the moment let them enjoy being young. With a unique wisdom, words for 'love' in Indonesian are based on roots of 'pity' and 'compassion' and I have always found it hard to fall in love with abstract nouns, for me they have to become people I meet before I can really commit to them. These three hopefuls *are* freedom. Side by side they look like a series of fine wood samples my husband Karl kept nailed to the wall of his workshop – glowing mahogany, delicate rosewood and smoky, burred walnut. It is odd that war, that engenders violence, hatred and inhumanity, also gives birth to so much compassion, love and self-sacrifice.

We set off in an old Panhard, once some Dutch burgher's pride and joy but now a smoky wreck with rustholes in the floor and a cracked windscreen. There can be nothing sadder than a patched whitewall tyre with its mixture of pretension and confessed poverty, like a doilie on a tin plate. The British have established a strong, defensive perimeter around the centre of Surabaya, centred on Rembrandt Square, using the Indian army – all mugs of *chai* and big, tombstone teeth – whose black skins and hairiness scare the Javanese but it seems we are not heading that way and lurch away from the city through a blasted landscape of flattened huts and pools of industrial waste. The Japanese radio studio in the city is not our goal then but an abandoned cement factory that boils with mosquitoes even at midday. We round the corner of some sort of silo and there is a Japanese truck like a huge steel box, bristling with aerials and covered with cement dust for camouflage and with great holes where something like tracer fire has passed clean through it. For some reason, they are known as 'banzai boxes'. If it had been a chest of drawers, my husband, Karl, would have described it as 'well loved'. It is the work of a few minutes to hydraulically raise the main aerial and crank up the generator. As the boys grin their encouragement and light each other's celebratory cigarettes, a young Madurese Marconi technician slaps a pair of headphones over my ears and I am live, on air – walking on air – speaking to the world, the first-ever English-language broadcast of Rebel Radio Indonesia.

'We the Indonesian people hereby declare the independence of Indonesia ...' Not much to the Independence Proclamation really. Sjahrir – soon to be Prime Minister – had written something much fancier that the others had hacked to pieces. Reviewers are hell. Certainly not a lot to show for a whole night's wrangling and rewriting. Just a couple of lines more about the rest being sorted out as and when and then that's it. Nowadays it sounds all a bit slapdash. Typical politics, I suppose. A brave, sweeping declaration followed by a load of vague mumbled ifs and buts that can't be pinned down and so make it unenforceable.

We can't leave it like that of course. I think of what the boys have just been saying in the garden with blood on their faces and roses in their hands so I have to make up some sort of speech about the glorious struggle that is to come and the two colours of our new flag symbolising just about anything you care to hold dear – earth and sky, martyrs' blood and innocence, socialism and Islam, body and soul, female and male, some stuff I half remember about Diponegoro fighting under red and white of the old Majapahit Empire during the Java War that so nearly chased the Dutch out in the last century. I'm not sure whether it's true and Diponegoro was a religious lunatic anyway that any decent Indonesian government would end up shooting but it sounds good so I mix it all in any old how, my audience are hardly going to rush off and look up the references in a library. I have always been the sort of cook who just throws everything into a pot and stirs, hoping a handful of chilli will cover up the cracks. I confess, I get a little carried away. But my muddled news bulletin is a great success. It seems that clarity of thought is not required in this job, being a terrible obstacle to both oratory and to patriotism.

At the end of it, the boys hug me and fist the air, exuding the sweet-tea odour of Asian sweat. A wrinkled old woman dressed in rags, a woman who has nothing – not even teeth – limps across the yard to bring me real tea and three stale biscuits arranged on a doilie laid on a chipped enamel plate, smiles and bids me eat. In Java you must never eat off a cracked plate. It is terribly bad luck. But a chipped enamel plate? I did not know. Time would tell.

My performance catches the attention of the highest level of the Pemuda. Soetomo, our leader, Bung Tomo himself, sends for me. Uki, Lukman and Reza are ecstatic to be boys in the gang of teacher's pet.

* * *

Soetomo, Indonesia's foremost boy scout. As I recall, he was only the nation's second-ever 'Garuda scout', with more badges swarming up his sleeve than a market stall has cockroaches and the spit-cleanest woggle in the business. He is a local Surabaya boy who once worked, like me, as a journalist. But things have moved on. Now he is head of the Barisan Pemberontakan, the young rebels, and his wild eyes and fearless voice are immediate icons of revolt. On his cap, he wears a single, red badge showing the horns of a wild bull, symbol of the Pemuda.

We meet on the shady porch of the Simpang Club, formerly the lush watering-hole of high Dutch administrators, a weird, riverside building with fine shady gardens that looks as if a church has collided with an Ancient Greek temple and the bits have got muddled up. The Dutch drape their gardens in classical statues, the Chinese in lions. Bung Tomo uses cute, young men in poses of military alertness. As I climb out of the old Panhard, he leaps to his feet, bows stiffly and hisses, thumbs down his trouser seams. Japanese military training dies hard. We sit. Tea is brought with revolutionary fervour, together with what look very much like the same three wizened biscuits from the 'banzai-box'. He ignores them, crossing his legs vampishly and letting his clove cigarette curl lavishly away in smoke. I have not allowed for the club's change in circumstances – seized by Pemuda with the Dutch all chased away – and am overdressed in my one good frock. Western dress always makes me look out of proportion. I should have worn my batik sarong. I look him over and slip off my earrings.

He bears a handgun glamorously strapped on his hip, creaking with shiny leather and has the long, untamed hair that is the mark of the young 'extremists'. Many have vowed not to cut it until Indonesia is free, a further blow to those poor barbers with red and white poles that have been victims of the Eurasian 'dogs of the Dutch' as they are called in Soetomo's fiery speeches. Lukman has told me that is part of his being a *jago*, a village 'cockerel' with superhuman strength and magical powers. Lukman goes misty-eyed whenever he talks of Soetomo. He gets a lump in his throat and maybe in his trousers. But the *jago* is just a stage presence. In person, Soetomo is no wild man, rather shy and with the smile of a choirboy, forever pushing or tossing his wind-blown hair out of his eyes. They call him Bung Tomo, 'big brother Tomo', but he is more 'little brother' being only 25 years old and sparely built but then many of his forces are literally schoolboys – or would be if they were ever allowed to go to school by the colonists. He has eyes that burn like hot coals and a mouth made for kissing babies, the sort that reunites, in women, their two strongest urges, that to breastfeed and that to have sex. He is simply beautiful despite the scraggy beard that so contrasts with the small, almost girlish features. What a shame that being a *jago* involves forswearing all sexual contact with women! But then, perhaps it is as well. Men always reduce all the different kinds of love to mere grunting, ferrety sex so that they all quickly come to the same sticky end.

'Sister K'tut, I have heard your talk,' he says, 'on my Rebel Radio. I could not follow all of it. What, for example is an *eejit*? But I especially liked the bit about Diponegoro. You know I am a descendant of his?' He preens briefly. 'It is from him I have my powers. You are a fellow artist, a true orator, and I admire you. Thank you for bringing the news of our freedom to the world. From Surabaya it has echoed around the islands and the planet. They have staged Proclamations in all the major cities.'

'I'm not a dog of the Dutch then?'

He laughs, waves the suggestion away in clove-scented smoke. 'Nooo. You are a tiger of the Indonesian people. You know that in the old days, the kings organised fights between tigers and buffaloes for entertainment. The tigers were supposed to be the Dutch and the buffaloes our own people. Tigers were fierce and cunning and had great claws but buffaloes were strong and patient and waited till the tiger had worn himself out with its roaring and clawing before impaling it on those great horns and stamping it to death. The buffalo *always* won in the end. All those *eejits* who were so keen to be of mixed blood when the Japanese arrived and dodge the camps are now of pure, Dutch blood again and some of that blood will have to be spilt to purge our land of lies and betrayal. The mist of resistance has condensed into solid form. Ours will not be a freedom won under a full moon and in the perfume of roses and jasmine. It will not be won around a polished conference table in a palace but over a Dutch butcher's block. And there will be accounts to settle with the Timorese and Ambonese who have thrown their lot in with the Dutch.'

A truck rumbles past, bearing cheering adolescents with raised fists and bamboo spears, boys simply enjoying smashing things up. I remember only too well the pleasures of the Glasgow tram riots and the ghost of Ham swims fleetingly into view. The air around them boils with a sweaty haze of cocked testosterone that could take fire at any minute. Bung Tomo smiles and waves back, looks embarrassed at his own celebrity. The gleaming, white walls of the club building are a provocation to youth and they have been daubing them with slogans in the red paint that they have all over their hands and clothes for lack of accessible, Dutch or collaborators' blood. A dusty banner across the entrance reads, more demurely, 'Once and forever the Indonesian Republic' like a Californian advertisement for diamond engagement rings. From round the back, come screams of laughter from the men washing in the river, splashing each other and joining in rough boys' games. Bung Tomo looks wistfully in that direction then turns back to me. He wants to go out and play.

'I want you to work with us, to go on the radio. Women are as just as good revolutionaries as men. The whores and pimps on the docks are already all loyal workers for the revolution, luring the troops away from duty, so why not you?' He laughs.

'You mean, in the revolutionary struggle, women are just men with knobs on – or rather off?' Many of the dockside whores were really men anyway – that fine old, Asian tradition of transvestism.

'What? Perhaps. Now we have access to new, shortwave equipment, we can reach far out. It is not like the old days in Jakarta. There they only had a rickety old transmitter hidden round the back of the hospital mortuary and used the stink of the corpses to keep the Dutch away. Even in death the patriots fought on over the air for the cause. But it took a week before some of the outer islands and the British Parliament knew of the Proclamation. The Dutch can use such delays against us. Moreover, the British and the Indians are in our city and we must divide them, weaken them, get them out. Many of them do not want to be here at all. The Indians are throwing the British out of India and everyone is tired and wants to go home. You speak their language. You will know what to say.'

'Bung. All my life I have been the friend of oppressed peoples. It would be an honour. The British cannot win. They are like men trying to sweep up leaves in a gale.'

'I like that. I will use it. The old men like Soekarno and Hatta say it is unreasonable for a mob like us to fight an organised army but the Japanese taught us that reason is a Western idea not an Asian one. More important is spirit. The Japanese had it and now we have it too.' He pushed something across the table. 'You had better wear this. It may save your life.' It was another armband, this time red and white and bearing the words, '*Merdeka atau mati*', 'Liberty or death'. As employment contracts go, it left a lot to be desired. 'It's from the same factory that used to make armbands for the Japanese. As we speak, we are moving against them and taking over their installations and stores. By the end of the day, we will have tanks!' His bright, young face glows with excitement. There it is again. Every growing boy wants to have his own tank. 'You must excuse me. I have to go and see Moestopo.' His pained face is eloquent. Moestopo is the former dentist now in charge of the Japanese-trained regular forces. Moestopo was said to like the idea of inflicting pain, a professional hazard perhaps. He teaches the militias to dip the tips of their spears into horse dung to create infected wounds and to eat cats so they can see at night – a visionary of sorts then. As well as pimps and whores and schoolboys, cats too can be heroes of the revolution and the uneaten parts receive honourable burial. Why shouldn't I join them? What else had I to do?

I move into the Oranje hotel and keep my ears open, cat-like. At the very least I steal copies of foreign or divisional newspapers and scan them for information to be used on the air.

The strange sort of truce that was brokered between the British and the local Pemuda after the flag incident – by no less than Soekarno and Hatta themselves – is still just about holding but every night is punctuated by gunshots and the reverberation of distant explosions. By agreement, the Japanese guard has been replaced by a tense Indonesian one. He has been tipped off. When I walk past he winks in a most obvious manner that the whites see – fortunately – as the sort of impertinent, sexual harassment they are protecting their own women from.

At the bar is mostly a mix of Dutch and Americans, the former from the camps, the latter from various newspapers – the Antara news agency is just across the street and newsmen are lazy but ever-thirsty creatures. That is almost certainly why the flag incident was blown up into an iconic event to mark the start of the fighting. If they'd had to walk to the end of the street to see it, it would have gone unnoticed. With the first I flaunt my Japanese scars and with the second my American accent. They relax around me and flap their mouths loosely over Skat and poker.

The Dutch rage against the British for not attacking the rebels so they can go back to their whitewashed lives of polite lawns and neatly trimmed servants but if you listen carefully it is clear that even those that have survived as married couples know there is no going back. Relationships have shrivelled and died, feelings become numbed by all that has happened under the Japanese. Everywhere life has become a temporary expedient, stripped of all sense of permanence, and everyone is just getting by. One evening, an American chain-smoker with an economics degree drops the information that the amount they give the Dutch in Marshal Aid exactly balances what they are spending to recoup their colonies. The land of the free is paying to hold the East in subjection. The fact sticks in my mind. I file it away. That will come in use much later.

'It is nothing but a few hotheads,' one Harlem banker maintains cigar-puffing. 'The Javanese are like children, easily led astray by a few bad apples. But they soon smarten up their ideas when the headmaster cracks his cane.'

Van Mook, the Dutch governor had said much the same thing. In fact, he said all sorts of dumb things about how the Indonesians were 'too nice' to fight him. And when he stumbled off the boat from Australia at Batavia – sorry Jakarta now – without his glasses, he saw the crowds holding up banners and was touched by such a warm welcome. 'What do they say?' he asked tearfully.

'Death to Van Mook, Your Excellency,' came the answer.

That night at a rally at the Simpang Club I see these 'few hotheads'. I slip away from the Oranje and rendezvous with Uki and Lukman who drive me there. The gardens are lit up with a thousand blazing, resin torches. The Japanese blackout is ignored. The speech will be carried echoing out into the streets on the loudspeakers they set up through the city to spread their own propaganda. The torchlights gleam on a vast, bobbing sea of shiny brown skin, white teeth, flashing eyes, excitement radiates out from their faces, happiness. How many thousands more tailing away into the darkness? I cannot tell. Perhaps it is the whole of Indonesia here this night feeling their essential humanity restored. Uki and Lukman sandwich me on either side as we ease into that hot, human maelstrom and I feel myself gripped by its tides and eddies and sucked into the swaying rhythm of that great, primeval force, a part of it, its blood my blood, its breath my own and I surrender to it as it boils through my lungs and veins. 'Merdeka! Merdeka!' Merdeka is not a philosophy or a set of arguments, it is a dizzying drug, a visceral mutation as irreversible

73

as the caterpillar becoming a butterfly and I feel my own bones abruptly dissolve, reconsolidate and click into new, immutable forms designed for a different purpose in a different world. There can be no going back now – for Indonesia or for me.

Bung Tomo is in fine form. He stands high on an improvised stage behind the big, square box of the microphone waving his wiry fist into the night sky. The British have dropped leaflets demanding that the Pemuda lay down their arms and surrender, thus abrogating the agreement they have just made. The city is erupting in rage. His fury rolls out in fine, thundering phrases. 'As long as the wild bull buffaloes of Indonesia have red blood capable of making a scrap of red and white cloth, that long shall we refuse to surrender to anyone.' The wild bulls around us roar and paw at their native soil, full of red blood. The ground shakes with their stamping feet and their bellowing throats. '*Merdeka! Merdeka!*'

Chapter Six

You remember that iconic black and white photo of Bung Tomo? Everyone knows it. The one where he looks like one of those paintings from the French Revolution? He's in uniform, one hand raised to the heavens, the famous thin moustache and flying hair, mouth crying out to the world against injustice. It's the picture of a man so charismatic he could have started his own mass movement in an empty room. He's shot from below and over him is a visually interesting umbrella swirling in what you know must be red and white raspberry ripple and the eyes are blazing into the crowd. Everyone assumes it was taken on November 9th when he made that stirring speech about the wild bulls. Actually, it was taken much later when we were in a little mountain town and by me. For months, there would be no time for speeches or photographs after that last night. Out of the blue, under the red and the white, the issues had suddenly become black and white and we were fighting for our lives.

Matters first came to a head on the 30th October. In the finest traditions of the British army it was a five-star, gold-braided, world-class cock-up. In fact it was a combination of more cock-ups than a chicken farmer sees in a year down on the farm.

At the Oranje hotel, I was booked in under the name of Miss Manxi, an homage to my Isle of Man origins – well – alleged origins. The hotel had had its ups and downs. First the Pemuda had come and dragged everyone away for interrogation and stripped it bare, then the Dutch had turned up with a truck and it had been freshly furnished with goods taken from some magical, mystical Japanese Ali Baba warehouse rumoured to exist down by the docks. Most of the stuff must have been looted by them from the houses of rich Chinese – all dragons and silk tassels – so that the whole place looked like a tart's parlour in flickering candle- and lamplight. A snazzy, walnut radio set with gold knobs stood on the bar, leaking Western music that sounded like an orchestrated stiff upper lip. I was drinking with a Dutch liaison officer, Wim, who was getting a little too friendly. He was young, blond, probably missed his mother and his pink, pig-faced girlfriend back in Leiden. I peeled his hand from my arm like a slug off a leaf.

'You're drunk.'

''Course I'm bloody drunk, Manxi. What else is there to do in bloody Surabaya? Listen to the bloody wireless?' He nodded at the bar-top god.

I laughed. 'It depends what station you listen to.' It was silly of me but I couldn't resist it.

He scowled into his glass of beer as into a crystal ball. 'I have to spend half my day reading reports on that damned Rebel Radio. It's stirring up the young bloods, whipping them up to god knows what atrocities. Thank God those collaborators Soekarno and The Mad Hatta went on the government station and tried to calm them down but they won't listen to them. It's that extremist Bung Tomo they heed.' The old men in Jakarta still trying to keep their hands clean, sitting on the fence, helping the Dutch to build yet more fences. For Wim all Indonesians were either Jap collaborators or extremists – both excluded as fit partners in any negotiation. 'Yesterday, one of Tomo's gangs threw hand grenades into a convoy of trucks transporting starving women and children to a feeding station. The Mahrattas, the Indians, fought to defend them till their last bullet but it was a mob of hundreds of crazed people shouting for blood, fighting their way over the bodies with knives and guns and spears to get at them. One of them was swinging a swordfish jaw over his head as a weapon for Christ's sake! And they've started chopping up the Indians they take prisoner – alive. We found a bunch of them, roped together with British troops, floating in the river with their eyes gouged out and their dicks chopped off. And I won't tell you what they did to the survivors of a forced landing of one of our planes out in the countryside.'

'Is it fair to blame the radio for that?' I stirred a little more Scots into my accent, twanged an American vowel or two. You could never be too careful. There would be no more sloppy, red flags from me.

He gulped beer, belched, wiped his mouth on the back of a hand and shook his head wearily. 'You haven't read the transcripts. And they've got this new woman – Surabaya Sue they call her – who pours out the most poisonous filth in English. We've put a price on her head.' He looked at me with incredulous, drink-bleared eyes. For a moment I thought the penny had dropped. But no. He went back to his beer and looked vacantly through the window.

Surabaya Sue! I had my own call sign just like Tokyo Rose. I would use it on air tonight. I had a broadcast in two hours.

'How much?'

'What?'

'The price on her head. How much?'

'Ten thousand guilders.'

It was a fortune! I thought what I could do with it and drifted off into daydreams of cashing myself in. But then, of course, I would be dead.

'You know why this revolution will fail?'

I sighed, called back to dull reality – very dull reality. 'Please enlighten me Wim dear.'

'Well it's because – in every successful anti-colonial rebellion there's ever been, the occupiers always assume the educated and Westernised locals will support them because they have more in common with them than with the unwashed natives. But they never do. You see, they're the new elite, the ones with most to gain from independence so they can get their own hands in the till. Look at America. The revolution was all about a bunch of greedy, local lawyers not wanting to pay their share of taxes and getting a bigger cut of the graft. The extremists have made a fatal mistake by alienating just those people, the Chinese, the Eurasians, the mulattos, the – what do they call them? – *blasteran*. By attacking them and killing them in their thousands they've made sure they're a hundred percent with us. We can't lose. We've got the elite. We've got all the brains.' He drank contentedly. 'Another thing. We're not supposed to bring in Dutch troops but I've got a little plan.' He tapped the side of his nose squiffily.

'Do tell, darling.' I put his hand back on my arm. It was like lifting a dead dog.

'What I'm gonna do, see, is bring in Dutch troops, black them up like Indians and pass them off under the noses of the rebels as Mahrattas. They won't even know we're here till it's too late.'

'Isn't that a bit daft? Why not just slip them into British uniforms? Wouldn't that be easier? Isn't that what you are, Dutch in a British uniform?'

He paused, mouth agape, eyes swimming, blinking. 'Bloody hell, you're right! I hadn't thought of that.' One of the elite with brains – he swivelled and blinked out through the window, rubbing his eyes and squinting. 'Snow?' he said suddenly, rising unsteadily to his feet, pointing out into darkness in trembling disbelief. 'What the hell? It's snow.' He turned to the crowd. 'Snow in Surabaya! It's a miracle! It's an omen of our restoration!'

It was impossible yet true. Great, white flakes were twirling down past the glass into the tropical garden, pale ghosts in the weak light. Out he rushed, the rest of us following to see this wonder. We looked up into the night sky, the whole, surrounding city velvety dark from the lack of reliable electricity but the hills aglow with a sliver of moon. The stars were that odd golden colour they sometimes have in Java but now we were smacked in the face by – not snow – but another drop of onion-skin leaflets, more like lavatory paper than snow, toppling down from on high, out of the heavens, riding the breaths of wind from the sea. Moonlight and snow was a romantic combination, moonlight and toilet paper lacked the same appeal. From overhead came the drone of a circling aircraft. Wim crouched to pick up a leaflet and nearly toppled drunkenly onto his front. He wheezed back up on his knees and held it to the lamplight leaking out through the window, struggling to read the print. A great grin lit up his flushed face.

'It's a final ultimatum from the Brits. They've given the rebels 48 hours to disarm and surrender or they will attack. No more buggering about. They're finally going to fight the natives for us!' He broke into a little dance of joy, lumbered around in an elephantine jig. The other Dutch hugged each other and laughed beguiled – no doubt – by those visions of houses and estates restored and pattering, newly deferential servants. This was a journalistic scoop falling right into my lap so I bent and scooped and sidled off, unobserved, into darkness clutching a sheet, Indonesian one side, English the other. There at the end of the road a rickshaw was waiting, pulled up in the shadows under a mango tree, the driver lolling in the seat with his feet up on the handlebars, his presence betrayed only by the glowworm circle of his cigarette.

'*Merdeka atau mati*,' I murmur.

There is a line of white teeth. '*Merdeka atau mati*. Climb in sister.' Uki flings aside the cigarette, clambers into the saddle and leans down on the pedals and we whisper away towards Rebel Radio. He is dressed as a rickshaw driver in old shorts and a torn vest and has very fine thighs filmed with sweat. My appreciation is purely aesthetic, not sexual. An artist learns to grab such glimpses of beauty in an ugly world.

It seems that, while local commanders had negotiated a perfectly satisfactory ceasefire with the Indonesian forces to allow the evacuation of prisoners of war, the brass in India and Jakarta had arranged for more leaflets to be dropped demanding their immediate surrender and didn't think to tell anyone in Surabaya. This looked like treachery to Bung Tomo and the result was renewed attacks on the Indian troops stationed at various strategic but isolated points around the city. Posts were overrun. People were butchered in the streets. The British commander, Brigadier Mallaby, drove to the International Building which was one such hotspot and tried to stop the fighting as had been negotiated with Soekarno and Hatta, bringing news of the latest ceasefire agreement. There are various accounts of what happened next. I know now that everyone lies in official reports. But I was there the next day with Uki and Lukman getting copy to pass on to the international press. I *saw*.

* * *

It was a hot day by the Red Bridge and everyone was trigger-happy. The Indians were scared. The Indonesians were furious. There had been a lot of potshotting about and the fronts of the building were all pockmarked with bullets but now things had settled down with the Indonesians all busy eating rice behind their sandbags and the Indians drinking tea inside the office block behind theirs. The sun on the square in front of the Dutch buildings hit you like a flatiron and to be caught on its exposed emptiness was certain death. Mallaby drove up with some local liaison people, a little Union Jack fluttering on the bonnet of the car, and parked right under a sign that said, 'Once and for ever the Indonesian Republic'. I don't know why he did that. Drivers are taught to always park in the shade and maybe that was it. Not a great slogan but it was an even worse choice of parking spot. It meant that every time someone looked at Mallaby, they saw the sign, saw his English flag and got all riled up again. His car was immediately surrounded by a mob, pushing and shoving, shouting and waving banners and he didn't help by poking at people with that silly, little stick English officers carry. I don't think he was in any danger but perhaps the Indians couldn't see that because of the sign being in the way. Anyway, the opening shot didn't come from either them or the Indonesians. It came from one of the other buildings. A white man was skulking along one of the upper balconies, taking advantage of the height to get a free line of fire. I quite clearly saw him rise on one knee and shoot at the Pemuda forces, bringing down a youth at the front then swivel and fire at the Indians, toppling a trooper behind a machine gun before throwing himself down behind the balustrade. He must be one of the Dutch vigilantes, shooting at both sides, as they often did, hoping to get something going. Well it worked. The Indians panicked and fired – some say into the air but I saw men falling and screaming, a young boy shot through the leg, blood pumping like a geyser. I will never forget the look of sheer terror on his face, astonished at the sudden revelation of his own mortality. And then all hell broke loose.

Lukman grabbed me and dragged me behind a car, bullets pinging over our heads and glass cascading down from the shot-up windows. Uki was face down in the dust but – with relief – I saw him move and make a successful dash for a pile of sandbags at the edge of the river as someone behind us opened up with a heavy machine gun and soon bits of the International Bank Building – a nice, modern piece of cast concrete – were flying in all directions. We made our way to join Uki in the long grass and, as the firing died down again, all settled in for a long wait, Lukman pulling his hat down over his eyes and taking a nap with creditable aplomb. Then, as in a dream, a young schoolboy, carrying a rifle and wearing some fantastical outfit of red and white and with a headband of silver lamé ripped from some lady's best frock, walked out from cover and slowly swaggered up to the British car – bullets from the Indians flying around him but he immune. This did not surprise the Javanese in the least. Everyone knows there are people who have magic, *ilmu kedotan*, that makes them bulletproof and that they were doing a good trade in the city. A great cry of 'Wah!' went up in admiration of him. The slim boy gripped the doorframe and swung light-footed in the window of the car as you might to have a cheery conversation with a neighbour then suddenly stepped back and raised his rifle one-handed, let off a few casual shots and turned balletically on one heel to walk away, holding the gun high in the air. A hand appeared at the window, groped blindly and tossed a grenade out of the car towards him and there came a great explosion that humped the whole vehicle off the ground and – as the smoke cleared – flames licked out at the rear with a great Whoosh! The back door towards us opened with a screech of metal, falling off its hinges as in a circus act for clowns and two British soldiers stumbled out, coughing and crawling with comically smoke-blackened faces. Uki raised his rifle to fire and took long, careful aim but I pushed down the barrel, leaving the squint still on his surprised face. The men scrambled down the riverbank and waded out into the corpse-strewn river, sweat running down their foreheads and blank terror in their eyes. Soon they were gone, doubtless incredulous to be still alive.

'No, Uki,' I said. 'Let them go. Otherwise they will say it was a cowardly ambush. Information is everything in a fight like this. Let the truth be known.'

* * *

'It was an ambush,' whined Wim, my Dutch 'friend'. 'A bloody cowardly ambush. You know they chopped the head off poor Mallaby's corpse? The Brits keep trying to spread oil over troubled waters and the rebels just keep setting fire to it. They're just a bunch of gangsters using the revolution as an excuse to go round killing and robbing people. Anyway, the whole Republic thing was just an invention of the Japanese to cause trouble because they lost the war. Sour *sake*. And the Brits have always envied us our Indies possessions, which is why they do nothing. They try to keep things from us but all their secretaries are good Dutch girls so we get to know everything the bastards are up to. Not English are you?

'American.'

'There you are then.' He signalled the Oranje barman for a refill. 'There's a hundred thousand troublemakers flooded into the city from all over the island just in the past two weeks. Kids,

Muslim lunatics. I've read the reports. The imams have declared it a holy war, all good Muslims must kill and maim and so on. They knew damned well Mallaby's team were unarmed, insisted on it, except for allowing them a grenade each.'

'Why a grenade each? Doesn't that sound a bit odd to you for a mission to announce a ceasefire?'

He stared at me blankly across the table, put his glass down and grabbed as it toppled on the edge, proud with raised, carved dragons. Chinese furniture is made for intimidation not comfort or convenience. 'What? Well that's hardly the point now is it? Do you know I passed by the Red Bridge with a patrol today. Mallaby's car's still there all burnt out but, would you believe it, the thieving buggers have already stripped it bare – wheels, tyres, bulbs from the headlights – all gone. They'd nick anything round here.' He sat back in the uncomfy chair nicked from the Japanese warehouse that had nicked it from a Chinese merchant's house in a whole country the Dutch had nicked and lit another cigarette. 'The good news is that the British are coming. It seems that for once they actually meant what they said in that leaflet drop. Had it from my friend Derek today. Do you know Derek? Ripping chap. Artistic, like you. Tried to show me his etchings but they were wasted on me, I'm afraid ...'

I had met him all right, at the Oranje Hotel, a failed actor, who had told me the dunderhead, British commander in Jakarta was drunk all the time and his chief interest was in staying as close to the bar in the Officers' Mess as possible, only being enticed away by the stream of women he had to procure for him as his ADC. Derek was a sweet-faced man with what I thought a typical Javanese Eurasian face – a cute little nose and that unmistakable, thick, black, Indo hair that fell over one eye in a delicious cow-lick. And a fellow artist to boot. His name was Derek but I heard that he afterwards changed it to Dirk – Dirk Bogarde. It was the first time a man had invited me to his room to see his etchings and actually shown me etchings. They were curiously old-maidish sketches of quaint little buildings with the odd local with a 'good face'. And some constipated-looking male nudes.

'... Anyway, the Brits've finally decided to do the right thing. Another week and they'll have 25,000 troops, naval vessels and the air force – all on their way from Singapore. Those rebel bastards will get what's coming to them. Boy will they be surprised.' He smiled and blew smoke in satisfaction, seeing them going down like ninepins in his mind. 'Then we'll put the whole so-called government on trial as collaborators with the Japanese and shoot the lot of them.'

'Really?' I said, putting my hand on his arm like Mae West and a 'my hero' gleam in my eyes. 'How wonderful, Wim darling. Do tell me more.'

* * *

The heavy, naval bombardment from the offshore fleet began at dawn and, as the guns boomed and shook the city like an earthquake, the British bombers came in over an inappropriate rising sun – Mosquitoes and Thunderbolts – raining down not leaflets this time but death and destruction south of the river. They say some 500 bombs whistled down onto undefended Surabaya and ripped it apart in flowers of flame. Then tanks and armoured cars lumbered off the ships and snarled down the wide Dutch avenues from the docks and into the narrow maze that was the native town. Everyone grabbed the children and the old ladies and poured out into the streets that were immediately clogged with screaming, panicking people, falling on each other and trampling everything underfoot except the urge for self-preservation. This was the Japanese invasion all over again and, now the Japs had surrendered, no one had imagined to go through it a second time. The British had expected to take the Indonesian forces by surprise and cut them off in large numbers but it was as if they somehow knew all about the Allies' plans and kept open the routes for a staged retreat into the hills. Battle-hardened British troops followed in the shelter of the advancing Shermans and then it was hand-to-hand fighting – dirty, messy and vicious – as they cleared the city street-by-street and house-by-house at bayonet point. Both sides had scores to settle. The Indonesians fired back with captured Japanese artillery but no one had shown them how to set the fuses on the shells first and they just bounced off. The Brits joked that their orders must be 'Ready, Fire, Aim.' Ironically, Moestopo, the notional Indonesian commander, had gone off to Gresik in a huff because the old men in Jakarta wouldn't let him fight the British and stopped him every time he tried. Now such a fight would change from being an unauthorised ceasefire violation to an act of national heroism. The British had Dunkirk as their own heroic defeat. We would have Surabaya. After such an effusion of blood there could be no turning back and every death fertilised the blooms of freedom. That's from one of my broadcasts by the way. Rather fine I thought.

It took three weeks for the British to drive the rebels and most of the starving, civilian population from the city. Out at the cement factory, fuelled by an unbroken stream not of ADC-procured women but of warm, weak tea, we gave it back to them hot and strong over the airwaves. The tea was brought by the same little, old lady who had brought the biscuits after my first broadcast. No one knew who she was or where she got the tea from.

'Hundreds upon hundreds were killed. Streets ran with blood, women and children lay dead in the gutters. *Kampongs* were in flames, and the people fled in panic to the relative safety of the rice fields. But the Indonesians did not surrender.' It was getting a little hard to find anything fresh to say but that, I suppose, is the nature of war. It seldom pleases by its sheer novelty.

The boys, Uki, Lukman and Reza, were fretting at being assigned to guard the radio station instead of flinging themselves, outgunned, on the Indians in some pointless act of sacrificial courage. This was seen as all my fault of course. Occasionally they would fire in frustration at aircraft overhead, far out of range but attracting their unwelcome attention, or chase away refugees desperate to get any sort of roof over their heads, Mostly, they just sat slumped against a wall and gazed glumly at the pall of smoke rising in the distance as if watching their own youth blowing away and listened to the dull crump of artillery and the rattle of machine guns that made such an evocative background to my own broadcasts. They dreamed of bigger weapons and to compensate for the lack of them, began to draw them intricately on the walls in an act of military masturbation, like the boys the Japanese allowed to parade around with solid wooden rifles on their shoulders during their own occupation. It struck me how very much better we had got at killing people during the few years of the war with all sorts of new tricks. What was needed was anti-aircraft guns, anti-tank weapons, mines. What they sent us was a writer. It is sometimes hard not to suspect the military of having a wicked sense of humour.

He wandered in after about a week, a thin, dark man of about twenty holding a notepad, dressed in an immaculate shirt and with shorts whose creases were sharp enough to hone the pencils in his top pocket. The whites of his eyes were beautifully clear, unlike our own, yellow from fever and dirt. He said his name was Idrus from the new revolutionary government office of literature and his accent said he was a Minang from Sumatra. He had a clear and polished way of speaking – an intellectual – and he spoke Javanese in the polite and elaborately embroidered *kromo*, form that the revolution had almost outlawed as hostile to its egalitarian spirit – as well as very good English. The boys were intrigued, never having seen anyone quite like this before and gathered round to peer at him.

'You are young like us,' they sneered. 'Not old like sister K'tut. Why do you not pick up a gun and fight?' Reza waved his rifle in demonstration. 'You use a lot of Dutch words. Are you a friend of the Dutch?'

The writer looked around at the snug and peaceful installation we had created beside the crazed concrete wall, the colourful awning set up against the sun, the cushions to rest on, the mugs of tea brought by the shuffling old lady, the card game abandoned on the table in boredom and said mildly, 'We all do what we can with what we have been given by God. I fight with words.'

'We too fight with words,' insisted Lukman, chest-beating and shrugging his rifle over one shoulder. 'We have written "*Merdeka atau mati*" on at least a thousand walls.'

Idrus smiled wanly. 'I congratulate you, brother. You might say then that all our writers struggle to emulate your own achievement.'

Lukman glowed and swaggered away to ask what 'emulate' meant but froze when he heard, over his shoulder, 'Of course. We should remember that you did not actually make up those words. The alliteration, the vocalic ending, the balance on either side of 'atau', all suggest a man who had a way with words and a piece of paper to hand. He might even have had to put away his rifle for a minute or two to write them down.'

Lukman turned back with a loud sigh, hands dangling loose by his sides like a gunfighter. He pushed out his chin. 'We have been warned to look out for spies and to shoot them on sight. How do we know you are not a spy? To me you look like a spy.'

'You are a journalist, you say?' I intervened, hastily, pulling Idrus into the shelter and gesturing towards a cushion. He remained standing as the boys stared in coldly from outside. I remembered that Lukman liked to have nice, clear enemies. We were all a little paranoid.

'No, not really. I work as an editor in Bata– ... Jakarta. I also write. It seemed to me that this fight would be something worth writing about, swordplay turned into wordplay.' Offensively good English then.

'I imagine you will want to go to the front right away,' I urged, offering a cigarette then turning him round and pointing. 'You will want first-hand experience, to see the facts.'

He smiled again as he waved out the flame of the match and inhaled in a smooth, aristocratic gesture and turned back. 'Maybe that would be just the pornography of violence. The facts are not the same as the truth, sister. The truth lies beyond the mere facts and all good fiction is a lie that tells the truth. Perhaps there is more truth to be found here than at the front. But then the whole world lives by stories so perhaps even truth is not enough. In the final analysis, it is only the stories we tell ourselves that keep us going. Politics is always ultimately about either hope or fear. We do hope. The Dutch do fear. That is why we shall win.'

'But you would not want people to say that you had never really been there, that you did not know.'

The old woman shuffled in with tea, yet more tea. Idrus thanked her politely and settled back on a cushion. The setting sun was drawn into the cracks in the wall above his head, transforming them into bloody arteries. 'They will say that anyway. Your young friends seem very eager for a fight – any fight. It is always easier to know what you are fighting *against* rather than what you are fighting *for*.'

'When you are fighting an army of Indians, it is hard not to behave like cowboys.'

His face lit up. 'That's good! Do you mind if I use that? Perhaps that's the sort of truth I have been looking for. After all, even a true story is still just a story. It needs shape. Point. A dominant image. Cowboys and Indians.' He leaned forward and grasped my hand softly between his two. 'Thank you, sister.'

Chapter Seven

The order to retreat to Malang came three days later. The boys returned from a briefing in town with the news and an American jeep, roaring into the yard in a cloud of dust with great grins on their faces. It was not quite a tank, but still ...

'Where did you get it?'

Uki blushed. 'Oh, umm. We found it. It didn't seem to belong to anyone. So ...' He shrugged. 'We've got petrol for it,' he pleaded. It was the way a little boy would justify bringing home a stray puppy that he desperately wanted to keep.

It was the work of minutes to pack up the few things we owned and a mere half hour more for the boys to decorate the jeep with red and white flags and ribbons to their satisfaction. The 'banzai-box' would follow at its own speed. Black rain clouds were fermenting overhead and unleashed themselves as we set off. I shall never forget that drive in the rain. The road was clogged with terrified civilians, bullock carts of wounded, rickshaws, grinding army trucks, heaving over the potholes. There were little groups of deserting Japanese and mutinous Indian troops with '*Merdeka atau mati*' armbands. Occasionally, enemy planes would be heard circling overhead, triggering a new panic and a stampede for trees and ditches. A near-naked woman ran by, screaming and clutching a baby covered with blood. And it went on and on for mile after weary mile with the rain licking at the refugees' trembling legs and shoulders and endless honking to get them out of our path. We were soon all soaked, beyond caring, hungry, exhausted. And the eyes of those people on foot, tramping through the mud, seared through my heart like daggers – envious but uncomplaining, registering my white skin and my privileged seat in a jeep as a sign that nothing had changed. Yet everything had changed. I wanted to shout it out against the cynical gaze of the old women and the hurt, reproachful eyes of the sobbing children. And then another plane would come overhead and people would start running again, wild-eyed, banging against the jeep, nearly falling under its wheels in their terror, hearing the whistling bombs once more in their heads. It's not true that you never hear the bomb that kills you. I've seen it happen.

And then we began the long climb from the hot, coastal plains up into the hills and mountains, volcanoes belching smoke on all sides as if eager to join in the destruction. The air cooled and thinned around us – becoming what Ma would call *dreich* – and we started to shiver in mist as we crawled through abandoned tea plantations, the neglected bushes already sprouting into lovely but unproductive trees, the gullies full of possessions that the fleeing had simply jettisoned in despair as impossible to carry any further. And now the rain had stopped, you could see the tears on the people's faces. Going downhill is at least as onerous as going up as all the weight has to be constantly braked by the legs and by the time Malang came into view, laid out before us, we had gathered up half a dozen more lost souls in various stages of physical and mental collapse, arranged on the edges and the bonnet of the jeep, so the driver could barely see the road ahead. One man was clutching two cheap Balinese carvings, one under each arm, the standard tourist rubbish, depicting a man in a headcloth and a woman in a dance headdress. What did they mean to him? Home? A memory of love? He hung on to them as if they meant life itself and shook and shook and shook.

Malang had become one great encampment of tents and strings of washing, hiding under a layer of swirling woodsmoke. Flocks of wild children fluttered amongst the ruins like swallows, briefly coalescing into packs that would swirl and swarm with sudden purpose. We drove through the centre, dropping off our passengers to wander in lost confusion and out the other side into one of the neat clutches of Dutch villas that crawled up the hillside. A white bungalow with pointed gables, its door smashed down and contents looted, suited us best. One of the rooms had been set up as a strongroom with a great steel door that had resisted amateur attempts to gain entry. Reza had at it more professionally with a will and a sticky tank bomb in the hope of treasure. The blast was misjudged and brought down part of the kitchen wall but what he found was much better than treasure, sacks of rice and an incongruous, slightly singed fur coat that they insisted I wear at night against the mountain chill, turning me into a moth-eaten bear. All quite unnecessary, I thought. In the climate of revolutionary Malang, many are cold but few are frozen. The garden was thickly planted with dense mango trees that would help to hide our radio mast. In case of circling Mustang spotter aircraft we could quickly down-scope like a U-boat captain in a crash-dive. It took the technical crew a day to reach us but two more days to find us in all the chaos, then Rebel Radio went back on the air. 'Indonesia – once free, forever free.'

* * *

Broadcasting can be like shouting down a well and receiving no answering echo. Yet two incidents showed the value of our work. Given that we dared have no fixed abode, we scarcely expected fan mail. But one day, despite the capricious functioning of the mail service, Uki rushed in with an envelope with the name 'Surabaya Sue' on it. It was no ordinary envelope, thick and creamy and full of military self-confidence. In the top, left corner, it bore the name of the Republic of Indonesia in simple classic script, final concrete proof of the existence of that mystical object of our desire. At that stage we had not yet got around to having overwrought Garuda birds plastered over everything official. The boys gathered round.

'Open it K'tut. It must be from Gnub Onrak.'

'Who?'

Reza grimaced. 'Bung Karno. That is what he is called here in *boso walikan*. All the Pemuda use it here in Gnalam. You turn words back to front. It confuses spies.'

'Well, it confuses me too, so stop it. Perhaps we should leave it until this evening when I can read it in private,' I teased, laying it, unopened, in my lap like a ticking time-bomb. 'It is addressed to me. It might be something personal – a marriage proposal for instance. Is General Soedirman married?'

'Open it! Please!'

'... or perhaps it is a command for me to leave Indonesia. My travel documents are a little out of order, you know.'

'Please.'

'... or it could be a tax demand. Can they send you a tax demand when you don't get a salary?'

'Sister K'tut, pleeeease!'

I eased open the flap gently. Dutch envelope glue had never worked very well in the steamy tropics and, anyway, it seemed a crime to tear it in a world where so few things were crisp and new and unsullied. They all stared breathless and unblinking at the folded sheet of plump paper inside that I teased out to spring back into shape. I had seen that spellbound expression before. It was like the men in the speakeasies back in America when the bump and grind dancer was finally getting down to shaking the real nitty gritty right in their faces.

I glanced at the signature. 'It's not from Bung Karno.' They groaned in disappointment. Reza slapped his thigh and turned away. Little Uki pouted. 'It's from General Namridoes.' I watched, grinning, as they rolled it around backwards in their heads. Soedirman, the new commander-in-chief! Their mouths gaped.

'Whaaat?' They had all perked up again. 'What does he say? Is there anything about us?'

'Dear Miss Surabaya, I am writing to thank you and the team of Rebel Radio for your fine work during the Battle of Surabaya that shares its name with you ...' – It was the first time we had heard the expression. We had become part of history. The Battle of Surabaya. '... and your services to the Indonesian people. I would wish you to know that your work has not gone without good effects. Although some 15,000 of our people were lost in the fight against the aggressors and only 600 Allied troops, more than 700 Mahrattas deserted, many citing your broadcasts as the reason. In addition, a contingent of Scottish gunners have come over to our side and are now working as artillery trainers in the Siliwangi Division. Please use this information in your future broadcasts. We wish you every, continuing success.' I scanned quickly. The rest was all verbiage, 'our victory certain', 'our cause just', 'given our people a new sense of purpose and self-respect', '*Merdeka*!' – in fact the sort of stuff I churned out myself by the yard. 'Right, boys,' I said. 'Too long have we lived like mice. This evening we do a special broadcast – one of victory – the victory of the Battle of Surabaya.'

That night, we walked back from the studio box in darkness, mango leaves rustling under our feet, still pumped high with excitement. The boys wanted to go off and look for girls in the town, feeling their oats and the urge to sow them widely. There were plenty of girls around nowadays, selling the only thing they had to sell and, of course, the boys – who had no money – would try to replace cash with charm. They had plenty of that. The girls loved their long, patriotic hair and tight uniforms. Young blood called out to young blood and male muscle under stretched fabric has a mute appeal all of its own. Some boys claimed to have magical, warrior powers so the girls wouldn't get pregnant. Occasionally, girls would come to me from the town, as the repository of all western scientific knowledge, and ask me what was the most effective form of contraception. In our circumstances what could I say? 'A sour face,' was the best I could offer them. It was just life reasserting itself and no one could think any the worse of either side.

'You should come too, sister,' giggled Lukman. 'Perhaps it is time you had a man. Not one of us, of course, we are too young. But perhaps we could find you one of those Indian deserters, all black and hairy.' He shuddered and dropped his voice to a panting whisper. 'They are very beeeg,' he grinned and gestured with his hands two feet apart, popping his eyes naughtily as in a Balinese dance. 'But they smell bad.'

'Yes,' grinned dark, little Uki. 'But you know they say men are like fruit. The black ones are juicier. There is that Captain Rashid who has deserted from the Indians and is on the radio in Bandung. Perhaps you could get together and … broadcast something. They say he has a beautiful moustache like the handlebars of a bicycle.'

'A kind thought, Lukman, Uki, but I have taken a holy oath of chastity.' Everyone stopped, suddenly solemn. Javanese view such things seriously.

'What oath is that, sister?'

'I have sworn an oath not to sleep with Bung Tomo until

Indonesia is free. It is a great disappointment to him.' *Then* they laughed.

That exultant broadcast raised our stock to such a degree that, a few days later, I was kidnapped. Kidnapping was fashionable at the time. Hatta and Soekarno had been kidnapped by the Pemuda to force the Proclamation of Independence. The Prime Minister, Sjahrir, was kidnapped by a rival faction until they were made to let him go. The Dutch would kidnap the whole republican government and be made to give it back. But most people who were kidnapped did not come back – ever. The rivers were clogged with the bodies of kidnapped Ambonese killed by republicans, Christians killed by Muslims, Muslims killed by communists, rebels killed by Dutch and Chinese killed by just about everyone. Most trigger-happy were members of the colonial army, newly freed from the Japanese camps and sadly embittered. Up around Tegal, there were rumours of kidnappings and massacres of the aristocrats and government officials who had sent the people's sons away to be slave labour for the Japanese and almost certainly to a horrible death – having been encouraged by Bung Karno to do so. I was unbelievably lucky. I was kidnapped by people who were fans of a sort.

They turned up one morning in a jeep, dressed as three young men from one of the Pemuda groups. In those days there were so many splinter groups on both sides and everyone was playing alphabet soup what with the SEAC, NICA, RAPWI, PETA, BKR, TKR, PNI, PKI, PPKI, PPPKI and all the groups changing their names and merging and resplitting like Hollywood couples. The names, of course, had promptly spawned more demotic interpretations among the determinedly monoglot British soldiery in their world of *jankers* and *fizzers* – Screw Every Asian Cunt, Nutless Idle Crap Army, Rape All Pretty Women in Indonesia and so on – an outpouring of foul schoolboy wit. The point is you never quite knew who anyone really was. The British and Dutch had got some of their vehicles straight from the Americans and not bothered to paint out the stars so that many of the Pemuda actually believed they were at war with America. They had come, they said, to take me to Bung Tomo's headquarters for a meeting. And no one thought anything more of it. But when we got to the centre of town, they suddenly swerved off in another direction.

'What's this?' I asked. 'This isn't the way to Bung Tomo's HQ.'

'It's moved,' they grinned at each other evilly. 'Security.'

That kept me quiet for another few miles as we headed off into the hills and then I really began to smell a rat as the town fell away and even bamboo huts became scarce as the vegetation closed in from either side of the road until it brushed against the flanks of the jeep. Perhaps they thought I was Dutch and intended to do something about it. I slithered the *Merdeka atau mati* armband out of my pocket and slipped it on, reached forward and tapped the driver on the shoulder so they would all see it. There were two ways to go. I could use the hanky-waving skills I had taught young Eunice Pringle back in LA or stamp my foot like a *grande dame*. I decided the latter would make me look too Dutch so I turned on the waterworks. I flung myself at the young captor to my left and began to wail.

'Oh where are you taking me? I'm a poor helpless woman. So alooone.'

They were appalled and exchanged horrified looks. 'Please don't distress yourself, mother. We are taking you to Tretes, to the radio station there. We have no one who can broadcast for us in English and everybody wants to listen to you. You will be safer there. You have been kidnapped by admirers.'

'Mother?' I shrieked, deeply insulted, and clipped him sharply round the ear. 'Mother? How old do you think I am? At the very most I am "big sister" to you boys.'

They laughed. We were friends.

* * *

The radio station was a real guerrilla *kampung* up in the hills, a filthy tangle of shacks and camp fires and tough, little horses coming and going at all hours bearing food and ammunition. Java, at that time, was riddled with different factions with separate militias who were under no central control. Some were loyal to particular political parties. Some fought under the banner of Islam or Christianity or Communism or Socialism. Some were loyal only to their local leader. They were fighting to create a new world and no ideas were too crazy to command belief somewhere.

This one was led by a self-styled colonel – mid-fifties, body rapidly turning pear-shaped, mulish but with little, piggy eyes – red-rimmed like piss holes in the snow – and a worrying facial twitch. He had a fat lower lip that was permanently wet, like a great, slimy slug.

'*Merdeka*!' I shouted, always a good bet.

'*Bebas*!' he replied, finger-wagging and giggled. Ah! Now that wasn't a good sign. *Bebas* is 'liberated'. Only the communists answered like that, making a pedantic distinction between independence and liberation – implying the former was just the start of the latter, a bloody, social revolution to follow on the heels of the political one with social hierarchy and privilege put to the sword. Then he confirmed my assessment with the words, 'Welcome comrade. Have you heard the great news? The parasitic rajahs of East Sumatra have all been executed in the just wrath of the proletariat and their wealth liberated for the people! Come and eat.' He gestured at a table where rice, fish and other, half-forgotten pleasures were laid out, liberated no doubt from the parasitic, local farmers. I could see my broadcasts would be moving strongly to the left and the red and the white would be pure red from now on. For the moment, I accepted it. Life is too short for the making of puff pastry or worrying about those things that cannot be changed. At least the food was better here than the endless plain meals of gritty rice and raunchy chilli of the Pemuda. No wonder many more died of the shits than the shells but such food was the red and the white, the blood and the bone of Indonesia. All these fearless defenders of the proletariat looked sleek and well-fed and the colonel contemplated the men around his table smugly.

Before the revolution, Colonel Soejanto had lived mainly by plying his crowbar around the back windows of his neighbours' houses and his forces still got cash mostly by plundering the wealthy Chinese of his patch. The fact that his men now wore nice, matching, black uniforms was neither here nor there. They were clearly bad boys and he was probably both mad and very dangerous. I soon learned that if he was crossed to the slightest degree, petulance would flicker across his jowls and people would start running before the fragile dam of his rage burst. My first broadcast that night was adjudged insufficiently socialist in tone.

'So what are you going to do,' I asked, 'shoot me?'

For once, he was stunned. Then. 'Look at it this way, K'tut,' he whispered gently, hissing like a snake, 'unless you can learn to fit in, we shall take away your armband – maybe we could even paint you up in the Dutch colours – and dump you in the middle of republican territory. I don't think you'd last very long out there. It could be very nasty.' He giggled again. The sound made the hair stand up on the back of my neck.

The communists had always enjoyed using sticks more than carrots. So I learned to fit in. I made it a grim joke. The Americans and British became 'the imperialist forces of reaction'. The Dutch became 'the running dogs of the slavering, capitalist hyenas'. Their every action was prefaced with, 'In a last desperate effort to avoid the inevitable fate predicted for them by scientific Marxism ...' or 'In defiance of universal justice and the interests of the people ...' As a good ally of the Soviet Union, I raged against the fearful, old men who thought they could talk the Dutch into independence with endless conferences instead of bowing to 'the irresistible force of class struggle as revealed by Marxist-Leninist thought.' It was clear that by now the Brits just wanted a piece of paper – any piece of paper – to cover their modesty as they ran away from 'the ultimate dictatorship of the proletariat.' And Soekarno and Hatta became 'the guilty, elitist collaborators with the Japanese fascist, occupation regime, their hands stained with the blood of a million of our brothers and sisters'. By the stringing-together of such expressions, my broadcasts became almost content-free and the Colonel was absolutely delighted with them.

And then salvation finally came. One evening, I had wandered down the track away from the main studio to enjoy a cigarette and a little precious solitude. I found an occasional cigarette added welcome city flavour to the pure mountain air and in war everybody smokes, just as a way of proving to themselves that they are still alive. Suddenly, two figures stepped out of the mosquito-buzzing shadows.

'Don't be afraid, K'etut. It is only us.' Reza and little Uki! Their grins lit up the darkness. 'We've heard your broadcasts, comrade K'tut. We've been waiting for two days for you to come out. We've got the jeep hidden down the road. We've come to liberate you and take you home as booty.'

Home! The word brought tears to my eyes. I was shaking with a rush of repressed emotions. We all hugged, then I hitched up my sarong in a most unladylike fashion and started running for my life. Whatever people may say, smoking is good for your health.

The next day I went back on the air for Rebel Radio. In my captivity, I had fallen foul of all manner of minor infections and skin diseases. I had not realised how much we depended on Reza and his ground-up herbs and simples to stay healthy. The skin was flaking off my soles, leaving great, bleeding sores and the toes were turning black so that I was scarcely mobile and had to be virtually carried to the microphone. And yesterday's cross-country race had done my feet no good at all. But Reza prepared an ointment of ground seaslugs that stank like a week-old corpse, driving everyone else from the broadcasting booth and soon my toes were back on their feet. And then the silent, old lady from the Surabaya cement factory shuffled in with a cup of weak tea. Somehow she had found us like a homing pigeon and simply resumed doing what she did. We still had no idea who she was but the biscuits seemed to have disappeared as a casualty of war. Home! In any war a sense of belonging becomes even more precious.

A while later, the Red Colonel was one of thousands killed by the national army as they snuffed out the independent Indonesian Soviet Republic declared by communist rebels around Madiun. I wrote a piece for a leftie Australian newspaper about it, all about these 'snarling traitors to the glorious people's revolution'. Somehow I couldn't stop those old words and expressions from the past creeping back into it. Apparently the Americans picked it up and – mysteriously – liked it. President Soekarno was no longer a dangerous collaborator. Now he was a valiant anti-communist and a bulwark against the new foe.

* * *

The revolutionary struggle had already lasted too long for Bung Tomo. By now his vow to eschew barbers had turned him into a little fuzzball with so much hair and beard that he resembled nothing so much as the stern Old Testament prophets of the Wee Free Kirk that still lurked in the nooks of my memory from childhood and Sunday school. The Dutch had put a price on his head – rather more than on mine – and were said to have dedicated squads seeking to track him down and kill him. So, people said, he had numerous suicidally hairy lookalikes leading them a merry dance over all of east Java. Come to think of it, anyone could be lurking under all that smelly fluff. I wondered whether anyone had checked recently. Then I saw the blazing eyes and there could be no doubt it was still him. He was sitting in one corner – a little huffily I thought – at a big meeting of leaders of the revolutionary struggle in the fair city of Yogyakarta and he kept dragging his fingers through his lion's mane and checking his knees furtively for dislodged fleas. The government had moved there from Jakarta after an attempt by Dutch gunmen to assassinate Prime Minister Sjahrir. Oddly, the republicans left Sjahrir behind in Jakarta when they moved.

At the front were the dapper 'old men' that Bung Tomo so despised, Soekarno and Hatta, delivering a smooth and well-manicured account of the Indonesian struggle to the world's press. Bung Karno was, of course, not old at all, being in his early forties and devilishly handsome in his gleaming, white uniform and *peci* hat. The sudden sprouting of those little black hats to replace batik headcloths had been the first visible sign of the Republic coming into being. As a public relations exercise, it was important that Indonesia be seen as modern, progressive, forward-looking, which is why I had been summoned to Yogya and abandoned my sarong for a fancy frock and high heels and had my newly blonde hair all shooshed up and my bosom jacked up to Sumatra but Bung Tomo seemed to take our immaculate grooming as both a form of betrayal of the revolution and a personal affront and stonily ignored my discreet, little waves of the hand. Thus do people end up foolishly bickering more over symbols of things than the reality of the things themselves. Or perhaps he simply no longer recognised *me* in my new disguise as an international vamp. I had been summoned to the new republican capital when it moved and helped out in everything from writing Bung Karno's English speeches – like the present one – to acting as interpreter for the various ministers and broadcasting on the new Radio Free Indonesia.

We were in the *Merdeka* room of the Merdeka Hotel, very probably on *Merdeka* Street that led off *Merdeka* Square and holding copies of the *Merdeka* newspaper. The boys busy renaming Indonesia and purging it of Dutch hadn't really got into their stride yet and only death would lend enough granitic solidity to names like Soekarno, Hatta and Soedirman to make them available for topographical use all over the archipelago. They had spread crisply handsome, young officers around the place to show Indonesia had clean linen and good teeth but their old Japanese-style uniforms were a PR disaster with the Westerners, summoning up all sorts of unhelpful associations. I must have another word with Bung K. I had written his speech by pasting together bits of Abraham Lincoln and Thomas Paine because it was vital to stop all the communist jargon and give them something that appealed to the liberal democracies. And after the usual applause, it was my job to circulate, guide and deftly direct the journalists' assessments as the wasp-waisted waiters dispensed drink and smiles. Bung Tomo, I noted, had slipped away, taking his easily outraged modesty with him, like the priest who leaves before the wake really gets going and he becomes an embarrassment. Apparently he had made some injudicious remarks about the politicians who were talking to the Dutch, struggling to give away again the gains made by the Indonesian armed forces – or in Bung Tomo's own terms, 'The young men fight like wild bulls. The old men talk like castrated goats.' When the Japanese had decided to take back Bandung to meet the terms of their agreement with the Allies, Bung Tomo had sent the Bandung boys a crate of lipstick as a sneering comment on their lack of manliness. God knows how much makeup they got when the British moved in to replace the Japanese and the 'old men' urged them to co-operate to avoid bloodshed and simply evacuate the southern sector. They had replied by complying but setting fire to it first. Nasty yes, but Indonesians are practical people. I was sure that makeup hadn't been wasted and gifts from it were now making terrible inroads into the virtue of the Bandung ladies. I wondered how Lukman, Reza and Uki were getting on. I missed them like a mother hen her chicks.

I was dutifully lecturing some brittle bimbo from *The Washington Times* or the *Wichita Gazette* or some such rag on the parallels between the American and Indonesian struggles for liberty and she seemed to be taking to it like a hangman to rope and scribbling away happily. Out of the corner of my eye, I could see the bosses glad-handing their way round the room, taking care of the business interests with clasped hands and big smiles. Bung Karno was offering cigarettes, the odd whispered joke, the occasional declaration of sincere affection that went straight to the solar plexus. He was master of all that. Were they *Merdeka* brand cigarettes in those days or have I invented that? I cannot be expected to remember everything. The Republic was desperately, almost comically, short of money. Its entire gold reserves were kept in a shoe box under a bed upstairs and the booze at the party was from a huge Japanese cache unearthed by chance the previous month. Otherwise we would have been drinking water. The Japanese had smashed everything before they withdrew so we were living like barbarians building campfires in abandoned Roman villas. Even the glasses for the reception had been borrowed from local, Chinese restaurants. None of them matched.

'Say honey. Ain't you that guerrilla lady that lives out in the jungle with all those half-naked boys?' She fluttered fake lashes with fake modesty and licked her pencil eloquently. 'Even if there are certain ... compensations out there, you sure must miss the comforts of home.'

'Look it's not a matter of ...'

I tried, as always, to redirect the conversation back to the outrageousness of the colonial system, the Atlantic Charter, universal human rights, but it was hopeless. Some pools are too shallow to register the impact when even the biggest rock is heaved in. A colleague appeared over her shoulder.

'Miss Tantri?' He drained his glass, immediately grabbed another from a passing tray and indicated my own. 'Gin and tonic, huh? Must make a nice change from those endless Molotov cocktails you're so used to lobbing around.'

'Well, as a matter of fact I have never been involved in any act of overt violence.'

A third appeared, rubber-necking between the other two.

'Did you say Tantri? You Surabaya Sue? Wow! The wild woman of Indonesia? Gee, can I get your autograph for my folks?' He shoved a notepad and pencil in my face. 'Could you maybe draw that dagger thing dripping with blood you see on the walls and something about death to all whites? And then sign "with love to Wayne".'

Others started gathering round, pushing and shoving, plucking at me like I was a pile of pullovers in a sale. One of those horsey, over-finished New England sorority sisters who wear tweed skirts and blazers elbowed her way through and started asking about where my family were from, as if I was the sort that got hung up in family trees. I felt like a lone, triggering crystal in a super-saturated solution of boredom. I saw Bung Karno look over at the noisy mob and frown in mid-oration, upstaged, downwinded, losing his thread and his audience. He wouldn't like that. People joked that the most dangerous place to be in Indonesia was standing between Bung Karno and a camera.

A few weeks later we saw the result of the conference when a bundle of American magazines flopped limply onto the press office floor. How many lives had been risked to get them to us? Very little about liberty or death but lots about me. Added to that, the bimbo reporter had managed to get my name wrong so that I appeared mysteriously not as Tantri but as someone pretending to be Miss Daventry. Perhaps that was just as well since the article was rife with Nudge! Nudge! insinuations that I was having hot, steamy jungle sex with the entire Diponegoro Division and possibly Wink! Wink! occasional underage orang utangs. I would have preferred it had they simply put it in Ma's raw Glaswegian and said that I 'banged like a shithouse door'. Why do women play men's game by snarling at each other in terms of their sexual availability? Even worse, she got Bung Karno's name wrong –

for some reason having got hold of the idea that he was called Achmad! And that damned silly name stalked him through the Western press for the rest of his days. Now *that* he really would not like.

* * *

From the first, I advised Bung Karno against accepting the Linggadjati agreement. Most of our conversations occurred as I was giving him painting lessons, our canvases standing side by side in the shade of a small open-sided pavilion. The main problem was his irritating habit of humming 'Yankee Doodle Dandy' under his breath as we worked. It became tooth-grindingly annoying. Palaces are always full of mirrors. I don't know why. Perhaps it is a tacit admission that ninety percent of power is stolen glitter and phony illusion. Whatever the reason, Bung Karno was beguiled by them. They distracted and obsessed him. He just couldn't leave them alone, always preening and checking his teeth. Out here there were no mirrors, just reality, which he never really cared for.

You might say that I was the first official artist to the Indonesian Republic. Since the principal aim of the republican administration was to just wear out the patience of the Dutch until they simply went away like my despairing parents had done, one of the great secrets of the presidency was that there wasn't much for him to actually *do*. His principal task was to just *be*. Bung Karno was an enthusiastic rather than an accomplished painter – self-taught – but the thirst was in him from the first though I learned quickly that he was easily bored. Only he had a taste for portraits of beautiful women rather than bowls of fruit and that all started as a boy when he collected cigarette cards of Hollywood stars. They say that by the end he had the largest portrait collection of naked women in the world, by all the best artists. But I have always regarded the gossip about his rampant sexuality as overstated. That story that the KGB filmed him in at an orgy in Moscow and showed him the film in a blackmail attempt only to be asked by him for more copies to show around – that never seemed to me to ring true. The proof is that in all out time together, he never showed the slightest sign of sexual interest in *me*.

But then sharp-eyed Mrs. Soekarno, Fatmawati, herself a third wife after all, saw to it that, when together, we painted nothing but bunches of chastely plucked, native, Indonesian flowers arranged in tall Chinese vases and some saw in this a metaphor of her influence on foreign policy. In those days every detail was overinterpreted and while the Dutch viewed everything in terms of the sinister and calculated chess moves of *Realpolitik*, the palace was thick with mystical augurers, wafting numerologists, necromancers, astrologers and scruters of entrails and portents of all kinds who looked back to the ancient Hindu myths and prophecies so that the president's every action was as closely studied and soothsaid by his own supporters as the bowel movements of Louis XIV. And the principal requirement of government reports was to have auspicious numbers of sections and paragraphs and so on which explains why so many of them were full of nothing. Even our painting got involved and was closely observed by a squad of pencil-licking bookies' runners. If Bung Karno chose a green background in a picture, that was a reference to Loro Kidul, the Goddess of the South Seas, and so the Sultan of Yogya – our host and one of her mystical husbands. A dab of red from the hand of one of Balinese ancestry, meant that he had doubts about the loyalty of the army. Too much white meant he thought palace treachery was afoot. Or maybe it was the other way round and what deep meaning lay behind his decision to paint only five flowers when there were actually six in that vase?

The British army had finally forced the Dutch to the negotiating table by the simple expedient of threatening to pick up their ball and go home in a sulk if they didn't. The result was the Linggadjati agreement, a recognition by the Dutch of Indonesian sovereignty over Java, Madura and Sumatra in return for some vague agreement to form some sort of joint realm under the Dutch crown.

I mercilessly painted in a bilious frangipani on my canvas and nagged. 'The problem, Bung, is that all the terms of Linggadjati remain undefined. It can be twisted to mean anything the Dutch like.'

He touched in a sinuous stem with flickering brush on his own. 'Maybe so, K'tut, but therein lies its advantage for us too. Now *we* can twist it to mean exactly what *we* want. The Dutch will try to nibble away at it from their side, we from ours. It moves the conflict away from pitched battles where we can never win and every time they protest to us, they are admitting that we exist. That's why I stacked the National Committee to get it through.' He pointed a paintbrush at me. 'It is the sleep of reason that produces war.' That line would be coming up in a speech soon. I had written it.

'But it will also lead to internal disputes as the different local groups twist it for *their* own ends.' I reached over to his canvas and straightened the flower stem by diminishing the highlights.

He sighed and compromised by shading in a pale offshoot that concealed the stem entirely, creating a façade of consensus. 'Then I act the great statesman, above factional quarrels, and speak as the voice of the people. The more they fight, the more they need Soekarno. The people know where Soekarno's heart is. Ducks flock together but eagles fly alone.' Bung Karno always managed to swim in the lethal currents and tides of Asian politics without quite getting his hair wet. 'You know that thing I always do in speeches when I play with the crowd? I ask ...' He lay down brush and palette, puffed out his chest and intoned like a priest, his hand creeping up unconsciously into the grandiloquent gestures of the demagogue. '"Shall I settle for ninety percent *merdeka*?" And they all shout "Nooo!" And then I do, "Ninety-two percent *merdeka*, then?" And they all howl "Nooo!" And then I look puzzled and go, "Well, what about ninety-five percent *merdeka*?" And so on up, teasing them with "ninety-nine and a haaalf percent merdeka?" Negotiating as if I am buying mangoes in the market and then – when I get to a hundred – only then do they all shout "Yes!"' Then I say, "How much? I can't hear you – louder." And they roar, "A hundred percent!!" and I say, "What? I still can't hear you – louder." And they scream, "A hundred percent!!!"'

It was true. The big cheeses all had very different oratorical styles. Bung Karno liked to joke and play. Bung Hatta loved his abstract nouns. Bung Tomo referred to the shedding of bodily fluids rather more than was strictly necessary.

'Yes, Bung, but you know that's an old trick from Western pantomime. Usually, it's the hero who is stalked by some great danger that the crowd can see but he can't. And they scream "Behind you! Behind you!" but he can't see it because he's looking the wrong way. The more he looks, the more they scream and stamp, the less he sees. Maybe that's how it is with you.'

He chuckled and took up his brush again. 'Thank you, K'tut.' He waggled a finger at me. 'I will remember that. But things are getting better. Today I saw a sign – a rat in the palace.'

'A rat? A sign? You mean a sign from above? Or do you mean in a dream?'

He shook his head. 'A sign from above? A dream? What are you on about? No a real rat, all fat and glossy and running down the hall. Up till now the people were so hungry they were forced to catch and eat the rats and they had all but disappeared. I don't know how we held on to the deer in the palace park. If rats are coming back, then it shows there is food about and that means things are getting better.'

It was true. And rats were not the half of it. There had been all sorts of rumours about gangs of starving children and packs of savage dogs that had been seen stalking and preying on each other in the ruins, dogs eating children, children eating dogs. 'Now tell me some Hollywood gossip. You know I love gossip. Tell me that story again about the star, Lupe Velez, trying to have a fancy suicide and being found with her bare arse sticking up in the air and her head down the toilet after she killed herself in such a complicated and beautiful way. That makes me laugh. A lot of people have planned my funeral and being a president doesn't make you laugh a lot. One day I should like to visit Hollywood. Perhaps they will make a film of my life but who can play Soekarno?'

I realise it is totally futile to try to talk facts with someone who is a hopeless fantasist like Bung Karno. He loves my stories of Hollywood scandal. Naturally, I invent freely.

Chapter Eight

The Buginese sailing vessel had dropped anchor halfway between the island of Karimun Besar and Singapore. The water was calm, delivering just the odd, lazy splash against the hull and the wind was a mere gentle, ruffling zephyr. If the Dutch navy turned up, we would run northwest to British waters, if the British we would turn east towards Indonesian. At the moment there was just a greasy Singapore tug out there but what they were doing was quite interesting. From afar, it looked as if they were tipping shoal after shoal of silvery fish back into the water from great buckets. They glistened and gleamed and caught the sun as they tumbled in with a fat splash. Only through the glasses could I see it was not fish at all but guns and that there was a Brit in a khaki uniform worrying over some sort of list with a pencil. There were too many guns in Asia, too may shells, too many mines. Now the big war was over, governments were dumping them by the hundred thousand and the cheapest and easiest thing to do was chuck them in the sea.

'You see, Ketut,' said Ah Beng. 'The water here very shallow because of the shoals. Soon as the Brits are gone, we send in the divers and the arms be deliver to your – ah – specification – all clean and grease and ready for use – good like new.' Ah Beng was a very handsome and plausible Chinese with a ceramic complexion and pencil-straight black hair and no emotional expressions at all.

'When?' I asked.

'We have to sell your opium first. I keep tell you. At the moment it drug on the market. Because it opium you think I talk poppycock?' People say the Chinese have no sense of humour. Don't believe it. It's just that they have a very bad sense of humour if Ah Beng's was anything to go by. We had to use agents like this all over the world. Because Holland was still the recognised authority and had imposed a blockade, they were often, legally speaking, engaged in smuggling. Sometimes this meant they were men of the highest, ideological commitment, sometimes they were crooks and the Republic must have lost a fortune in thefts and doublecrossings. The revolutionary government had had some difficulty in finding an honest agent in the US. There, I had been able to help with my American contacts and they were now represented – bizarrely, I admit, but efficiently – by Matty Fox, the producer who turned Universal Pictures around. Bung Karno loved the Hollywood connection. Joe Kennedy had already burnt his fingers and his bridges in diplomatic service otherwise I might have dropped him a line. I wondered if he had forgiven me for the Louella indiscretions.

This trip was a total nightmare. The Minister of Defence had sent me on a terrifying blockade-busting flight via Sumatra where the stockpile of government opium was hidden deep in caves. Opium was a government monopoly in Indonesia in those days and had only been banned in Singapore by the Japanese, so it was a moot point whether that regulation was still valid. Other Indonesian envoys were trading sugar, vanilla, quinine and birds' nests all over the East, anything to keep the Republic's finances afloat. We had to dodge Dutch fighters and a terrible, tropical storm in a wobbly old Dakota run by air pirates and short of fuel, load up the plane and land across the causeway in Malaya, truck the cargo into the city to Ah Beng's warehouse and it would be sold and ultimately converted into guns and an unused British field hospital to be shipped back via a small port in

Thailand. The hidden costs, the bribes, storage charges, transport, the commissions, took massive bites out of my dwindling budget while delay followed delay. The price of the guns was always going up, the value of the opium down. The particular guns I wanted were suddenly in short supply while it was now the wrong season for opium, the wrong kind of opium, the wrong trademark that people did not trust. I knew absolutely nothing of either commodity. Of course, no one gave receipts or proper documents. It was painfully obvious that I would never talk my way out of allegations of stealing when I got back to Yogya – if I got back – with what would almost certainly be the wrong guns. And always there were more delays. Much of my purchased stock was sold off by British quartermasters who then had to arrange for fires in the stores to cover up the losses. There had already been fires all over Singapore and the military police were getting suspicious, not having received a cut.

Its task finished, the tug started its engine, coughed, gobbed out dirty water, belched smoke, pirouetted and headed back for Singapore. One of the coolies gave us a cheery wave with a length of rope.

'Do they know what we're doing?'

Ah Beng turned and laughed. 'Of course they know. They our men. Why else you think they kindly dumping them in such shallow water so they so easily recover? You almost can reach down and pull them out from here.'

They slipped me ashore near Changi Point. I waded to the beach with my frock tucked up in my drawers like a little girl paddling in the Clyde and memsahibed my way back to Scotts Road, bullying myself aboard an army truck of returning nurses who chattered with medical boldness about their boyfriends. I was staying in the bland villa of a Javanese sympathiser who was keeping his head down. There had been fighting between Javanese – *romushas* stranded by the war – and Malays out in Geylang around the Happy World Amusement Park and I was hardly living high on the hog myself, being dependent on Ah Beng and the unsold opium for money but determined not to borrow more than absolutely essential at his usurious rates.

That evening there was a phone call. I had a mysterious visitor. He entered somewhat unusually for a senior diplomat of advancing years – over the back wall of the garden and landed on a banana tree – and arrived puffing and sweaty, with torn trousers but giggling. It was Abdul Monem, Egyptian special emissary of the Arab League. We settled him in with a glass of cool lemonade and he straightened his tie and drew himself up to his full height on the overstuffed sofa and bowed over his paunch.

'Madam K'tut. I am Mohamed Abdul Monem, here as the special envoy of King Farouk and the Arab League to extend official recognition to the Republic of Indonesia and offer the establishment of full, diplomatic relations.' Then he collapsed miserably down into the cushions. 'Unfortunately the Dutch refuse to let me in so I am stuck. Any ideas?' We gave him more lemonade.

This was a major diplomatic coup. It could be the unblocking of the logjam that would bring dozens of other countries to recognise the Indonesian Republic and influence the UN in its attempts to bring pressure on the Dutch. It was the same old dilemma, diplomacy or guns? This time it had to be diplomacy. The next day I set to with Ah Beng, touring the harbour, investigating the cost of finding a boat to dodge the blockade or maybe sailing to Yogyakarta via the Philippines. Everything was locked down tight by the Brits. Then we discovered that the British and Dutch authorities had granted special permission for a Dakota that would carry some of the starving and stranded Javanese back through Dutch airspace to Yogya and hatched a plan to hide Monem amongst them. That fell through for fear the British would find out and stop the rest of the mercy flights. Depressed, I went out to a street stall and dug through my pockets for a few, last cents to buy a bowl of noodles. I had been scrounging lunch money from Mr. Monem for days and now I was so poor I had to haggle the price of noodles down.

In such a situation, there was only one thing to do. I went back to the villa, dressed myself up to the nines, painted my face and drove out to the airfield in the biggest, shiniest car I could borrow. There, I grandly chartered a spanking, new plane from a Philippines operation, disdainfully signed a phony cheque on behalf of the Indonesian Republic for $10,000 and Mr. Monem and I did a Glaswegian, moonlit flit from Kalang under the very noses of the authorities, our illegal plane taxiing to the end of the runway with its propellers still turning as we ran from the bushes and scrambled aboard. In a trice, we had turned and were barrelling back along the airstrip, as all hell broke loose around the airfield, and flying far out beyond Sumatra at full speed so as to be out of range of Dutch fighters.

At Maguwo, in Yogya, the airstrip was covered with parked trucks to prevent any unannounced Dutch visits and we had an anxious ten minutes of circling in God-given cloud as the strip was cleared for our unannounced landing, while scanning the horizon for forewarned fighters that might be lurking at our only possible destination. I have to say they did Mr. Monem proud with bands and pomp and salutes and a big bunfight at the palace. His chubby, little face glowed with unalloyed joy at the speeches of mutual love and support. The two American pilots were the life and soul of the party, relieved, no doubt, to have made it alive. I wonder if they ever got paid. I sure as hell didn't.

Chapter Nine

One day I was summoned to the office of the Minister of Defence, Amir Sjarifuddin. The minister's quarters had just been moved to a new building from the ground floor of the Merdeka Hotel where I also lived and my courier was a stern, young officer called Suharto who arrived in a long-nosed Chrysler and clearly missed the days of Japanese, gratuitous face-slapping. From his glowering, silent intimidation, I feared I was being arrested for some capital crime and past horrors flooded back so that I arrived at the defence building a quivering wreck.

As we drew up the officer turned to me. 'Sister K'tut. This is not a taxi service. Petrol is short and expensive. As a foreigner, I hope you will be willing to demonstrate your loyalty to the Republic by making a donation towards your transport costs.' I looked up and saw the driver rolling his eyes and grinning at me in the rear-view mirror. He had seen all this before then. Having dressed in haste, I only had a few, scruffy Japanese notes with me. I handed them over in a bunched fist. He looked down on them in sneering disbelief but pocketed them anyway. It was the first time I had ever been mugged. It is strange to think that this same Suharto would be one of the executioners of Bung Amir but a short while afterwards.

Several cups of water inhaled in the waiting room and a few gulped-down cigarettes somewhat revived me, even though hungering and thirsting Muslims frowned on my blatant disregard of religion for it was the arid fasting month and they would take nothing till dusk. The building was buzzing with stiff-legged military and secretaries running in and out, jeeps screeching to a halt every few minutes and people shouting in the stairwells. It was unlike any ministry I had ever seen, tingling with an excitement that was near-panic. Normally they are places of slow time.

I already knew Amir as a gentle communist – in fact both a Christian convert and a tolerant communist – with the face of a benevolent owl. Bung Karno believed there were only two forms of religion – the differences between Muslim, Christian, Hindu etc. were irrelevant – those forms of belief hostile to life and those supportive of it. It was one his sacred Five Principles of Indonesian nationhood that we had all learned to chant back at him together with a lot of other pieties whose feet barely touched the ground. This was probably at the height of leftist party power when half the ministries seemed to be occupied by openly communist PKI members. Like all men who smoke pipes, Amir always had a need of jackets with pockets full of accessories, matches, pipe-cleaners, poking implements, tobacco pouches that gave him a permanent look of being weighed down and harassed. I had visited his office before and it was exactly what you would expect of an Oxbridge don, all scribbled notes and stacks of periodicals menacing a terminal bookslide. Propped in one corner was the violin that he played beautifully. At any moment I could be offered a glass of sherry and a mildly reproving but helpful comment on my last essay.

I was shown into it, a weird still centre of peace and calm. The door closed and we were back to the slow, ministerial time of a man who was being blatantly by-passed and kept out of the loop. Amir swivelled in his chair, plumed fragrant smoke like a volcano and smiled impishly. The room was stiflingly hot, the furniture careworn and heavily Dutch, the sort that seemed to disapprove of you. His Dutch diplomas were carefully framed on the wall behind his chair – if you wanted to insult someone in their own language you had better be fluent in it – and beside them was the mounted analysis of his urine sample from a fashionable Amsterdam clinic. There were, it seemed, many paths to distinction. The scars from his encounter with the Japanese he still bore on his body. 'Do sit down K'tut. Would you care for a glass of ... water?'

'Water? No thank you Bung Amir. It would be unkind to ask a fasting person to bring me water.' Of course, he was a Christian and I would be assumed to be the same. In Indonesia, only the criminally insane have no religion and Bung Karno was careful to doff his *peci* equally to all faiths though not everyone, even in Yogya, practised what Bung Karno preached. Even the mystical goddess of the South Sea was to be included. Since all the rulers of Java had some sort of relationship with her – father, husband, lover – Bung Karno let it be known that he rendezvoused with her in a hotel room on the coast every Wednesday afternoon as a modern business man would his mistress.

Amir looked thoughtfully at his pipe and laid it down, cupped in a Javanese tourist ashtray that swarmed with curlicued flowers. He was a very trim smoker. The stem was never wet with saliva or sticky residue as when other men smoked pipes. 'I really should give this thing up, a habit I acquired as a student in Holland. Pipe tobacco is the whole problem of Indonesia in one small tin. The Dutch grow it for nothing here using child labour. The children become addicted to nicotine from touching the leaves while their parents starve to death. They export it, blend it, package it, charge import duty and sell it back to us for a fortune. We make cigarettes and cigars in Sumatra and Semarang. Why not pipe tobacco that tastes like this?' He looked crestfallen. 'Of course, the factories would now be in Dutch hands again.'

'Dutch hands? Has something happened?'

He ran his unDutch hands through tired hair and gestured at the outer door. 'Reports are coming in that the Dutch have attacked again, claiming violation of the Linggadjati agreement. It started at dawn. Yesterday. They've seized the principal ports in Sumatra and are advancing on all fronts in Java and pushing down from the north with heavy armour and non-stop airstrikes. They will be bombing us here any time now. Clearly this has been planned for months.' He shook his head in frustration. 'The mistake was allowing the Japanese to disband their local defence forces after the surrender so we had to build an army from scratch instead of just taking one over. Oh, I warned Soekarno and Hatta but you know you could take them to a restaurant and the only way you could get those two to stop just talking about the menu and actually decide what they wanted to eat was to get a Pemuda to hold a knife to their throats. Bung Karno likes to see himself as a thinker but he is really just a dreamer. I once wrote...' He pointed vaguely to some article, printed somewhere, lying in that heap there and shut his mouth. It was not the moment for disloyalty. 'Our forces are heavily out-gunned as usual but they are striking back and slowing down the Dutch, attacking stretched lines of supply but we have to spare them from suicidal acts. The army must be saved for total guerrilla warfare if that is what it comes to. It is all in the hands of the soldiers now.' He pointed at his stacked desk. 'At least we are still churning out papers and not yet burning them.' For an intellectual the ultimate cry of hope and despair.

'But what am I doing here? Do you want me to go back on the radio? Is that it?' I was already editing the text in my head. 'Treachery', 'Stab in the back' – or, 'Gallant, barefoot patriots crushed under the iron heel of tyranny'. Yes, that was better, classier.

'No. No. We have others for that, white people like Coast and Bondan who are useless at anything else. Some people don't help to carry luggage. They *are* luggage. No, what we have in mind for you is rather special as far as luggage goes.'

* * *

'Wim, darling! How lovely to see you. What a super surprise!' He was in the bar of the Hotel des Indes in Jakarta, where I was told he would be and clutching a beer to his bosom like it was a long-lost friend. Being a real long-lost friend, however, I went unclutched. The hotel was struggling back into civilian business after its various wartime requisitionings though a little understaffed owing to Pemuda reprisals against any Indonesian working there. Recently a pastry sous-chef had been fricasseed alive. I remembered that, during their occupation, Hatta had been installed in the hotel by the Japanese and found it hard to get served by the local staff who became deaf and blind to his every need. Around us all white faces again now, of course, a shock after Yogya, and a battered-looking palm court Eurasian orchestra, shiny at cuff and collar, sawing away at a syrupy version of the old hit 'Terang Bulan,' 'moonlight.' And on every table it was the raw white gleam of old-fashioned but serviceable linen. What I could have done with a few modern textiles! It was clear Wim had been in the bar for hours. 'You're drunk,' I said, sliding into a chair at his table and picking up our conversation pretty much where we had left off in Surabaya.

'Manxi? What the hell are you doing here? I hardly recognised you. Thought you were dead as a matter of fact. I sort of assumed you'd been gang-raped and your head cut off in the usual way. Maybe not in that order. 'Course I'm drunk. What else is there to do in a shithole like Batavia? Except maybe sex. And you can only do that so many times a day and I've done it but I find I can drink steadily from dawn till dusk, pace myself right. You can't do that with sex.' He swatted away a fat fly that was circling his beer. Two barflies, one glass then.

I was as nervous as a dog in a Chinese restaurant. In theory, no one knew that Manxi was Surabaya Sue. But after those pictures they had published from Yogya ... I had dyed my hair again – gone back to red and pulled it back into a bun of disapproval – wore a blind woman's dark glasses and was dressed as a Dutch housewife in some sort of dreadful, flowery housecoat thing. Most cunning, I was clumping around in a pair of ghastly flat shoes, almost clogs really, that changed my height and the way I walked and on my head I had the sort of sunhat bonnet affair one of the Voortrekkers might have worn to goad an ox-cart across the *veldt*. Just to be on the safe side I had even turned up the American accent a notch or two. To think I had risked my life in the mountains for years – for this. In my bag nestled some fake identity papers the ministry had given me but who knew how long they would withstand proper scrutiny. My real security lay in a white face. The Javanese barman, too young and intelligent-looking, was hovering with ears apout and showing far too much attention to our conversation for someone not supposed to speak English. Obviously a Pemuda spy. He should be more careful. I ordered a beer and shooed him away.

'I see the uniform's Dutch now, Wim.' He also had one of those pseudo-American haircuts that are just one step short of a scalping, perhaps the revenge of Red Indian barbers.

He shrugged down at the shoulder flashes. 'Now all the Brits have run away again – just like they did in Malaya – it makes me less obvious.' Yes, I thought, and when they left they waved their fists in the air and shouted '*Merdeka*!' to the dock workers and that was the Seaforth Highlanders, the same regiment that began the first British occupation of Java under Stamford Raffles in the previous century. 'You don't want to stand out in a crowd these days.'

I certainly didn't. I took off the dark glasses.

'So did you come here straight from Surabaya?'

He glugged more beer and gave a soft, ladylike belch. 'Like hell I did. Semarang first. Another mess, another shithole. The Brits had disarmed the Japs and then realised they couldn't deal with the extremists on their own, so they rearmed them and they really got stuck in. Tough, little buggers as you've every reason to know. Nasty business, each side massacring the other, Eurasians crucified and chucked in the river, little Chinese girls raped to death. But the Japs came through and, in the end, the Brits tried to give the Jap commander the DSO for services to the British Empire! When something like that sounds reasonable, it's the world that's gone crazy. Perhaps you think this is not a joking matter but the Indies has taught me that people are never more ridiculous than when they are being totally serious.' He narrowed his eyes and nodded, trying to look as wise as an owl and ending up just looking as tight as one – ridiculous. 'The politicians back home wouldn't have it of course – the medal I mean. Now The Hague is trying to give away all the gains just made by the Dutch army in the last "police action". They've stopped our advance before we could finish the job – frightened of America and the UN. Gutless bastards! Another week and we'd have swept the extremists into the sea. There's a difference between pouring oil on troubled waters and pouring it on raging flames. All that vicious fighting in Surabaya may have come as a bit of a shock to some of *us* but you can be sure it scared Soekarno to death, showed him he wasn't in control of anything. Now we have the Van Mook line with Java split into a leaky sandwich between us and the republicans but that won't hold. You'll see. It's only a matter of time. So where were you?'

I was in mid-gulp and started coughing. When it had stopped, 'Oh here, there. It was all confused after the fighting in Surabaya. I just kept my head down. Then I was up in Bandung for a bit. Oddly, I thought I'd try Semarang. I always liked it there but I'm having trouble with my stuff. A friend looked after my house here during the war and the extremists burned half of Bandung down so there's nothing left up there. They won't let me take everything I need back to Semarang – something to do with keeping the roads clear for military transport. I can't get through the road blocks. They tell me I need some sort of a priority pass. Can you help, darling?'

He shrugged. 'Sure, why not? I can give you a chit. No need for clear roads now that those windy sods have caved in ...' He was off on a rant again. I tuned out and studied the bar. This was a dangerous place. You never knew who you might meet. A man had come in, wearing some sort of shiny, green uniform, hawkish but smugly handsome, late twenties, looking somehow newly minted and heading towards us with a worrying fixity of purpose. As his shadow fell over the table, Wim looked up, lit up, stood up.

'Turk!' He stretched out his hand and they did one of those firm, manly double-grip things. 'Manxi, this is my friend Turk Westerling!' said with pride, almost infatuation. The man smiled a languorous lounge lizard smile and bestowed a handshake. Nasty piggy eyes. Cold hands. Who had hands that cold in the Indies – Indonesia? 'Sit down, Turk. Join us.'

The lizard smile turned into a shark's. 'No time, I'm afraid. I have to go to HQ. The enquiry. Why else would I be dressed like this? I came to pick up my lawyer.' A point across the room followed by a martyred look. 'I just wanted to wish you luck with the new project. I gather it's ... proceeding. Keep me informed. See you around.' He nodded and shot me a look that lingered just long enough to seem threatening, telling me I had been filed away somewhere, then walked across to a table of civilians who all leapt to their feet and began pounding him eagerly on the back and contesting with each other the right to stand him a drink. They looked the sort of crew who made a lot of money doing something very boring.

'Marvellous man,' breathed Wim. 'Marvellous! Do you know Mountbatten picked him as his personal bodyguard and the rebels have put a price of 20,000 English pounds on his head? They call him Turk because he was raised in Istanbul. They know how to treat rebels there. Do you know, in a few short months he saved South Celebes from the extremists they sent over from Java.' He lowered his voice. 'And he always says his chief weapon was a golf club.' He tittered.

I frowned. 'A golf club?'

Wim nodded and whispered. 'Interrogation. Getting the terrorists to betray each other with a few well-applied golfing shots without using the *usual* golf balls – if you get my meaning – and then mowing them down like dogs. Apparently, in any village, after a demonstration drive or two, even the toughest nut would crack as our Turk carefully teed him up. So – one way or another – they all ended up spilling their guts.' A snigger. Then, bitterly, 'But are the government grateful? Do you know what they've done? They've started a secret inquiry into what went on while he was out there, set the bloody, blood-sucking lawyers on him. They're trying to pretend they didn't know and they'll hang him out to dry. That man's a hero! Think how many lives he saved in Celebes, think how many innocent villagers he protected from those Javanese thugs in the Pemuda.'

I felt dizzy and revolted but stuck to my main clause as they taught me at school. 'What's your new project, Wim darling? Your friend said you had one.'

He tapped the side of his nose with an unsteady finger. 'Ah, can't talk about that one. Very hush-hush.'

I pouted. 'You can tell me all about your brave friend but you won't tell me how clever you are? But darling that's just not fair. You have the right to be proud of yourself too.'

He brightened. 'I do, don't I? All right. Hey, here's an idea. Instead of telling you, I'll show you.' He grabbed his beret from the spare chair and drained his beer. 'Come on. I've got a jeep outside.'

I hesitated and looked across the room. One man was standing, demonstrating golfing swings, with lots of elephantine bum-wiggling, to the hysterical laughter of the rest. Westerling was simpering and blushing like a girl being paid her first compliment.

Then suddenly, a man I knew walked in and sidled over to the bar, laying out big braggadocio gestures on every side like a round of drinks. He was more rotund, more confident-looking and in an American colonel's uniform but there could be no mistaking him with that clenched-buttock, shake-your-sticking-balls-loose–with-gravity walk. It was Bob Koke, my old enemy from the Bali hotel trade. I slipped my dark glasses back on and crushed my bonnet down hastily over my face.

'Let's go,' I said.

* * *

I was expecting the ride from Hell. With all the beer he had drunk, Wim shouldn't have been driving a jeep at all. Close up his breath smelled like that of a cat I once had. But I was wrong. He drove like a little, old lady on her way to church, respecting others' rights of way, slowing at every intersection, courteously allowing pedestrians to step out in front of him. He even stopped for two heavily laden Indonesians to cross with a pig slung between them on poles.

The city had changed since my last visit. Everything had a makeshift, unshaven, wartime look and there was khaki everywhere. The only relief lay in the Jakarta trams that were daubed with paint patches in all kinds of cheerful colours to cover up the *Merdeka* slogans. The Pemuda no longer rode free of charge and, most striking of all, the conductors had resumed bowing to every Dutch passenger. And even white people wore the oddest combinations of clothes, anything to maintain basic decency – evening jackets over nightdresses, dress shirts over pyjamas so that the whole city looked on its way to a weird ball of bacchanalian disorder. Yogya was a different world where colonialism was already but a dim memory, a brief interlude blown away by a great wind of change. Here, it still lay on every hand. But then here the mutilated and injured of war had been filed neatly away whereas in Yogya, you saw them on every corner, young men with torn bodies and missing arms and legs or shattered faces, reduced to begging on the streets. What both shared was that every road was gap-toothed with fire-scorched buildings. But here alone there was business on every empty lot, bustling trade, life reasserting itself at the imperial trot, vigorous weeds pushing up through the broken concrete.

Much has been written about the plight of the Chinese after the Dutch surrender of WWII, subjected to every form of terror and despoliation, first by the Japanese and then by the revolutionaries. Even families that had been in Java for centuries were still not regarded as properly Indonesian. Lukman had once shrugged the whole thing off. 'A mongrel can give birth in a stable, that doesn't make mutts into horses' and snorted with fine, equine disdain through flared nostrils. But business is business and some Chinese played an essential part in the battle for the young Republic. In Surabaya, an important part in the supply chain had been the Chinese dealer who had negotiated to buy the steady supply of empty beer bottles from the British barracks. It was a nice, little earner for the quartermaster-sergeant and went straight into his back pocket. Only during the fighting did the Brits realise that the bottles were being shipped into the countryside to be sold to the Pemuda and made into Molotov cocktails to be thrown back at the British camps. Empty bottles were strategic military equipment and Karl and Ma would have made a killing in Surabaya. The trade was more important than it might seem. There was one particular little Indian officer, a tank commander called Zia ul-Haq, who stirred up endless trouble for the Brits. It was not that he particularly objected to Molotov cocktails being thrown at his tanks but non-halal Molotov cocktails were just not on, especially from fellow Muslims. It was exactly the sort of thing that had triggered the Indian Mutiny and its ghost put the wind up the British generals.

We were in Kota, Chinatown, and ideograms snarled up the sides of every building. Goods were stacked out on the pavements, hung from walls, strung up in doorways, everything from tin baths to fighting cocks. We pulled up in front of an old Chinese godown surrounded on all sides by a modern chainlink fence and with armed sentries outside, black Ambonese of the colonial army, many still bearing the marks of the Japanese camps where they had been treated even worse than the Dutch. Wim flashed a pass and was saluted in through the gate and parked against one wall. We walked down a gloomy corridor whose walls and floor were stained with a hundred past sins of incontinence. Wim's boots made odd sucking sounds on the lino paint. I couldn't help wondering if this was another place where Westerling had so cheerily practised his golfing shots. Then, into a cavernously shuttered space full of hot, still air and the smell of mildew with dust dancing in the slashed sunlight. Crates of military hardware lay stacked everywhere, stamped with long serial numbers, and other machines of death draped with tarpaulins with just their steel snouts protruding, great green and yellow drums embossed with stencilled skulls and crossbones and – suddenly – rows and rows of smiling Balinese carvings, laid out on shelves. I recognised the form, of course, the standard pair of male bust with teased-up headcloth and female with flared dance headdress, staples of the tourist trade. I had seen a thousand in my time on Bali. Gathered together like this they looked like a headhunter's hoard. I thought of Westerling again and shuddered.

Wim stopped and pointed with pride. 'Mine,' he said simply. 'Fresh in from Singers.'

I didn't quite know what to say. 'Yours? Are you a collector, Wim? Or do you mean you made them yourself? And why would anyone import Balinese carvings from Singapore? Are you going into the tourist trade?'

He shook his head unwisely and staggered under the impact. 'No. I mean I invented them, my idea. Look closer.'

I picked one up, looked at the top, the bottom, could see nothing out of the ordinary. A tourist carving like so many others. Junk.

Wim sniggered. 'Can't tell, can you? What do you think they

are made of?'

I shrugged. 'Some sort of softwood. They use anything these days.'

'Composition C-3, the latest plastic explosive.'

I nearly dropped it. Laid it hastily back on the shelf.

'No need to worry. It's totally inert until you set it off with a fuse. You can play football with it till then. I shouldn't eat it though if I were you or put it too near an open fire. It's raw explosive mixed with sawdust as a phlegmatizer.'

'A what?'

He preened in insider knowledge. 'A phlegmatizer – a technical term of the trade. It makes the explosive phlegmatic, stable ... and painted down so you can't tell the difference from wood. Clever eh? You can carry these all over the shop and no one would ever suspect, stand them on the sideboard, let the maid dust them if you want to. Then, when you need to use one, you just drill a small hole, pop in a pencil fuse and boom! Up goes a railway bridge!'

I suddenly remembered the man astride the jeep bonnet on the road from Surabaya, clutching his two carvings in the mist and rain like they were very life to him. A saboteur?

'How lovely, Wim. What other toys have you got?'

He reached in another box, drew out a bottle of extra-hot chilli sauce. 'Make any meal go with a bang.' I raised quizzical eyebrows. He waggled it at me. 'Try to twist the top off here – see – and you start a five second fuse before it explodes. The idea is that blokes would bend down, trying to get the stiff top off, hold it against their laps to get more grip and boom! They become Westerling-proof! Only problem is most of the Javanese I know would think that chilli that actually blew your balls off was just the sign of a good batch!' He laughed. 'But you could be sure no

Dutchman would be fooling around with it.'

'Oh my God!' I manged to hang a smile on my face. 'I mean – how clever, darling. Did you really invent these all by yourself?'

He doodled coyly with his left foot in the dust and fluttered his eyelashes bashfully. 'Oh, it's been an uphill struggle,' he sighed. 'One shipment of our mango hand grenades went astray and ended up issued to native troops as rations. That ended rather badly. Very badly in fact.'

'Never mind, Wim dear. You'll come through. You're a very dogged sort of chap.'

'Dogeared?' He pouted. 'Why would you say that – call me dogeared?'

'Not dogeared. I said "dogged".'

'Dog*head*? … What?' He looked confused, crestfallen and hung over. 'Oh Hell, forget it. Let's go and get a drink.' He brightened. 'Hair of the dog and all that.'

* * *

In the whole Nakamura affair, the only person whose relative honesty seemed beyond question was Thio Wie Koen, the Chinese 'fence' and professional criminal who handled the stolen goods, and he was banged up in jail. The Americans and the British, of course, were ultimately to blame for the whole mess or maybe the Japanese for the suddenness of their surrender which brings us full circle. After they dropped the atom bombs the Americans dumped the whole problem of the Jap forces in Indonesia in the laps of the Brits who were in no position to do much about them. Even the local surrender in Singapore had to be policed by Japanese troops like turkeys mixing their own stuffing. So the Jap army in the Indies was left high and dry with no means of survival. It is not to be expected that a bunch of heavily armed and very hungry young men would allow themselves to starve to death so they hit upon a relatively benign solution. As the Indonesians were busy declaring their independence up one end of town – through the good offices of the Japanese navy – up the other end, the Japanese army commander ordered the Kempeitai to seize the contents of the government pawnshops so that they could be used to finance the maintenance of their troops. Captain Hiroshi Nakamura obligingly removed some ten steel trunks and five crates stuffed with gold and jewellery and great bundles of cash and took them to headquarters.

But then, not quite. On the way, he admitted dropping off some ten million dollars' worth at his mistress's house, a leggy, Eurasian beauty known as Carla Wolff. What happened to the bulk of the loot was not known. Some thought that maybe it was converted into rice for the troops. Others that it just disappeared into kitbags and melted away back to Japan. Of course rumours about the treasure took on a life of their own for Indonesians love gossip. Occasionally someone would claim to know it was buried in Menteng and a wild crowd would suddenly appear in a flash with hoes on their shoulders and dig up all the gardens, heedless of the owners' protests. Or maybe it was in Bandung where harmless squatters would have their shacks knocked down by rampaging treasure-seekers. I know where it was. It never got to HQ at all.

Miss Wolff was not the sharpest blade on the penknife. She immediately started wearing diamonds to do the shopping and talking to the neighbours about eating her breakfast off gold plates and sleeping on a gold bed. Ears were pricked. Local snitches grassed to the Dutch who laughed at the whole idea of chests of gold and jewels. The Brits, who had been raised on

Treasure Island, paid more attention and soon poor Carla found her house ransacked by excited military police reliving their boyhood fantasies. Western men are prone to that in the tropics, as I know all too well. Perhaps it's something to do with going back into short trousers. After all, the process of male maturation is best seen as growing up in mastery of a peashooter only to have – at adolescence – a scary bazooka thrust into your hands without a revised manual. No wonder men are prey to constant anxiety. A few hours of being slapped around in a chair back at HQ prompted Carla to draw the boys a treasure map – of her own free will – and they romped off through the city with it, on a no-girls-allowed adventure, yodelling with joy. Thio Wie Koen whose house lay in the crosshairs of the X on the map was infinitely obliging, handing over bundles of worthless Dutch guilders that, as an honest and innocent banker, he had been asked to sit on and had stashed in an enormous, antique, iron safe. The Brits brought in a crane and carried the whole thing off – safe and all – for the photographers and dramatic courtroom display as a symbol of evil. Various people were convicted of miscellaneous deeds of ungodliness, Nakamura got a sentence of ten years and served hardly any of it and a long bicker began about how much more of what was by now known as 'Nakamura's gold' had disappeared into Dutch and British pockets along the long, judicial pathway. The newspapers adored the story. It had sex, gold, corruption, a little judicious, judicial violence, even a huge diamond hidden inside the hollow heel of a crashing, British army boot. Carla loved all the publicity and was much photographed – sheathed in silk but still leggily provocative – and managed to make the world's oldest profession once more exotic and mysterious though she had to swop her gold bed for a prison straw paliasse for a while. The Brits were shown in the newspapers handing over the remnant of the treasure to the Dutch – absurdly regarded as the legal owners. The real legal owners were of course ignored. Carla found a new rich friend and got herself a smart, new hairdo. Many hands dipped into many pies and many years later, one of Carla's frequent daughters would be married to an Indonesian Foreign Minister. Everything died down nicely. Business as usual. Then the Black Fan moved in.

Towards the end of the war, Nakamura had been involved with this secret organisation which is why the Brits had first been interested in him – that and the fact that he was the interpreter between the Japanese and the Indonesians throughout the Proclamation of Independence affair. The Black Fan were set up to fight the Allies, under Japanese leadership, if the shit ever hit the other metaphorical fan and the West attacked Java. It had never been activated but still existed because trying to officially dissolve something that did not officially exist was like trying to shoot a ghost but – like everything else – it had shivered into a thousand factions as different groups reinterpreted its purpose. In Surabaya, it had been hijacked by the Eurasians – now calling themselves 'Dutch' again – and been a particular focus of Bung Tomo's rage. It was likely they were behind the flag incident at the Oranje Hotel. In Jakarta, the Black Fan stood by the Republic yet regarded themselves as rightful heirs to Nakamura's golden inheritance. A short visit to Thio Wie Koen's house and Westerling-type interviews with his domestics established that the garden of the abandoned house next door was the place to dig. They dug – or rather the servants did. The Black Fan found the rest of the treasure and seized it. Not wanting to waste perfectly good holes, they then shot the servants and pushed them in and fired the house out of sheer bad habit. The treasure was clearly unsafe and useless in Jakarta. It had to be got to the republican capital, Yogya, to be used to keep the war going. That was now to be my job.

* * *

The bar of the Hotel des Indes was not the brightest place to hold a secret rendezvous. I had no idea who I was supposed to be meeting. It was evening and the servants were pattering around, preparing for the dinner rush. The *rijstaffel* here was justly famous, dozens of small but delicious Indonesian dishes – served with an aristocratic disregard for the washing-up involved – that you mixed and matched to your own taste. Looking around, I could see no one who was an obvious contact. Perhaps that was the point. They were the sort of burghers for whom the hardships of the Indies once more amounted to having to keep the liqueur chocolates in the fridge. Even Wim was not around, probably neglecting his drinking to keep up his sexual quota for the day.

Parched air was blowing in from the veranda carrying sounds of the city with it and rustling the potted palms and the dogged, old orchestra were back on with – oh no! – 'Terang Bulan'. The singer was a very pretty, kohl-eyed Eurasian girl in a black *cheongsam*. At one stage in her act, she sashayed around the room among the indifferent patrons like Fanlight Fanny. Their minds were wholly on their stomachs and they swatted her away, bending over their plates of asparagus soup that looked and smelled uncannily like the product of an elephant's hot ejaculation. She paused by my table, fixed me very firmly in the eye and sang the first verse again – out of place:

The full moon is shining on the edge of the river.
A crocodile is floating and people think it's dead.

Don't believe what people say.
They are brave enough to swear an oath but are afraid
of death.

I realised for the first time what a thoroughly weird song it was. She ran her fan coquettishly across my face, a fan made of ostrich feathers dyed black – a black fan. Very subtle.

The band took a break in a clatter of musical instruments and thin applause. The singer gave me another significant look over her shoulder and walked off, swinging her hips the way Charlie Chaplin did his cane. Somehow, it came out all wrong and, in that sheath dress, she ended up looking like a penguin. Still, I had seen *Casablanca* and knew how these nightclub vamps worked. I followed.

The dressing room was really a poky cupboard. I pushed through the door behind her and she turned and stared back at me, gimlet-eyed – the inevitable cocked cigarette wafting smoke, heat melting the makeup on her face and making her look like a failed waxwork. It was a place where – apart from allegedly beautiful singing stars – they also stored unwanted parasols for the veranda. Somehow they had squeezed a dressing table in too. Queen Wilhelmina looked doubtfully down at us from a cheap print on the wall.

'Password,' she said.

That pulled me up short. 'Password? No one told me anything about a bloody password. What's the point? We both know what's what. Let's get on with it.'

'Password. Listen sister, it's a dog-eat-dog world out there. No tickee, no washee. Password.' She had seen *Casablanca* too and let her lip curl Bogartishly.

I thought desperately. '*Merdeka*,' I said.

She laughed. 'You see. You knew it all the time.' Oh my God! She reached back and took a derisively small handbag from the dressing table, fished in it and pulled out a piece of paper. 'Here's the address. Make sure you're not followed. Go there now. They're waiting. Memorise the address and eat it.' They were treating me to dinner of a sort then. She sucked on her lip nastily. 'Christ, they said you were a plain-looking woman but in that frock you look like the bride of Frankenstein.' A veritable film buff. 'And the shoes, darling. The shoooes!'

* * *

The rickshaw driver was not happy. 'You should not be out alone at night, madam. It is not safe for you. It is not safe for me either to have you in my rickshaw. There is madness about.' He was the usual wisp of a man with incredible power in his legs, a sort of human praying mantis.

It did not seem unsafe. Nowhere in Indonesia ever seemed unsafe to me. We had left behind the thronged streets, teeming with the roadside stalls of sunset and lit by a thousand smoky lamps and were in one of the well-heeled areas of Jakarta, though he barefoot, me in clogs and the tyres hushed by deep, soft dust underfoot. Bungalows set back in lush grounds, curving, country roads like in the American deep south but brightly lit, big shade trees, the odd smart Dutch sentry patrolling and no lights on inside with everyone tucked up safely in bed by 9 o'clock at night. It was the sort of well-ordered place where you used to find a dozen convicted murderers from the jail shaving the grass with huge, razor-sharp machetes while guarded by one small man with a stick. They probably still had night watchmen here who pottered about signalling 'All's Well' by the tinkling of bamboo gongs. Security is never a fact but an assumption. Most of these houses had been requisitioned by Japanese – now gone – and their current ownership would be a matter of some confusion, since much of the seized Dutch property had been hastily sold on by the Japanese to the Chinese. And now everyone had ended up feeling entitled but dangerously outraged. We pulled up outside a white building looking like a child's drawing of a house, complete with bay windows and a chimney that can never have been used except by Santa. It was much further than I had thought. I had negotiated hard with the rickshaw driver and I paid him double what I had promised to slake my guilt. He stared down at it in incredulity. No one had ever done that before. 'Merdeka,' I said in explanation.

I walked down a concrete path, a faint but grateful wind hissing through the palms overhead, my pseudo-clogs echoing off into darkness. Some great insect of the night whirred past like a clockwork toy and made me duck. No sign of life inside. I stood on the step and hesitated. I could stand there all night. Taking my courage and the doorknocker in both hands, I rapped loudly and heard it ricochet through the house. Something about the sound said it was empty. Nothing stirred. There was a poem somewhere about this – travellers knocking on moonlit doors. Tell them I came and no one answered. I felt relief and turned to go but old notions of duty and loyalty flooded back, not so easily dismissed. I knocked again, then tried the door. Bugger! It was unlocked. That meant I had to go in. Of course – as in every horror movie – the light switch did not work, mere futile clicking, but there seemed to be a sort of dull glow under a door at the end of the passage. Every instinct was to creep, holding my breath – perhaps there was a huge hole in the floor just waiting for me to fall through – but if there was anyone intent on doing me harm, they knew

I was here and were well prepared so that mere creeping would not save me. So instead I clogged heartily down the corridor and threw open the door.

'*Merdeka*!' It was truly a word for all occasions.

Three astonished, brown faces looked up at me. One paused in the act of bringing a cigarette to his lips. They were sitting round a table, playing cards in an otherwise bare room. Curtains whose hideous pattern was an offence against Nature were tightly drawn over the windows. The players must have been there some time since the cigarette fug would have smoked kippers. On the table lay two huge revolvers that you could have beaten a buffalo to death with but no one moved a hand towards them. Then the furthest figure leapt up, sending his chair crashing to the ground and his face broke into a ravishing smile.

'Sister K'tut!'

'Uki! How? When? What are you doing here?' At first I had not recognised him dressed in a sarong and *peci* hat.

He laughed. 'Let me look at you, K'tut. Wah! In that outfit, with those shoes ... you look like a miniature Dutch housewife – except you don't look angry.'

'But how did you ...?'

'I grew up in Jakarta until I was sent to the Koranic school in Surabaya. I got a message that my mother was ill so I came back here. Here too there is fighting to be done.' He looked older, thinner, wearier. In Bali, a mark of maturity is to file down your teeth. The world seemed to have taken a file to Uki's whole body and spirit.

'What of Lukman and Reza?'

His face fell. 'Lukman went north to Madiun, to the communists. Reza is still in Malang. He married a girl there and left the army. I think she was a nice girl. He always wanted to be a farmer and make things grow. Oh, sorry. Let me introduce my Uncle Wirno and Pak Dion, they are in charge of the operation.'

We shook hands, muttered greetings, the usual Asian wet fish handshake and hands pressed to hearts. Two older men, quieter, reflective types. Dion looked at me hard, got straight down to business. Only Uki offered me a seat. 'We needed Uki to make sure you were who you claimed to be. Otherwise we wouldn't have bothered with a silly boy like him.' He sneered at Uki who seemed to shrivel in his gaze. Not a nice man. 'Now we've done that, this is the plan. We have to move fast. Here, too many people are getting interested, especially that commie queer Tan Melaka and his nancy boys.' His lip curled in contempt. To avoid wasting the tail end of the look he threw it at Uki. I could tell that Pak Dion and I would not be chums.

Uncle Wirno chimed in. 'As we told them in Yogya, the Nakamura loot is hidden in four big jerrycans. We filled them up with the gold and jewellery and poured hot wax over them, leaving just a few inches at the top for a separate compartment that is filled with petrol. If anyone looks inside all they will see is petrol. The weight is right. If they slosh it around all they will hear is petrol. We hang the cans on the outside of the truck. Inside, the truck's filled with Dutch furniture which is all anyone will search if we are stopped. You unload the stuff in Semarang and then you have to slip across the Van Mook line into republican territory and on to Yogya, on horse and on foot. It won't be easy.'

'You could do that yourselves. And what do I have to do?'

'The whole of North Java is locked up tight as a drum. We expect you to get the travel permit from your Dutch friend – without that we can do nothing – and you sit up front and show your big, ugly, white face, slap the stupid natives around if they dare come near and scream at the troops at the roadblocks if they so much as touch your precious stuff.'

Uki giggled, 'Just like in Surabaya really.'

Pak Dion snuffed out the laughter with a single, searing look, took a final drag on his cigarette and crushed it out angrily. 'I hope for your sake you are not a spy. Uki says you are not but he is just a stupid boy who knows nothing. And don't think of getting lost. You won't see us but we'll be watching and we have eyes everywhere.'

Uncle Wirno nodded and tapped the revolver with one finger. 'Watching,' he said softly. 'Eyes everywhere.' Then he spoiled it all by putting on bottle-bottom glasses and blearing down at the cards like a blind owl.

* * *

Two days later we set off, myself, Uki and a big, silent Ambonese called Andrew – a rare thing in those days, a Christian, Ambonese republican – who did all the driving since Uki was still learning and I had to be too grand to drive for myself. Uki mostly dozed voluptuously on a hideous, carved sofa in the back in a pose reminiscent of Mae West. He was like a camel building up a massive hump of sleep under the canvas top. It was not quite seemly for such a white woman as me to sit so close to such a black man as Andrew and on the same bench seat but what the hell! There was a war on and I was well aware that the only way for a democracy to overcome the contradictions of running an empire was a desperate, extreme racism. Just sitting was a violently revolutionary act.

The first few checkpoints with sleepy, colonial troops were easy enough. Andrew could joke with them in their own language and I could see from their eyes that some of their jokes involved me. Water off a duck's back. At the outermost perimeter of the city, the roadblocks were manned by pink conscripts straight from Holland and a little more finicky and very, very jumpy. It would have been better if I had spoken Dutch but I did my snotty American act and I did it well, trumping their Dutch snottiness with my transatlantic own. I complained loudly at being stopped at all, at being made to get out of the truck, at being made to stand in the hot sun, at having my goods turned over. I dropped Wim's name and the nickname of the governor and – God help me – Turk Westerling's for good measure. Right on top of the pile of my worldy goods I flaunted the two fake Balinese carvings Wim had given me as a disconcerting, last-minute present. You never knew, someone might recognise them as a *laissez-passer*. I had suggested flying a Dutch flag but my companions balked at that. Still, our little act left the troops grinning like Cheshire cats and rolling their eyes in our dust, glad to see the back of us. The jerrycans, lashed to the outside and clanging at every pothole, were mercifully ignored. There were, I suddenly realised, five of them not four. Of course, one of them really was for petrol.

Then we were out on the open road, taking the southern, less-militarised route, and we all felt the atmosphere lift just to be out of Jakarta in a cool sunny day that got even cooler as we headed for the heights of Puncak. A short while ago, this would have been too dangerous a route, since the area swarmed with militia who delighted in shooting up the road and burning down the houses when there was no traffic to occupy their minds but, in accordance with the latest ceasefire, republican forces had withdrawn to the other side of the Van Mook line and now once more mist clustered and curdled peacefully in the hollows of the tea plantations as it had for a hundred years. Andrew was not a great conversationalist, it was true, but he liked to sing. Unfortunately, all he knew was hymns. The first slopes prompted

'Rock of Ages' in a fine, ebony, baritone voice that made the hair on your neck stand up. His rendition of 'Abide with Me' in Dutch was completely unironic and as we ground down the escarpment he embarked on a tune that – in English – would have urged the hills of the north to rejoice. It was infectious. Shrugging off my Wee Free constraint, I joined in. Then I treated him to a solo rendition of 'Oh God Our Help in Ages Past' and he replied with an unseasonal but spirited version of 'We Three Kings of Orient Are' with horn accompaniment. Poor Uki can never have been subjected so intensively to the sounds of the Christian faith.

It was a day of easy travelling. We even stopped off along the way to bathe in the hot springs and eat our leaf bundles of fried rice with our fingers. It began to feel like a holiday but then another lorry pulled up with excess of macho panache and out spilled a bunch of new Dutch recruits, knees unbrowned and overly boisterous with too much blood and sperm in them. They looked sneeringly at us as we ate together in unsegregated harmony and without benefit of cutlery, made monkey gestures and pissed impudently against the trees as if in our faces, while we stared back at them blankly. I could see Uki beginning to heat up. Luckily we were completely unarmed but that just made us feel more vulnerable. We could not afford any trouble. We packed up and left to hoots and jeers. We had not gone fifty yards when we heard the rat-a-tat-tat of automatic fire behind us. At first, I thought it was more boyish exuberance, then I looked back and saw green-clad figures bursting out of the tree cover and spraying bullets at the screaming boys who had stupidly posted no guards like real amateurs. Then came the sharp bang of a grenade and their lorry went up in a sheet of flame that sent a gust of hot air and a stench of roasting flesh over us. Andrew started braking and peering in the mirror – not the thing to do when people were shooting.

'Go!' I screamed. 'Go!'

He stamped on the accelerator and we fish-tailed away. After some hours of silent rumination Andrew reached a conclusion. 'The outer islands do not want to fight for *Merdeka*,' he said. 'Maybe they would like it but they lack the anger. Only the Javanese have the anger and, when the Dutch have gone, we fear to be ruled by them in their anger.' He nodded glumly but soon revived us somewhat by singing a Dutch version of 'Onward Christian Soldiers' in a voice that merged into the bass growl of the engine. Even little Uki joined in, bravely lah-lahing the chorus from the back of the truck.

* * *

Bandung had been blasted apart by peacekeeping. The whole south of the city was a windblown desert since the withdrawing militia had fired it in patriotic pique. Admittedly that was where most of the Chinese had lived so the act was double-edged. I spent the night in a filthy hotel room that still smelled of smoke while the boys had a better time of it on the cool veranda and kept me awake with snores that sounded like a herd of foraging bush elephants. The hotel staff counted it a mark of my nasty American meanness and suspicious nature that I insisted on the jerrycans being stored inside my room. We actresses must suffer such things for our art.

We set off before dawn, the truck still stinking of human barbeque, determined to make it to Semarang the same day. It was hopeless. Much of the road surface had been ripped up by manoeuvring tanks and heavy rains had completed the work of destruction. Aircraft circled threateningly overhead. We spent hours grinding through the mud, in the midst of heavy traffic, both military and civilian, our souls unuplifted by Andrew's hymns. At several points we got stuck. The tyres were old and worn and would not grip despite our pushing and throwing branches under the spinning wheels that covered us in slurry from top to toe. We finally decided to head north to join up with the coastal road and it was night before we reached Pekalongan. Perhaps that was just as well. By dawn's early light the devastation caused by recent events was clear – the ousting of the feudal regents who had sent the people's sons off to die in Japanese labour camps and the massacre of the Chinese and the collaborating government officials. Fresh, new graves sprouted everywhere. Some of them were local boys the Japanese had tested new and untried vaccines on. This bloodsoaked interregnum was referred to in smooth bureaucratese as the 'Three Regions Movement'. The Indonesian army had put it down after a vicious battle only to now have the Dutch move back in, Shiva's weary wheel going full circle with divinely gripping tyres. There was another reason we stayed the night. Having only one functioning jerrycan for fuel, we now ran out of petrol.

Ironically, as we should have learned from our cargo, petrol was worth its weight in gold here. The next morning, after a stale breakfast of mildewed rice porridge, we scoured the market and sidled up to the hotel staff with heavy hints of still heavier tips. Petrol? No chance, they sneered. It was not like that first time, back in Bali, where the gods led me to run out of fuel outside Nura's palace. Here we were just stranded in Hell and without hope of redemption. Finally, Andrew discovered a platoon of fellow-Ambonese colonial troops camping on the beach. Two windblown hymns later our problem was solved in the idiom of armies everywhere. 'It fell off the back of a truck,' he grinned, tying the petrol securely onto the back of our own.

The endless fields changed from sugar cane to tobacco and back again as we bowled along a well-maintained road. Brightly dressed workers teemed between the rows of crops, indistinguishable from the flowers, as in a romantic Dutch 'Beautiful Indies' painting, while the light glinted off the nearby sea that freshened both the earth and the air with its neatly marcelled waves. It did not look like a country at war with itself. From afar, sunlight gleamed on the roofs of the well-proportioned city buildings and monuments, a fine example of colonial town-planning. Only when seen from much nearer would it all prove as raddled by time and neglect as poor, dear Gloria Swanson had in close-up.

The roadblocks were tighter here. The Dutch were enforcing a blockade of republican areas, cutting them off from imports of food and stifling exports with their warships cruising just over the horizon in angry vigilance. At the entry to the city was a guard post where my goods were thoroughly rifled, the hideous sofa turned upside down and prodded forensically and Wim's travel permit treated with extreme suspicion by the officer in charge – to the point of telephone calls to HQ. It had been a mistake to have the signature of someone with too high a rank on it. I must have underestimated Wim. A young lieutenant returned and gave a smart salute. Wim must have done his stuff. 'Proceed. You are lucky there have been no attacks on this road all week. Otherwise we would not let you through. Why does your truck smell so bad? Have you been transporting rotten meat?' A sad truth, nowadays human flesh was just meat. We said nothing but shrugged and smiled politely. They stamped our passes. It was no longer the moment for stamping my feet.

We had been given an address out in the cool garden suburb of Candi Baru – duly decoded, memorised and the paper it was written on eaten. The Indonesians had an obsession with sending us coded messages, communicating in great chains of z's, k's and w's that looked like the world's longest Polish surnames. It could take hours to translate the simplest, trivial note. Old Joe Kennedy had a better approach, 'put nothing in writing' but then he had secret names for everything and everyone. He was always and everywhere 'The Big Boss' – in capitals – while Gloria was 'the vehicle.' Architect Karsten's original, non-racial principle for Candi Baru had somewhat crumbled under pressure of war and the Chinese had flocked together here in a vain search for security. They were happy to see a new, white face apparently moving in, a hopeful sign that their troubles were finally over. No one seemed to know exactly what was to happen now so we settled down to wait in our fine villa with its Balinese carvings on the sideboard and listened to the slow ticking of the hall clock. God knows we had enough furniture. The truck was parked as far away as security allowed and downwind, as its sweet stench of human flesh steadily ripened in the sun. Only after three days did we find the severed human hand trapped in the folds of the canvas roof, blueish-black and swollen up like a curry puff, with the shrivelled tendons pulling the fingers into an obscene gesture – I suppose that's what you call having the last word like Ma with her unpaid gas bill all those years ago – after which the stink finally began to dissipate on the wind. It should be easy enough to slip through the line and make our way home to Yogya. Home? Yes it was home now.

To pass the time, I began to tame the garden, cutting back the intrusive weeds, weighing in on the side of aromatic frangipani and bougainvillea. No matter how much it was insulted, the world of plants always came back. A beacon of hope for the new republic. But somehow the weeds always sprouted far more vigorously than the cultivars. Not so hopeful then. Or perhaps it was just proletarian plants triumphing over useless aristocrats, native plants over outsiders. Politics was everywhere and there was no escape even in the rustling flower borders any more than on the strikebound plantations and estates. Of course, it was only a matter of days before the gossip started amongst the neighbours. It was the usual sexual tittle-tattle, all whispers and sniggers, the nonsense chatter that a single woman suffers in a house full of men whenever undergarments of both sexes appear mingled on the washing line – what you might call 'oral' sex in its truest sense. I cared not a hoot but it was bad for us to be noticed so I got in an ancient, female maid whose busybody pottering guaranteed the chastity and due hierarchy of sleeping arrangements and kept the knickers unentangled. And as soon as she left every afternoon I took Andrew to bed with me.

Ladies, a hard man is good to find and – as the white folks back in America used to say – it's true what they say about Dixie! That young man had been greatly blessed and was happy to share that blessing with me, a body that was a *smorgasbord* of unknown tastes and textures. The kinky hair not at all like a doormat but wonderfully soft and silky. There were no passionate avowals between us, they were not needed. It was not exactly romantic love but simply a matter of nature reasserting itself inside the house as it was outside and it was a time of honeyed madness, friendly, uncomplicated, even funny – a time of musky nighttime warmth and the comfort of waking to the sound of another human heartbeat caught in the morning flutter of the windblown curtains and I astonished myself by behaving like a schoolgirl – baking cakes, giggling, putting bright flowers in jamjars. I remembered fondly my joking about my womanly needs with the boys in Malang the night of our 'victory' broadcast when they were feeling their oats and off tom-catting. Those needs had finally come home to roost. One dawn, I woke up at cockcrow laughing from my sleep at an old joke that had popped into my head from girls' school. 'Q: Why should you always ask for boy jelly babies in the sweet shop? A: Because with boy jelly babies you always get that delicious, little bit extra!' But I wonder, was it even about sex? After all, for generations women have been having sex with men for the much realer comfort of sleeping with them.

Initially, little Uki was shocked by the new arrangement, like a teenager whose mother still shows green shoots of sexual life but after a few days he came to me, took a deep breath and made a resolute and manly declaration. 'Big sister,' he blushed. 'You are not a beautiful woman, so you cannot hope for a real Indonesian man who is Sundanese or Javanese. It is natural that you and Andrew are together. It is like the humping of buffalo.'

* * *

We set off at dawn, five of us, ourselves and two others come over from Yogya, slipping across the demarcation line and meeting up with a gnarled dwarf who was tending six tough and sceptical little horses tethered under a tamarind tree. We took the jerrycans and each a bundle containing a change of clothing and, for some reason, the Balinese carvings and abandoned ourselves to the embrace of fortune. Its first gift was two battered tommy guns and a cumbersome, Japanese rifle with only three bullets that we had to carry.

'Sister, you will ride. The rest of us will walk.' Andrew being the gentleman. The jerrycans were hitched onto the horses' backs, the guns slung over the men's shoulders.

'Nonsense,' I snapped. 'I'm not some frail, little china doll. I'll walk like the rest.'

He sighed. 'You walk too slowly. You will hold us back. It is better you ride. We must move fast. We may be followed.' I rode – on a saddle that was like sitting astride a bundle of chopped firewood. We were led along little, zigzagging mice trails that circled the villages and ducked under the trees and were obviously made for the use of smugglers. We travelled for days, camping at night under tarpaulins, avoiding roads and clattering across rivers on stony fords. The dwarf looked after the horses and navigation, while the two other Javanese did the cooking and spoke their own local language so that they could only reliably communicate via Uki. For me they had set aside some precious cans of British bully beef that I insisted we all share. We ate them with rice and chilli and hardly talked at all but lived surrounded by a cloud of iridescent, twittering birdsong. It was the mating season for them but not for us. Andrew and I kept our distance by unspoken agreement. Time and place are everything. We both knew that ours had passed.

It is no great way from Semarang to Yogya and there is a fine, main road that the Dutch always used, preferring to sail from Batavia to Semarang rather than taking the land route but we avoided it, heading out far to the east to make sure we were in secure, republican territory and skirting round Mount Merapi, a great, lowering, smoking, volcanic presence. Every time I asked how far we had to go there would be a long process of passing the message from Uki to the Javanese to the dwarf and the answer would come back – always the same. 'A little bit far still.' I had looked at Merapi from so many sides now I began to suspect that we were simply circling it endlessly but who can remember the silhouette of a conical volcano? It is like trying to remember the different sides of an orange.

We were coming down a slope, ricefields on one side, scrubby forest on the other – our steps softly tree-muffled and drowned in a skirl of rasping cicadas – when a series of sharp, metallic clicks told us we were no longer alone. We were surrounded and a dozen pairs of young, expressionless eyes were peering at us down a dozen gun barrels. It was like an uprising against the teachers by the third form.

'Hands up!'

Boys of that age have no experience of life and so no pity. The whole of Java was awash with starving, feral children, some acting as guerrillas, others as criminal gangs with no one sure any more where the line lay between the two. Perhaps there was no line any more. It is at such points that you become abruptly aware of how you must appear to others. A white woman – to villagers we are all 'Dutch' – and an Ambonese – both defined as 'the enemy' with their Javanese lackeys. They were as unconvincingly dressed as ourselves, some with British army blouses – complete with bullet holes and bloodstains worn like medals – one or two with Australian bush hats, some with overlarge Dutch boots and others barefoot – but all painfully skinny and underfed with great, soulful eyes that had seen too much. Some looked angry but others about to cry, as if a single, kind word would make them burst into tears. Gathered together they looked like the urchins' chorus from *Carmen*. I let Uki do the talking. A woman should not appear to be too pushy, too 'Dutch'.

I could see that Uki was not making much of an impression. There were language difficulties. He was disconnected and confused, lying of course about us and our mission, but had not had the sense to prepare something in advance to which he would stick, come hell or high water, which is always the secret of plausibility. Ask any politician. It was time to intervene.

I spoke in my very best Indonesian and smiled, smiled, smiled as I climbed very slowly off the horse. 'Excuse me.' They all turned and lowered their guns at the sound of a woman's voice. A very good sign. I put my hand gently around the shoulders of the smallest and gestured at the bundle of possessions tied in front of the saddle. He leant against me, starving for motherly love. Give me a bag of sweets and I'd have them all eating out of my hand in minutes. But, of course, I had no sweets. My voice choked. 'I have something here that may help. May I ...?' I dumped it on the ground so they could all see what was inside. No hidden guns or grenades. Nothing nasty. I dug out the letter from General Soedirman, carefully preserved and presented it to the young man who seemed to be the leader. He looked at the envelope and turned it over and returned it politely. Of course, they were local village boys. He could not read. None of them could. Now, they asserted, we would have to go and find a man of learning. In a village around here, I knew, that probably meant some illiterate and opinionated old imam who had mastered a few verses of the Koran off by heart and would have our infidel throats slit on a whim. Not a good idea.

'Wait!' I crouched and dug further. I pulled out a photograph of myself and Bung Karno smiling together at the conference in Yogya and held it out proudly. They gathered round and uttered 'Wah!' and burst into loud chatter, by now completely forgetting to point their lethal weapons at us. Alas it did not solve our problem. It was now clear we were people of such enormous eminence that we could not possibly be allowed to just pass quietly by. We must go off and meet the man of learning as an absolute necessity, perhaps we should be taken even further afield to meet a man of even greater learning. It was obvious we must either fight or go with them. We went, half guests, half prisoners, all keeping a sharp eye on each other.

It was a trek of several hours through patchy landscape and then yapping dogs announced a settlement of some sort through the rustling trees. We walked out into a clearing of beaten earth hedged in by simple, thatched huts. People tumbled out in various states of undress and stared at us. Only men. No women to be seen. And all armed. A bad sign. Everyone started talking at once and pointing in different directions. A curtain twitched back across the door of a hut and a big man emerged looking annoyed, wondering what all the noise was about. He straightened up. It was the man of learning. It was Lukman.

He had done well for himself, filled out, put on weight – no *taken* on weight – assumed an air of substance and sported a beard. He looked astonished.

'K'tut! Little brother Uki! How did you know where to find me?'

'Well ...'

* * *

'After Surabaya I began to think. I began to read.' His eyes were sore and watery from constant exposure to cookhouse woodsmoke, not from reading. 'I read the story, "Surabaya", written by that writer, Idrus, the one who came to see us at the cement factory. I think I would have shot him dead if he had still been around, I was so angry, but later I came to see that his sarcasm about things was right. The old men just want to put themselves in the place of the Dutch. They don't want things to really change. We must immediately nationalise all Dutch property and deport every last Eurasian, repudiate the national debt, redistribute the land to the peasants, throw off the Dutch queen, ban the use of the Dutch language, trams should be free but here there are no trams so we should have new trams in every village ...' Lukman went off on a rant, gathering up the loose threads of a whole lifetime's resentments, rattling over the points like one of his imaginary trams. We should have been sitting round a jolly camp fire, sharing confidences and memories in the flickering firelight but the night was too hot for a camp fire so we just sat in a circle and stared blankly at the empty centre as if we were looking at a pie with no filling.

'... and forbid the serving of potatoes in schools ... So why are you going to Yogya?'

Uki grinned and dropped his voice to a whisper. 'We have had an adventure. We are taking back ...'

'Vital information,' I interrupted and glared at Uki. 'We have been collecting information about the Dutch stance in the next round of negotiations, stuff our delegates need to know to strengthen their hand in The Hague. We must get it back to them as quickly as possible.' The fewer people who knew what we were up to the better. They might well decide they could find a better use for our cargo.

Lukman grinned and shook his head. 'You remember how Bung Tomo used to talk about the fiery Pemuda versus the old men and their endless conferences – wild, bull buffaloes versus bleating, castrated goats. Nothing has changed. Nothing. The politicians cannot be trusted. They are not the solution but part of the problem. Only the army can act as the guardians of the people's liberty. Only the army is honest.' He looked at the outer darkness where our horses were tethered and the jerrycans were stacked. 'You have much petrol there, sister, and this route belongs to us. Perhaps you will give me some? About half should do.'

Uki and I froze and looked at each other. 'It is not mine to give. It is urgent to get it to Yogya. They have tanks there that are desperate for fuel. They need it for the tanks to defend the city.'

'They also need it for the big, fancy saloons the old men drive around in, waving at everybody and smiling to themselves. What if I were just to take it? How would that be?'

'Tanks,' I urged. 'They need it for the tanks. You do not have tanks here.'

'No.' Sadly. Bitterly. 'Here we do not have tanks. Keep your petrol.' He got up and went huffily to bed, leaving us in a backwash of petrol-fuelled guilt.

The next morning when we got up, Lukman had already stalked off on patrol but one of his men was sent to accompany us to join up with the Yogya road that followed the southern coast in from the east. We clanked on with our jerrycans intact, sounding for all the world like medieval knights in armour.

'It is no trouble,' our escort smiled away our thanks when we reached the tarmac. 'No trouble is too great for friends of Pak Lukman. Did you know he is a hero of the Battle of Surabaya? There he led an attack that killed over a hundred Indians. Some he killed with his bare hands, others by just looking at them.' He raked us with his own blazing eyes in demonstration. 'Those boys are so brave – real men – not just talkers. We all live in their shadow. Wah!'

So Lukman had become a basilisk. Our lingering guilt evaporated like the mist in the sun and the absurdity of his words kept us smiling as far as the first roadblocks around the city. Even in those early days the Revolution was already being eaten alive by its own cancerous myths and I could feel myself being squeezed to fit into the narrow mould of official history till I came out like one of those identical jelly babies of my childhood. And, of course, all jelly babies had to be boy jelly babies with that little bit extra.

* * *

'K'tut, we owe you an enormous debt of gratitude. The contents of those three jerrycans will make a tremendous contribution to the war effort. It is a pity that Amir cannot be here to welcome you.' We were back in Yogya after a relatively easy final stretch on horseback, in the palace – Bung Karno in one of his spotless, white uniforms, sitting on an old, collapsing, rattan chair and flicking disdainful cigarette ash onto the red carpet. I remembered what Bung Amir had said about his inability to make choices. Maybe the uniform was a response to that. It was either on or off. Simple.

'Three? There were four. What happened ...?'

He shrugged and smiled – as ever – waving the inconvenience of precise accounting away as beneath his dignity. 'Three, four ... what's the difference? You will notice that half the cabinet have gone. Amir for instance. After he signed the Renville agreement with the Dutch, accepting the Van Mook line, there was no saving him politically. He knew that of course but he had to sign it so the international community would bring pressure on the Dutch and stop the attack. He sacrificed himself for the nation. So now he is no more.'

'Yes but if one of the jerrycans has gone missing ...' I sounded like someone singing that horrible roundel about green bottles hanging on walls they made us learn at school.

'I have a present for you, from the Indonesian people.' He reached elegantly into a jacket side pocket with the sort of smooth-handed gesture a dandy would use to slide out a slim, gold cigarette case. It was a slim, gold cigarette case with alternating bands of white, red and yellow metal. 'For you. We would wish you to have it as a memento.' He looked at me unblinkingly and smiled.

It was a bribe of course, to keep my mouth shut, to look the other way. Impossible to refuse without giving offence, a flattering sign that I was now an accepted insider, one of the family, one who spoke the language of give and take and due deference – the *real* language of Java. Once I took it, any shortfall in the accounting would be on my head as much as anyone else's. But surely it was too big to go through the mouth of a petrol can? It couldn't be part of the loot. I tried to remember the exact dimensions of the battered, old jerrycans but I couldn't be sure. The whole point about the jerrycan business is that you don't notice them. Prudence, good manners, covetousness – it was a breathtakingly beautiful object – all pushed me in the same direction. Anyway, wasn't President Soekarno in some sense the very incarnation of the Republic? No line could be drawn between him and it, as the Dutch had found out to their cost. There are times when too much thinking can be dangerous and ungracious and anyway, wasn't I due a little payback? In all the time I had been at the Republic's beck and call I had never received a penny in proper pay, just food and lodging and scraps like the palace dog.

'Thank you, Bung.' I received it with demurely lowered head and in both hands as a gift of consequence. It slipped ever so willingly and without friction into my bag – to be seen as the true authentication of my change of nationality. This was the way things were done here.

The tension disappeared. 'So who should I make my new Minister of Defence? Soedirman would have been the obvious choice and it was grotesque for a fighting soldier like him to die of tuberculosis, an old man's disease.' He sucked smoke into still-healthy lungs. It was an important decision since Bung Karno had the good sense to leave military decisions to military men and never interfered in them. 'It must be someone who listens to his men. I used to tell Soedirman that the most important thing an officer ever learns is how to say, "Carry on sergeant." Tell me who you would choose. Ah, wait, here is my wife.'

Fatmawati was a nice, down-to-earth woman and a good mother. You could imagine that story about her hand-stitching together the first flag of the Republic for the Proclamation of Independence might actually be true – as it clearly wasn't for poor, old Betsy Ross and Martha Washington. But then it seems it's everywhere a woman's job to sit and patiently sew things together while men strut around and rip them apart. And she scrubbed up nicely as the mother of Indonesia. As she walked towards us and turned her head, I noticed she was wearing a sumptuous, new pair of ruby earrings that literally glowed about her face. I tactfully forbore to admire them. Then badness overtook me. Perhaps it was some sort of a mental short-circuit between Bung Karno, Jane Russel and exploding busts.

'Actually, Bung, I have a present for you, two fine Balinese carvings that I picked up in Jakarta – very phlegmatic. One even looks like you. I'll send them over.'

I wonder if they are still there in the palace. It never occurred to me that someone might decide they were so ghastly that they should be used as kitchen fuel, which would have had interesting results. As curiosities, they are probably objects of some value now. Poor Wim's plans came to nothing again. No thousands of ready agents, eager to blow up railway bridges for the Dutch, ever existed across Indonesia and the military planners soon realised that they depended almost entirely on the reliable transport of supplies – much more so than the guerrillas. It wasn't like a rerun of their time in Holland under the Germans but the exact opposite. It should really have been Bung Tomo's boys blowing up the bridges. Had they realised this, they would have turned around and gone home in shame. Poor Wim, a sheep in wolf's clothing and a man for whom every silver lining had a hidden cloud.

Chapter Ten

There were two of them, one tall and thin, the other short and plump and they took it in turns like those Japanese slaps delivered first to the left, then the right of my face. Now, the tall one came back in, threw a limp, brown dossier down on the table and himself into a chair. He let his whole face sag and sighed. I had pushed my luck once too often, slipping into Singapore and sliding round the normal controls, only to be picked up by a shore patrol in Little India – convinced they had caught a dangerous spy – and dragged off in mid-samosa. I should never have lit up that clove cigarette in public.

'It won't do, Mrs. Pearson. You can't expect us to allow you to come and go from Singapore like this, just wandering in and out illegally and simply get away with it. Don't you see that the fact that you don't have a passport is not an excuse? It makes it worse. We already have enough on you to put you away for years then give you back to the Dutch since their territory is where you admit you came from. I think you need to co-operate with us.' The accent was Brit-ish but with White Commonwealth tonalities.

He let that one sink in and, when I made no response, hauled open the cover and stabbed at the page with a forefinger. A very neat forefinger that. Nice, clean nails, no smoker's patina of tar, unsullied by toil. Men's hands are always interesting, something of an obsession with me. They tell you a lot. Maybe he was higher up than he seemed on first view. 'When you were picked up in the city, in fact, you were bearing a passport of the Indonesian

Republic which we do not recognise.' He took out a fresh sheet of paper. 'Passport number one.' That made him smile. 'What is the reason for your visit to Singapore?'

'I am a refugee of British nationality. I am here precisely because I need to sort out this business of passports. Second, I wish to recuperate from the injuries I sustained in a Japanese prisoner-of-war camp. Third, I wish to write a book concerning my experiences. Fourth, I don't want to stay in Singapore. I want to go to Australia.' I watched as he wrote that down. Four points on four, tidy lines, he liked that.

He raised his eyebrows and drummed his fingers on the dossier. 'A book? Not political activity then? No guns? No opium or aeroplanes? No smuggled diplomats? Have you any evidence of that?'

'You will also have found in my luggage a manuscript that I wish to work on. In Australia, that is.'

He frowned and dug back in the file. 'Ah yes. Well, we'll have to take a look at that won't we? I'm afraid you have something of a notorious reputation, Mrs. Pearson, and it may take some time for us to...'

'Don't call me that. My name is K'tut Tantri.'

He smirked back at me and slipped his pen in his inside pocket. 'Well that's rather what we have to decide isn't it? The matter at issue. Who exactly you are and exactly what you've been up to.' He closed the file, stood up and whisked away, the door slamming and locking behind him. Being locked in alone made me feel like a child, shut in the coalhole back in Glasgow and I shivered despite the heat.

* * *

'Number one. James Hay Stuart Walker was your father. You lived at 30, Moss Street, Garston and he was a commercial traveller not a boilermaker or an archaeologist as you claim in your memoir. You didn't live in dire poverty in a tenement. Your circumstances were actually quite comfortable. You weren't an only child. Walker had kids by a previous. Don't you think we consult public records? A lot of security services have been interested in you.'

'Number one,' I said. 'James Walker was *not* my father. You will see from my birth certificate that Ma was three months pregnant at the time of the wedding. He may have been a commercial traveller at one stage. Mostly he just drank. When I was ten, he walked out on us and I took the train to Glasgow Central with the intention of looking for him, was overwhelmed by the crowds and stood there crying. A big policeman came up and was kind to me and they put out a search bulletin for him. When they found him in a bar he was so ashamed he came home and stayed off the booze for three months. Of course, that didn't stop him giving me a belting. As for poverty, what is the point of growing up in Glasgow if you can't sing a song of starvation, violence and rats. It would be like growing up in Paris and not living in the Eiffel Tower. In fact, we had to move frequently and ended up living in some nasty back alley full of dustbins. Like Queen Victoria, we were not a mews. Do you have a number two?'

He sighed again. 'Did you type this manuscript yourself or did someone write it for you? It's shopgirl fiction isn't it?'

'I did, though I prefer dictation. It frees one's mind from the concern with process.'

He frowned. 'So why so you write so much in the present tense? All this happened – if it happened – years ago.'

Now it was my turn to sigh. 'This is not a creative writing course. The present is the only reality. To be remembered at all, things have to be recalled into the present. Moreover, I have worked in the movies as a scriptwriter. Movies are the art form of our age and they exist only in the fleeting present. Attempts at any other tense on the silver screen are always cumbersome and affected and unconvincing. I am thinking of you and your friends in the past tense right now.'

He had to stop and think about that. 'All police reports are in the past tense because they're supposed to be real. I think that tells us something about the truth of your so-called memoir.'

'Police? Is that who you are? I confess I am a trifle disappointed. I imagined you were something much more glamorous.'

He glared. 'Okay, we'll come to the script-writing later. We've checked with the British records. There is no evidence of any Walker being involved in the Glasgow labour movement, as you claim.'

'Impossible!' I sneered. 'Sheer invention. Walker is a very common name. Why there were two other Walkers in the same class as me at school. Mere statistics dictate that there would be a Walker somewhere. If not, that would indicate that the records are incomplete or have been deliberately tampered with.'

He closed the folder irritably. 'Come off it. Who the hell would go to the trouble of changing your records, Mrs. Pearson?'

I smiled. 'As you yourself remarked, a lot of security services have been interested in me at one time or another. Now, do you think I might have a cup of tea? I'm afraid I have lost track of the passage of time in here, being, as we are, without windows and trapped in the present tense.'

* * *

'Why would you even admit to something like that business with

Ambassador Kennedy – conspiracy, perjury, Christ knows what else?' The short, fat one was back, Tweeledum. He was sweating as though he had been the person accused of all that. The beige dossier had grown a little thicker. He wore a ratty, old jacket with elbow patches, not a suit, so was presumably lower down the pecking order than Tweedledee. They had at least brought me tea today though with measly amounts of sugar and in one of those ghastly Works Department blue cups. In Java we take lots of sugar even in savoury dishes. But the tea came with a proper matching saucer and with two dry biscuits, no doilie. Unexpected.

'Isn't one of you supposed to be nice and the other one nasty. If you're both nasty to me, it isn't going to cut any ice. Anyway, it's all long ago and far away. Statute of limitations. I'm only a little, old lady. Quite harmless. Maybe I don't remember so well and it's just an *aide-memoire*. Remembering requires forgetting ninety percent of what actually occurred and it's hard to write a life without turning it into a story or even a morality tale. And you've decided in advance that my manuscript's all lies. Perhaps it is. How would you ever be able to tell?' I smirked. I was messing with him. If he couldn't be sure about something like this how could he be sure about anything?

'That's the trouble with lies, Mrs. Pearson. They're hard to remember unlike the truth. You tend to wander and contradict yourself.' He sipped his own tea delicately but his hand was shaking and he had one of those inexplicable spasms of the arm that hit you from time to time and sloshed it on his trousers. 'Jesus Christ! Would it surprise you to learn that there is no trace of anyone called Walker associated either with Senator Kennedy or the RKO studios?' The bureaucrat's answer to everything. Only believe the paper. He rubbed at his inside thigh sourly, saw me looking and blushed.

I remained demure. 'Who says I was using the name Walker? I was, after all, married.'

He frowned and looked down at the dossier. 'Ah yes, Mr. Pearson. Tell me about Mr. Pearson. This mysterious Mr. Pearson who allegedly gave you an American passport. Was it love at first sight? Did you perhaps meet on a tram?'

I smiled and set the smirky expression irritatingly on my face like a mask. That tactic had served me well at school. The headmistress had termed it 'subaltern insolence' in more than one school report. 'But I don't want to lapse into – what was it now your friend said? – "shopgirl fiction".' I waited until he tried for the cup again, then said. 'Mr. Pearson was a shortarse.' He coughed gratifyingly and got the dossier point blank with a mouthful of tea, hastily wiped it off with his handkerchief. 'Shortarses are frequently a little pushy. I speak as a shortarse myself. And,' I continued, 'he was of Swedish origin. People always imagine Swedes as walking, blond treetrunks. Well he wasn't. Yet his shoe size was still bigger than his IQ and he was fourteen years older than me.'

He pouted and pencilled a note.

'But he had a nice house and car and a flourishing, little furniture restoration business and he got on well with Ma.'

'Sounds as if Dr. Freud would have enjoyed your family.' The pencil circled, closed in for the kill, hit paper. 'Hmm. It is on record that you once claimed to have had two children by him, both tragically lost in a road accident while he was driving under the influence. As usual, no trace of any of this can be documented. What were their names?'

'Who?'

'The children. What were their names? You may be – as you yourself say – a "shortarse" but you tell tales that are tall enough for anyone.'

I'd had enough. My patience, as Herr Hitler used to say … It was time to do 'little-old-lady'.

The lace hankie is an indispensable prop to a woman on the make. I had tutored Eunice Pringle in the strategic use of it, to great effect, for her courtroom scene and, at the crucial moment, the silly girl had just chucked it down like a tarpaulin. Now, I fumbled mine blindly down from my sleeve, indicating scattiness and senile helplessness and pressed it hopelessly to my eyes. A lace hankie is non-absorbent – full of holes – nastily sharp-edged as a thing to wipe around sensitive membranes – and totally impractical – which is the message it carries about its owner. It just shouldn't be out there in a rough world to be sullied and torn. When you let it fall gently, it flutters like a pair of see-through panties. A lace hankie is fancy knickers for the nose and men respond accordingly. They can't help it. They have been trained that way. I dropped mine with great professionalism and clutched at my heart, the fluttering of the one reflected in the other. 'I can't … talk about that. It is just too painfuuul,' I wailed. 'My babies! My poor, poor babies!'

In a flash he was dithering up on his feet, looking as confused as the ninth leg of an octopus, ringing for a female wardress to tidy away the mess of tea and spilled emotions he had made. Anything to get away from the spectacle of this ghastly, womanish sentimentality that now made me fling myself across the desk in a state of collapse. I thought of going for the teacup but that too had been drained. No point in knocking it over now. I struggled to my feet, clasped my breasts, hooting out my grief for my lost sucklings, let my knees buckle and was led away clutching at the big, strapping girl who answered the call and took me away down the corridor. She was called Janice. Interviews for today were over.

It was a small and charmless room they took me to, not exactly a cell but not far short of it, the way a kept mistress is not quite a whore. Given my own biography, perhaps I should have avoided that thought. There was a small, hard bed, the sheets worn but clean – unmade from this morning. Clearly maid service was not included in the tariff. In one corner a washbasin with fly-blown mirror – probably a real one, unlike that in the interview room that no doubt concealed a camera and recording apparatus. The window incorporated three closely spaced, vertical mullions with glass in between, disguising bars as an architectural quirk. Through them lay a scrap of grass and a flagpole with the Union Jack run up and going a little ragged in one corner like the sheets. All those damned flags. I had slept in grass huts and on the backs of trucks, even leaning against a field gun or in a genuine prison cell with seething vermin and snarling guards. Yes, I had seen worse. It was a place designed not yet to humiliate and break you but – for the moment – to contain and observe. There was a barely concealed threat in the chipped plaster and the hole worn in the linoleum. I lay down on the bed and closed my eyes, turned my senses off and retreated back into my own head.

* * *

'It won't do I'm afraid, Mrs. Pearson.'

Today, it was the tall one, Tweedledee. He had a shaving cut under his chin and was wearing cufflinks not buttoned cuffs. Did he have a job interview? Or perhaps it was for me. No. I could see now he had a button missing on one cuff. He was wearing a plain, gold wedding ring. A neglected husband.

'Your wife,' I said, 'what's her name?'

He looked surprised. 'That is hardly to the point.'

'Then let me tell you about her.' He looked tired. I pictured his wearisome home life with the faded, resentful wife announced by his ring finger, as dry as a Javanese lawn in the hot season. 'English-born, a graduate, maybe in Eng. Lit. She will be resentful about being cleverer than you. Resentful about having to look after your two noisy kids. Resentful about the unfulfilling job she has had to take teaching in some down-at-heel secondary school to help pay the rent and the maid's wages. She'll be called something like Sarah. You see how easy it is to do your job.'

A shadow passed across his face, then surprise. Then it closed down again as he bit his tongue. 'We're not here to talk about me but you.' He blushed and raised the dossier in authority. It had got bigger since yesterday, probably with the transcripts hammered out by busy, little typists overnight. How many family dinners around Singapore had that ruined? 'Talking of names, why have *you* got so many?' He opened the dossier. 'Muriel Walker, Muriel Pearson, Manxi, Manx, Miss Tenchery, Mrs. Daventry, Miss Oestermann, Sally van de As – I like that one – Molly Rosenberg, Vannen, Vanine, Vanessa Modjokerto, Surabaya Sue and K'tut Tantri. Rather more than the average woman would need, I think.'

'I am not the average woman. Those are not all me and there are others you don't mention. I worked in Hollywood where names are a fluid medium. We are quite different people at different times. Don't you find yourself thinking back and being quite amazed at some of the things you have done in the past under different circumstances? Don't you find yourself thinking, "Can that really have been me?"' Clearly not. 'Why not have a different name for each of the different people you have been? I am under no obligation to maintain continuity of identity for the convenience of the Singaporean authorities. A lot of those names were made necessary by the prying of people just like you.'

There came a crash and a howl from behind the fake mirror. Someone had caught a finger in whatever whirring apparatus they had back there. He resisted looking over his shoulder and stared professionally down at the page. I awarded him house points for that.

'It's not just the names of people. Look at that film you mention so deliberately, the one that brought you to Asia. *Bali, the Last Paradise*. There's no such film. There never has been. I think you know there's no such film. The name's not quite right. It could be this or that film. The year's not quite right. Wasn't it 1934 not 1932? And the place is wrong. You sailed from New York not the West Coast. You intentionally confuse things at every possible opportunity just to muddy the waters. You're not going anywhere until we discover just who you are and just what you've done. If you co-operate this can be short and sweet. If you don't you'll find we can be quite unpleasant and your arse will back on a ship out of here so fast it won't touch the ground.'

I wasn't happy about that. All right, my arse was no longer the pert bubble it once was but it hardly dragged on the ground.

He sent me back to my room like a naughty child. I lay back and stared at the ceiling thinking that there would be more sleepless nights for my exploited typist fellow workers but not today. All that stuff about his wife, by the way, I got from Janice, the wardress who fetched me from my room and watched me eat in the staff canteen, a big, lonely woman in whom I easily detected one of those forlorn passions – for unworthy Tweedledee – that warm-hearted women like us are prone too. She talked about her mother's operation, her bitchy sister, her painful feet. I take it all in and forget nothing. I am a good listener. I should have done this for a living.

* * *

'Except,' said the fat one, Tweedledum, 'it didn't happen like that at all.' He sighed and reached into the dossier. He had the sort of smug world-weariness at the sins of lesser beings that suggested he might grow up to be a Conservative candidate. 'Do you think intelligence services don't talk to each other? We have a report here from the Dutch NEFIS.' He had those half-moon reading glasses that make you look down your nose, a pose that also fitted him. 'They checked into your background in Bali most carefully. The family of the Rajah of Bangli confirm here that they scarcely knew you, that you bullied your way in, brought by a tourist tout and that they rented you an old garage round the back of the palace enclosure, as they thought for your car, but then found you actually living there in fearful squalour. There was a suggestion of some sordid, sexual liaison with one of the family, if not both father and son – possibly overlapping as it were – that shame prevented their confirming. According to the Dutch the Balinese are big on shame.' He laid it down and looked at me with distaste. 'Unlike some.'

'Look,' I said, 'even you must realise that it is all a matter of interpretation. Of course my family in Bangli downplayed my connection with them. I was a freedom-fighter, an enemy of the Dutch. They weren't going to admit to something that could land them in jail or worse. And the Dutch have always been happy to smear me. As an insider, I'm sure you know how easily that's done. The Dutch always tried to stop any contact between outsiders and locals, lest it bring down the empire that was founded on separation and discrimination. In their own fevered imaginings, any woman who sat in a car beside her driver must be an adulteress about to be carried off to the harem and you can't imagine what a tight, smug, little community it was. Or perhaps you can. I don't think Singapore is so different. I can't tell you how often I had to suffer browbeatings by absurd, lecherous, little men of the colonial service, ogling me as they threatened to deport me as "undesirable". They all hated me because I saw right through them and they couldn't take that. The whole colonialist enterprise is founded upon a huge bluff, a terror that someone will point out that the Emperor isn't wearing any clothes and that the natives will laugh.' I was becoming a little heated.

'But *you* did more than laugh though, didn't you Mrs. Pearson? Very much more.'

'I've never denied it. I'm proud of what I did after the war.'

He scanned down the page again. 'We are talking about *before* the war and then *during* the war. It says here that Bangli is where the Dutch built their big lunatic asylum and that to say that someone is from Bangli is to imply that they are just plain mad. That must have been very tiresome for you. But that of course is just a joke and the Dutch aren't really known for their jokes are they? But maybe the Balinese are. I believe Tantri is a girl in the local version of the Arabian Nights who has to make up fairy stories to keep a nasty rajah amused and he only spares her life to find out what outrageous tale she will come up with next.'

We looked at each other and both laughed, our first moment of real, human contact. 'A little like us?' I suggested.

* * *

'Oh for Christ's sake, Mrs. Pearson. Boo bloody hoo! Give it a rest.' He threw the transcript down on the desk and rubbed his eyes, loosened his tie and yawned. 'There was no mortgaging of the ricefields in Bali by noble peasants so you could build your bloody hotel. There was no cornucopia of ancient coins laid at your feet. Moneylenders don't lend in ancient, silver dollars. Pull the other one.' Tweedledee is back and in a snotty mood. 'Do you really expect me to believe that a bunch of rice-farmers are going to sell their children into slavery for the crazy ambition of a foreigner which they could never even begin to understand?' He slurped at his morning coffee. Then made a face. I had been offered none.

'I ask you to believe nothing. I am simply telling you what happened. Is it so hard to believe that they saw me as their friend and helped me as I had helped them?'

'Frankly yes. For the Balinese to be as you describe them they would have had to have wings and a halo. I find no mention in your account of the island of the epidemics of smallpox, diphtheria and endemic starvation that were also part of the scene.'

'I see that you have never travelled in Indonesia. If you had, you would be far less ready to dismiss out of hand the possibility that other people might be kinder, less selfish and more open-minded than ourselves in the West, even in the midst of the greatest difficulties. If you travel far enough you get to a point where you are willing to believe almost anything. That is why it broadens the mind.'

He tutted and dealt out piles of stapled documents on the table top like a man setting up a game of patience. He teased one out.

'Right. Here is a statement that the Dutch acquired from the American OSS.' He passed it over. 'It's from a Mr. Bob Koke, an American from Hollywood, who invested in a hotel in Kuta just before the war. Apparently, his female business partner proved unreliable. His wife said that she tried to get her hooks into him but she was more a vampire than a vamp.' He looked up. 'I suppose that must be an American joke. There was a question of funds removed from a joint account, funds subsequently used to construct a rival establishment across the road. I believe that partner was you.'

'Bob was always jealous of me as was his ball-breaking wife. He was a tennis gigolo, all forehand smash and capped teeth – at least he put his money where his mouth was. He thought all he had to do was flash those china teeth and flutter his eyelashes and any woman would swoon. Well I didn't. His wife was a silly lobsick goose who thought she could paint – though certainly no oil painting herself. I had been a highly successful scriptwriter and journalist whereas he had merely "designed movie sets" and introduced Bali to the surf board. His idea for a hotel was limited to that ramshackle beach set he claimed to have created for *Mutiny on the Bounty*! I ask you. Who needs anyone to design a beach! In fact, I was never convinced that he had any genuine link with Hollywood at all. He was a sad fantasist who took colourful events from my own life to adorn his own rather dull biography. Why, I once heard him repeat a cruel wisecrack Joe Kennedy made to me about Gloria Swanson, as his own experience. In those days, when shooting the stars in close up, they would sometimes smear the lens with Vaseline or take them through gossamer tissue to hide any lines. "When we were filming *Queen Kelly*," Joe cracked, "we tried shooting poor, old Gloria through gauze but it was still no use. In the end, we had to use a Witney blanket!" Joe never wasted any time on Irish gallantry. Oh, I don't want to talk about it. It is all still too ...'

'"Painful?" I think, is the word you use.' He dealt out another wodge of papers with croupier coolness. 'Hmm! People who stayed in your own bungalows seem to have experienced something quite different from the fairyland, Balinese palace of your memoir. How about "a set of dirty native huts". I have here copies of reports from the Dutch secret service into the activities at

Manxi's bungalows just before the Japanese invasion – apparently a place of ill repute on the beach much used by hot-blooded, young Dutch flyers from the airbase right next door. There was some question of possible security leaks, found to be without substance and the report recommended turning a blind eye to the prostitution on the grounds of containment of an unavoidable evil.' He sat back, folded his arms, raised an eyebrow quizzically, tried not to look smug. 'So it seems that in the official view you were not just "undesirable" but "an unavoidable evil", Mrs. Pearson. Quite a compliment. And as for your fellow artists, they are also less than complimentary – regarding you and your work as something of a joke.' He scrabbled in another pile like a cat covering its excrement, pulled out more muck-raking vilification and pushed it across.

I refused to read it. I was unmoved. 'You are confusing the first hotel with the second. As for art, all great artists have been regarded as a joke, especially by their fellows, Picasso, Chagall, Henri Rousseau ... You don't know them? No I thought not. As it is, yapping reviewers do not interest me.'

'And yet ... And yet not a single one of your wonderful paintings has survived to speak out for you as an artist and explain what you were doing in Bali. How very odd.'

'There was so much confusion during the war. Wars and tropical climates are not kind to paintings. An artist is not be judged by quantity but quality. A single painting can change the world. Some of my pictures, I confess, I destroyed myself. I have always been my own fiercest critic.'

* * *

'I liked that bit about the wild sea releasing your innermost emotions,' said Tweedledee, briskly tapping his teeth with the edge of the transcript till it turned soggy, 'a sort of reverse pathetic fallacy. A touch of quality that. But look, you must stop going on about this great, romantic figure Prince Nura. You're not doing yourself any good with it. We know all about him. He was no great shakes, not even a little Valentino sheikh. He's reliably described as "short, dumpy, usefully unimaginative to the Dutch". He was never engaged in the rebellion, only had the most rudimentary education – oh and you *did* habitually sleep with him. Many witnesses confirm it.'

'Did I ever deny that? Why would I? Why all these questions?' I questioned. 'Is this a matter of just meeting immigration requirements or are you trying to psychoanalyse me? What is the interest to you of my prewar sleeping arrangements? God knows, they barely interest *me*. Or are your big brothers, America, Holland, pulling your strings? What's it all for?'

'It goes to the question of your reliability. The Dutch would like to get their hands on you. We must protect our citizens from dangerous elements. You are a notorious person.'

'Why thank you dear. That's exactly what the Dutch always used to say in my youth but you know, after a certain age people go glum and get respectable. I don't know why. It's nice to be still thought of that way at my time of life. It makes me feel like dear, old Mae West in her glory days. I expect the Japanese said much the same too when they tortured me but they were harder to understand.'

'You surely would not compare the Japanese methods with our own?' He blinked. It had actually hit home. He took a breath and shook his head. 'Would you care for some coffee? Sugar?'

Whatever he might say, Tweedledee was clearly troubled almost to the point of humanitarianism. I had got under his skin.

He nodded at Janice who lumbered to her feet and headed off down the corridor, a dreamy expression on her face. Had he just called her 'Sugar'? We women are such fools, building crystal castles on the basis of some man's long eyelashes and a suggestion of weightiness around the crotch.

'I merely meant that it brought it all back, that it was deeply upsetting. It took me years to forget and now you are demanding that I remember. The memory is a dangerous thing. If you look back at good times, you realise what you have lost. If you look back at bad times, it brings the horror back anew. In Indonesia at that time it was often dangerous to remember too much and you taught yourself to get out of the habit.'

'Not "painful" this time? That is what you usually say, isn't it, when you want to dodge a question?'

I felt anger well up inside up. I resisted it, knowing he was provoking me deliberately. 'Your methods may be different from the Japanese, the aims are the same. Interrogation has nothing to do with the elicitation of useful information. It's all about proving your own petty power. As you well know.'

'I had hoped that you might find it therapeutic, that it might strike a chord that would lead you to unburden yourself of the rest of the truth. And yet, Mrs. Pearson, we find, as usual, all sorts of odd gaps in what you choose to tell us. Why, for example, did you stay in Bali in the face of the Japanese invasion? Most Westerners found it prudent to leave – except the neutrals.'

'Who left and who stayed was a lottery. We used to talk a lot about the Dutch officers who had flown their mistresses out to Australia and left their wives behind. Where else was I to go? I had no means except for my hotel which – as it happened – the Japanese immediately destroyed. I had made Bali my home. I considered myself Balinese, so a sort of neutral.'

'Hmm. Bob Koke says here that, once he'd gone, your first thought was to march across the road and throw your weight about, grab his bit of the hotel and his car and scare his staff into submission by threatening to have them shot when your friends, the Japanese, arrived.'

'I told you Bob Koke and I weren't friends. He made that up.'

'Yet you held a British passport at that time? An American passport? Both?'

'I also have an Indonesian passport, as you know. In a world full of power-mad bureaucrats, you can never have too many passports.' Janice returned with the coffee and put it down on the desk in front of me with a wan smile. Most of it was in the saucer. She was a clumsy girl.

'Yes, I have that passport here before me. But not – crucially – from that time. How would it have been possible? There was no such thing as Indonesia for you to be a citizen of. So you were necessarily – as I said – British or American or both and any act of collaboration with the invading Japanese would have been an act of treason. And it seems there may well have been such acts.' He sighed and reached into the file again. The voice dropped to a machine gun rat-a-tat. 'Did you, or did you not, run the Bali hotel as a facility for Japanese military personnel?'

I laughed in his face. 'I did not – though it would have been a wonderful revenge. Apart from all their attempts to undermine my business, the Bali Hotel actually banned me from the grounds.'

'Yes. You said that. And did you, or did you not become the mistress of a Japanese naval officer, highly placed in the Balinese administration and subsequently found guilty of war crimes? You were seen frequently as a passenger in his car – a rather ostentatious and distinctive vehicle. There can be no mistake about it.'

'I most certainly did not. Major war crimes are seldom committed on the back seats of staff cars. I don't think you realise the position of women under a foreign occupation. As a man how could you? It was necessary for my work with the resistance to cultivate good relations with powerful people who could be used by us for our own ends. Propositions were often made that could not be flatly refused. In such circumstances a woman has to develop delaying tactics that might avoid confrontation and turn a situation suddenly dangerous. The world is not as straightforward as simple men may think – be they Western or Japanese.'

'Is that a yes or a no?'

'Women at that time were often forced into arrangements that they neither sought nor relished. Each side may well have had entirely different ideas of how voluntary a relationship might be.' I looked at Janice and she offered a furtive smile of encouragement. I sipped my coffee. Hang on. What was this? Somehow Janice had slipped a tot of whisky into it. Good girl! 'Lovely coffee, dear. Thank you.'

'So is that a yes or ...?'

'No. Absolutely no. The fact that I had to escape from Bali to Java hidden under the seat of a Chinese bus rather proves the point. I can only speak of any such relationship as seen from my own side, of course.' I balanced the coffee on my lap. I didn't want it getting too close to Tweedledee's flaring nostrils.

'Hmm. And then, after all this unpleasantness in prison of which you speak in such detail, the Japanese suddenly let you go. Now why do you imagine that was?'

I shrugged elaborately, nearly lost the coffee, caught it just in time. 'I imagine they had had their fun with me and saw no point in detaining me any more. Haven't you got a note about it there in all that stuff?'

'Well, oddly ...' He smirked and pulled out another sheet of paper and scanned it sceptically. 'It seems that you were not simply flung out into the street as one might have expected – or shot for real – but seen being politely escorted back to Surabaya on the train by a Japanese officer where you were admitted to a private room in the Simpang hospital. It doesn't say here what class of carriage you travelled in. The other details we have. And shortly afterwards, the Japanese radio started new, shortwave broadcasts of particularly offensive propaganda to Australia using the voice of a young woman with a marked Scots accent. Several people, including Bob Koke, identified that voice as yours.'

I smiled sourly. 'Enough of bloody Bob. He had every reason to bear me a grudge. We ended up in court over the hotel business. There was bad blood between us. And, as you can hear for yourself, I haven't got a Scottish accent.'

'Not now perhaps. But then ...? Some people can turn it on and off at will, you know – speak with forked tongue and all that. I think you mentioned earlier in your script that you had deliberately learned to imitate BBC English just for office use. A bit of a linguistic chamaeleon then. Let me play you a little to jog your memory.'

He went over to a table set up against the wall and twiddled with some knobs on an extraordinary gadget that recorded sound on a spool of tape instead of a shellac disc. A loud hiss, followed by thumping, martial music. Then a very young voice emerged, alternately swelling and shrinking through the fog and crosscut by moans as of some deep-sea creature. 'I want to talk to you about our Australian prisoners. You know we have thousands of them all over the East. You know how they were abandoned by the British in Singapore and Hong Kong and Batavia. They all ran away and left them. Many of the men who ran away are there with you, relying on your protection, claiming to be heroes. There is a saying here, "To survive the angry tiger you do not need to run faster than the tiger, only faster than the friend who stands beside you." This is not the war of our Australian prisoners and we look after them until we can send them home to you after the final Japanese victory. This is not your war either. It is a war made by your leaders for their own ends and it is an unjust war. There is no dishonour in you ending it right now so that we can all live in peace. You remember how good peace was? You remember what it was like to have your husbands and sons about you. The only people preventing that happy state are your own generals and politicians who have betrayed you. This a painful truth but a truth nonetheless ...'

'Nasty that – very. Oh, and there's your favourite word, "painful", again. Do you deny that that is your voice?'

'I think you don't know very much about Scottish accents,' I gulped. I would not cry. 'That one sounds rather Edinburgh to me.'

'Really? Yet all our experts say most definitely Glasgow.' He sat down, made a little steeple with his fingers and looked at me through it, blew a little gale across the roof ridge, huffing and puffing but not yet blowing my house down. 'Of course, perhaps I should mention that my elder brother was one of those Brits who ran away on the last troopship out – badly wounded of course. He lost a leg. Limped away rather than ran, then.' He slapped the cover of his folder shut, stood up and flounced out like a dancehall girl who has just had her bum pinched.

Just my luck to find one of those rare creatures that actually liked their siblings. What were the odds? Janice looked at me reproachfully and bit her nails, always a nasty habit. Now he was angry, her face said. All my fault.

Tweedledum sucked in his bottom lip and laid down the piece of paper he had been reading. 'But again it can't have been quite like that, can it?'

No Janice today. Perhaps she does not bother to sit in on dumpy, little Tweedledum. Perhaps unsexy Tweedledum with the currant bun face is thought not to need a chaperone to reign in his stallion sexuality in my presence.

'For once you have made the mistake of being specific, Mrs. Pearson, given us dates and places. There was no joyful liberation of Western women by smiling rebel forces, no *feu de joie* at the Ambarawa camp. Far from it. What really happened was that British soldiers arrived first and fought for their lives alongside Japanese troops against the mob of attacking Islamist Pemuda. There is a full report in the archives by Wing Commander Tull who was in charge of supplying the camp by airdrops from Dakotas, a necessary expedient since road supply was made impossible by hostile, local forces. Before thousands of witnesses, on 22nd November 1945, the rebel fighters broke through the defensive perimeter of the camp and drove the mainly Dutch civilians – starving women and children – into a compound where they mowed them down with machine gun fire and threw hand grenades among survivors before they could be driven off. They then maintained a steady bombardment of mortar fire on the undefended prisoners' compounds over the next few weeks, killing and wounding many more. Are you now admitting to being complicit in that horrendous war crime or were you not there at all, or were you just looking the other way?'

Hot and strong today. I spoke carefully. 'The revolution was not a single force. There were all sorts of groups with all sorts of different aims. Some were political extremists, others religious. You cannot imagine the confusion. Occasionally they fought with each other, sometimes they submerged their differences or switched allegiances. Yet behind it all was the belief that the world had been offered a final opportunity to begin afresh, that it was possible to keep an idea pure and realise it in all its virtue. I can only tell you that the young men who broke me out of Ambarawa were the finest kind of idealists who would never have been involved in any such atrocity – and there *were* Indonesian atrocities just as there were many Dutch. Surely you already know this or are you the innocent victim of British propaganda?'

Tweedledum smiled then blushed, ashamed of himself for his levity. 'Me, an innocent victim of propaganda? You will pardon me but, coming from you Mrs. Pearson, I really find that rather funny.'

* * *

Tweedledee looked down at the dossier like my old headmistress looking at a report on a recalcitrant pupil. 'A minor point. There was no radio broadcast of the Independence Proclamation. That was just PR – another word for lies. The famous, "authentic" recording was mocked up in a studio after the event. The picture of the actual Proclamation shows just a standard microphone not a radio mike and don't you think it's nice the way the declarers of independence stand around in Japanese poses of respect and submission with their hands in front of their balls?'

'The Japanese may have been midwives to the birth of independence, but the child is purely Indonesian.'

He snorted. 'But that's just by the way. So now we get to it. You have avoided the question. At the time of your own Proclamation broadcast what passport did you hold?' He paused, pen poised in mid-air, as if to administer the fatal blow.

'American, of course. I've already told you.'

'The marriage to Karl Pearson, yes. But had you formally renounced British nationality? That's the issue here.'

'I forget what it said on the form. In those days having more than one nationality was treated a bit like bigamy but I had abandoned it and it me, a bit like Karl. Surely you have your own records?'

'You see, if you hadn't, then any actions in support of the Indonesian fighters, in time of war, might be held to be treasonable and subject to the most severe penalties.'

'But the British and the Indonesians weren't at war. They never had been – "formally" as you say. The Second World War was over, all the neat pieces of paper had been signed and the bills were being sent out. And after the Oranje Hotel incident, the Brits and the Indonesians had come to terms and "formally" signed an agreement so that they were "formally" allies of some sort. I believe the agreement was that the two sides would keep out of each other's way and that the Brits would make no moves to disarm the patriots, an agreement they promptly broke. I was there, you see. I saw. I was at the Red Bridge that day, the day the real fighting began.'

'So you say. But you continued your activities *after* the fighting with the British had started, didn't you? This much-vaunted Indonesian patriotism of yours, I wonder if you didn't just think, "After all my acts of treason, the British and Americans will want to hang me and the Dutch shoot me, I'd better become an Indonesian nationalist since there's nowhere else to go." That's really what happened isn't it?'

'You mean I should have become even more loyal to the Brits *after* they started raining bombs down on my head, deliberately trying to kill *me*? But by then I had an Indonesian passport, you see. The fact that the Brits didn't recognise it is surely not my problem. I've told you. I was the first foreigner ever to get a passport from the Republic of Indonesia. They don't give them away with chewing gum. You look confused. Don't worry dear. I expect the records got lost. Is it time for lunch?'

* * *

'Very nice,' purred Tweedledee, resuming and looking down at my memoir. I'd had my usual NAAFI standard meat pie – other ranks for the use of – with Janice for company which is horribly clogging to the bowels – the pie I mean, not Janice, she is a very considerate listener – and most unsuitable to such a hot climate – again not Janice. I wondered whether the nobs got something better. I could really have used an afternoon doze. 'But not quite what happened I think. Somehow you never, ever, tell the whole story.' Oh yes, Janice is back. I should have said. She has had her hair done. She looks nice but has gone unconvincingly blonde. Perhaps she should have the eyebrows done too. They stayed black which is never a good look. I will suggest it at teatime when we have one of our all-girls-together chats.

'Those rallies at the Simpang Club for example. Not all the sort of chummy tea party you describe.' I started. Tea? Perhaps he was reading my mind. 'And Soetomo's oath about the hair was actually – let me see – ah yes – that he would not cut his hair "until all whites had been hurled into the sea". And that was to be taken very, very literally, it seems.' He pulled out a single sheet from the brown dossier. 'Let me read you now just one eye-witness account of what really went on at your Simpang Club. There are many more. The public business of the place was as a collection point for whites and Eurasians where they were then dragged out, killed and their corpses piled up on the club's outside dance floor. Perhaps you did not notice that during your nice tea? I quote. "Before each execution Soetomo mockingly asked the crowd what should be done with this enemy of the people. The crowd yelled "Kill!" after which the executioner named Rustam came forward and decapitated the victim with one stroke of his samurai sword. The victim was then left to the bloodthirstiness of boys 10, 11 and 12 years old who further mutilated the body. I can't say how many people were dispatched this way but it was certainly in the hundreds. From my position, I could see into the back of the garden where there was a tree on the riverbank. One by one, women were tied to the tree. According to the shouts of the executioners and spectators they had lived with Japanese. Peeping through the lashes of my downcast eyes, I saw a spectacle so shocking, repulsive and gruesome in its reality that it may never have been equalled in history. Completely absorbed in their grisly business, the executioners – the champions of liberty! – then thrust their bamboo spears into the genitals of their helpless victims with all their might. The heartrending screams and the collapsing and shaking of the body of the poor woman only drove the bloodlust of the executioners still higher. They drilled through a certain point in the abdomen with the bamboo spears just long enough so that the unfortunate woman gave up the ghost from her wounds and blood loss. Then the bodies were thrown in the Mas river round the back of the Simpang Club." So it wasn't used just for jolly bathtime fun between the romping boys as you suggest.'

He lay down the paper and put his hands together like a judge summing up. 'Later, it seems, your chum Soetomo ordered them to pile up the severed heads and corpses from the dancefloor and throw them in the sea. You are right, Mrs. Pearson. Japanese habits did die hard among the people they had trained and armed. But sometimes there is a little poetic justice. Admiration is a two-edged sword – no pun intended.' He scanned another piece of paper. 'Other witnesses swear they caught other Pemuda literally drinking the blood of murdered Japanese prisoners inside the Babutan jail, apparently as an expression of their regard for the military virtues they had imparted to them in training.' Janice had begun to sniffle into a handkerchief. He shot her a frown.

The meat pie rose up in a belch. I struggled to talk through it. Tweedledee would see it as weak, womanish nausea induced by his penny dreadful tales. 'All lies. Propaganda from the Allies. Typical, incredible falsehoods. I saw no such thing. They would do anything to discredit the movement. I don't believe a word of it. But you must remember there was very little reason left in the world at that time. There was no normality any more. Everyone had gone a little mad. The Dutch did very much worse.'

He shook his head irritably. 'I don't think that's the point. We are talking about your own complicity in war crimes here.'

'War crimes?' I boomed, Lady Bracknell's 'Handbag?' echoing in my head. 'War crimes? In that case what about the bombing of Surabaya?'

* * *

There was something in the wind – something judgemental. Both Tweedledum and Tweedledee were here, sitting to attention. A third chair stood empty in between. Unlike their own, that chair had arms, a boss's chair, then.

'Please sit down, Mrs, Pearson. We shan't keep you long. We are just waiting for our colleague.'

I sat as primly as possible. We stared at each other. The air became strained. Who were we waiting for, Churchill? I tapped my fingers and sighed, opened my mouth to say something. Then the door opened – we all turned – and in waltzed Janice. I giggled at the anti-climax and then she went and sat at the head of the table, put down the folder and looked up at me with a firm, businesslike expression I had never seen before. That wiped the smirk off my face.

'My staff and I have had a final discussion of your case Mrs. Pearson and feel it is time to make a recommendation to the minister based upon the evidence laid before us.' She tossed the fake blond hair back behind her ears and grinned at me. The little hussy! The two Tweedles chuckled at my obvious discomfort. I had been taken for a ride. Just what had I said to her in those moments of girl-girl intimacy over the meat pies and the cups of tea when I thought *I* was pumping *her*? I realised for the first time how insidiously I had been drawn back into an institutional sense of Britishness by the resonating memory of school dinners – seduced by the romance of stodge and boiled cabbage in the canteen. 'I'm afraid that everything you have presented to this panel is both mendacious and meretricious. We find that there is *prima facie* evidence of smuggling, infringement of immigration and foreign exchange regulations and arms and drug dealing. Further, we have proof of irregular, financial transactions of all sorts that would be of great concern to your Indonesian sponsors. Oh and perhaps we should not forget high treason and participation in war crimes.'

'So what are you going to do – hand me over to the Dutch, the Americans? Send me back to Blighty?' I found it hard to suppress a tremble in my voice.

'No, Mrs. Pearson. That would be a great waste of your talents. Such a record suggests to us that you are more than qualified to be a recruit for our own intelligence services. You have an excellent, inside knowledge of the current Indonesian leadership which is something that interests us greatly. I would suggest you come and work for us. We can arrange for that visit of yours to Australia to be made possible and for this file to find rest in a safe place away from the public eye.'

'Out of the question! The freedom of Indonesia is a noble cause to which I have dedicated years of loyal service, a cause for which I would lay down my very life. I couldn't possibly do anything that would harm my friends!'

Janice gave an I-told-you-so look to either side and clasped her hands together in her lap. She leaned forward and dropped her voice and spoke slowly and with emphasis as if to a dull-witted child. 'Nor would we ask you to. All we want is information. Surely, it would be of benefit to both nations to understand each other better and to avoid misunderstandings. Your Indonesian friends, as we see from your luggage, have left you high and dry and virtually penniless. We would be prepared to pay you, of course.'

'You insult me further by suggesting my loyalty is for sale? You think I would sell my honour to keep my comfort?' I stuck out my lower lip and flashed hostile outrage around the room. 'How much?'

* * *

The stateroom aboard the sleek SS *Marella* offered a rare interval of peace and prelaxation. It was the first time in years I had been cossetted with proper food and a luxurious bathroom with real, flowing, hot water and the effects on my physical and mental wellbeing were almost immediate but it also made me aware of how very tired and fragile I had let myself become. After all, I had come to the Indies in search of paradise and found war, revolution and death. I discovered a hidden passion for fancy cream cakes and the first time I ate high tea – the only truly civilised meal in the Western canon – I burst into tears in the china-tinkling saloon – as overwhelmed by a sense of loss and futility in the face of a rum baba as I had been by the nostalgia of a NAAFI meat-slime pie. After that, I kept mostly to my cabin, taking exercise on the deserted, nocturnal decks – letting the wind snatch away my terrors and enjoying anonymity, secure in the knowledge that no one knew who or where Surabaya Sue was. Left on my own in my cabin, I cried a lot.

There are few places better than Australia to bring you rapidly down to earth, for the Australians have always been the awkward squad of the British Empire with a permanently truculent set to their shoulders. It is as if the force of gravity is stronger there, keeping your feet more firmly on the ground, and the coarse Australian sun bleaches the flow and colour out of unctuous, British bullshit. Or perhaps it is just that it's a country full of red meat, thick and solid as common sense. As we tied up at Fremantle, I became aware of a strange rumbling outside and, peering through the porthole, saw a great crowd gathered round the gangplank. The dockers had turned out to welcome me, waving gay banners as vigorously and happily as the Jakartans of Van Mook's return. 'Good on ya, Sue!' 'Hands off Indonesia!' Alas no 'Death to Van Mook.' At the end of the world war, the 'wharfies' had blacked all Dutch vessels in support of the revolution and even rubbishing their own, treasured 'White Australia' policy to allow Indonesian dissidents to stay. The Dutch had been up to no good in Australia, imprisoning Indonesian sailors there who refused to work on their ships or serve in their army and trying to spirit 'troublemakers' away to prisons that were virtual death camps in New Guinea. There had been trouble at a Dutch military base. People had been shot. Attempts had been made to deport aboriginal wives. My wobbly travel documents did not permit me to descend the gangplank so I turned out on deck dutifully and strutted and waved to them in my best batik. I wasn't sure about that clenched fist *merdeka* salute and how it might go down here. Didn't Italian fascists do that?

Melbourne was a whirl of frustrated press attention, baying at me from the dockside. In Singapore, I had promised to refrain from all political activity but the government was tying itself into knots over whether it supported the Indonesians or not and whether they would even allow me to land in Sydney when the ship got there. As it was, I just flounced down the gangplank with six pieces of luggage and no passport and told the press to let the government know that my address would be the Australia Hotel if they wanted to see me. People were dying for accurate information about the Indonesian situation. How could I refuse them? Instead of peace and quiet it was noise and confusion. Questions were asked in parliament, ministers were hounded by press and opposition and I was grilled – fair barbied – by the media, giving talks, interviews, denying rumours about me circulated by the Dutch. I was a communist, a fascist, I had run a brothel in Bali, all that rubbish dredged up again. Being hard up, I arranged for most of this press attention to take place at restaurants and stuck them with the bill. God how I ate!

After a while, it was clear my moon was beginning to wane, coverage was slipping down from the quality press to the redtops and I was reduced to singing for my supper at one of the less fashionable Sydney yacht clubs in front of the starched shirts of the most conservative bunch in the city. They looked like a convention of bank branch managers and failed estate agents. Hardly any reporters had turned up, being by now familiar with my song. My audience was dozing, fuddled by drink. Then

I had a bright idea.

'I should like to announce ...' I said at the end, over the ruins of the salmon Wellington – the meal had been unfilling but I could get something better on the way home. I'd noticed a proper fish and chip place just down the road. '... that I have been touched by the sympathetic response of the Australian people to the plight of innocent Indonesians who ask for nothing more than to be left alone and in peace. However, some of your newspapers have been less than fair to me. All sorts of outrageous allegations have been made. I have therefore instructed my solicitors to begin proceedings for libel against some of the muck-raking Sydney press. I wish to let it be known here and now that I will not settle for less than a million US dollars in damages.'

That woke them up. There is something about the phrase 'a million dollars' that resonates like a teaspoon thrown into an empty teacup. One old buffer with a neatly regimented line of pens in his blazer badge pocket sat bolt upright and shouted, 'Why a million?'

'Because a girl has to live. I'm Surabaya Sue though I haven't got a Surabaya sou to my name so I'm suin'.'

It brought the house down. They laughed till their dentures dropped out. That little joke got me back on all the front pages even if I couldn't really raise enough cash even to pay for the stamp on a summons.

The news from Indonesia wasn't good. I scanned the newspapers compulsively. The Dutch were consolidating the Van Mook line. The communists were restive as the new government under Hatta tried to disband some of the wilder militia groups, stripped Bung Tomo of his armed support and reformed the national army under firmer, central government control. Civil war bristled and threatened on every island. At the turn of the year, there would be the menace of an Islamic secession under the Darul Islam movement and a full communist uprising in Madiun, put down by the army, with great bloodshed and hundreds if not thousands executed after the fighting. More people died there than in the Battle of Surabaya but censors would ensure Indonesia was not told about that. I feared for Lukman. In the midst of all this, the Australians decided that in the last three months I had tarred my own feathers enough with my communist supporters in the country to justify my deportation back on the SS *Marella* to Singapore. I went with regret. This time there were no flags and no banners and still no British passport.

Singapore was as keen to pass the parcel, or perhaps fling the hot potato, as Australia, and I was met off the ship by a blank-faced immigration officer from Sutton Coldfield with a terrible cold who hustled me immediately to the airport. Tweedledum and –dee and Janice made themselves scarce. They must have got a rocket for unloading so much trouble on Australia. At the airport, I was signed for by another blank-faced man from Dayton, Ohio, with a bad cough who handed me the flimsy ghost of an American passport stamped 'Valid for single re-entry into USA only' and escorted me to the very steps of a waiting aircraft that throbbed with impatience to be off. So I arrived 'home' and stood alone in the dark, windswept snow of New York, shivering in my thin, tropical frock and with my luggage ranged around me, coughing and sneezing and with my own coagulating snot sticking in my throat like an iced oyster – symptoms that were doubtless parting gifts from my Anglo-American, Singapore nannies. This time the word 'home' had a bitter aftertaste. Time for some home truths, then. I was ill, penniless and a certified leftie in a country floundering in a tidal backwash of anti-communist hysteria. It was Christmas. I was hungry.

Chapter Eleven

'I saw you that time in the Hotel des Indes. Don't think you got away with it. I recognised you right enough. But Christ! You've really piled on the pounds since Bali.' Bob Koke, CIA agent, in a white seersucker suit with a Panama hat on the hatstand. Clearly maintaining his tropical credentials although the leisurewear look and the Hawaiian shirts of Bali had now gone for good. We were sitting in a bland Washington office with a great, grey, steel desk, just down from the Capitol. A wall calendar showed a busty girl with deranged eyes sprawling on the wing of a bomber labelled 'Big Boy'. In post-war America everyone seemed to be working for the government and enslaved by phallic imagery in cars, architecture, even those great, shiny ashtrays like bombs they stood erect outside the elevators. The sign on the door said that this was where an accountant conducted his business but that was an awfully ambitious mirror for a legitimate accountant to have on his wall. Someone in the outer office was hammering away at a typewriter – the olive green, government-issue Corona they all use – another dead giveaway.

'I figured it was no business of the United States to get you shot for collaborating even if you deserved it. It would be a pretty shitty world where we only got what we deserved, wouldn't it? It was amnesty time anyway. Of course I *was* still a little ticked about the Bali deal but every little thing I did had to involve the Dutch and the Brits and Christ knows who else in triplicate and you would have made a helluva lot of paperwork. *You* always do.

In those days, if we'd wanted to, someone could have dropped the colonial army a couple of bucks to take you out one night with a machete in a dark street. Simpler times, Manxi.'

The typewriter went oddly silent when he stopped talking.

'Thank you for that.'

The typewriter clacked briefly again and stopped. They were clearly typing up our conversation live as it happened. I was an outside broadcast. There must be a bug somewhere. It was the straight version of that scene from *The Great Dictator* where Charlie Chaplin is dictating to a typist and there is a total but comical lack of fit between the length of his speech and the length of her typing. I had met Charlie when he came to Bali, a nice but unhappy man, uncomfortable in his own skin. I abruptly started up again, deliberately talking at breakneck speed.

'How long have you worked for the agency. In Bali? No? Later? Yes? Of course the CIA didn't exist then, did it? Like Indonesia. You were in an airforce uniform. The last time I saw you. Was that just a front? Maybe you can be both airforce and agency, I don't know. I don't know anything about spying or collaborating. As you saw, I'm just a simple girl who ran a hotel.'

The typewriter rattled along. The bell tinged like a streetcar careering out of control. Someone swore in a man's voice. Bob held up his hand.

'Whoa! Slow down, Manxi. Cool your engines. I was recruited after we left Bali for the States. They needed people who spoke Malay and only the Brits had them. I tried to get hold of you discreetly after that sighting in Jakarta but you'd left and nobody knew where you'd gone. That guy Wim you were with told me you'd talked about Semarang which was off the map to us. Nice guy. Smart as a whip too. Original thinker. Do you know he told me he ran this network of spies back in the Surabaya days?

He collected together this bunch of sweet, little old ladies who were just invisible to the Indonesians. They wandered in and out of everywhere with these little cups of tea they'd made. People thought just because they didn't have any teeth they couldn't speak Dutch and Javanese and Madurese and didn't have any ears. You wouldn't believe the stuff he picked up through them.' He swivelled forward in his chair and opened a brown dossier. Another of those damned dossiers. I wondered how much of the Singapore stuff had found its way in there. Not a lot by the look of it since it was quite slim.

'It says here you recently applied for an American passport that was refused?'

I nodded.

He made the rictus of a man afflicted with wind. 'Now that's kinda a double bind. If we give you one now, it means you were entitled to one during the war which makes some of the things you did treasonable. On the other hand we'd rather have you over there than over here. Those talks you give, those articles you write, they stir things up in a way we don't find helpful. We're very interested in Indonesia. Sure, since the republicans took out the commies in Madiun, we don't see any immediate danger. Of course the factory workers went on strike too and they caved in to them. But I guess you don't know how nasty industrial strikes can be like we do. But we'd like to know more about the current leadership. Fact is, up at the White House, they're screaming for gen so they can find a way out. Who's in? Who's out? Bung Karno. Who advises him these days? Is he stable? Can he be bought? What colour socks does he wear? Who's he sleeping with? We're real interested in his health. Do you figure you could get us a stool sample?'

I looked puzzled. 'A stool sample? He doesn't sit on a stool.'

'Oh come on Manxi, don't play dumb with me. Stool. Shit. Doody. Yeah. I assume the toilet arrangements are pretty informal.' He shrugged. 'OK, well maybe some blood, then. Throw a fit, punch him on the nose and make sure you get plenty of blood on your frock, whatever. Use some initiative. Sperm would be good too. Maybe you ain't got the tools for collecting that one, Manxi, looking more like a sperm whale yourself these days, though I hear he throws it around generously enough.'

'Look,' I said. 'I quite literally won't do shit for you.' Then, of course, the idea popped into my head that I might do just that. Mine or Bung K's, how could they tell the difference between two turds? Or maybe some thrusting young palace guard's or a wobbly, old gardener's? What would be the implications of a substitution and how could I best use it to knock the crap out of US foreign policy? I would have to think about that. 'If you're so keen on controlling things why don't you act a little smart yourself, do something useful and just threaten to cut off Marshall Aid till the Dutch return to the conference table. Sabre-rattling's no good. They know you're not dumb enough to get bogged down in any hopeless colonial war like the Brits did. I say, let your big bucks do the fighting. I'd rather be over there too but if you think I'm going to spy on my friends for you, you're badly mistaken. If I go, I go as a free agent. You should know that my love of Indonesia is so strong that I am almost to be seen as a victim of it.'

He smirked and flicked the dossier cover back and forth between his hands. 'That so? Really? A victim of it? I like that. Oh my! You know why Soekarno likes you? It's not a meeting of minds. It's because you're short. He's got this thing about tall people, anti-Dutch and all that. Intimidated. You may be short but I understood you'd always been ... flexible.' He looked down. 'That would let us be a little flexible too. Talking of big bucks,

I see you don't have a whole lot in your bank account at the moment and you're running up a lot of bills – taxes, utilities, telephone – my but you make some interesting phone calls, Manxi!' He looked back up. 'I guess the film industry ain't too kind to those of your particular political colour at the moment. Says here you've been scratching a living peddling cheap Balinese carvings around the souvenir stores. Your friend Wim gave me a pair. The Dutch were having some sort of a fire sale on 'em. Louise loves 'em. We didn't have time to take much when we had to get out of Kuta to avoid the Japs.'

'That hammy prick Ronald Reagan got me blacklisted after I bent his ear at Grauman's Chinese Theatre one night about Indonesia and he got on his high cowboy horse about sacred capitalism.'

'"The Gipper"? One of our loyalest Americans. A true patriot. But let me tell you a story, honey. Maybe you've been a little out of touch with developments in the Indies. You will know that the US managed to persuade the Dutch to stop their nonsense by pushing them into that ceasefire conference with the republicans on board the USS *Renville*. But now the Dutch've gone and done it again! A coupla days ago, they attacked the Indonesian positions all along the Van Mook line and dropped paratroops into Yogya. They've rounded up the republican government and shoved them off into exile on some godforsaken island called Bangka. The aim was to draw the national army into a fight and wipe them out but, instead of defending Yogya, they just withdrew and faded away into the jungle and the government was switched over to Sumatra. So the Dutch are left looking stupid and holding their own dicks – and the entire, republican government which is much the same thing. Now, what's interesting is they were able to pull it off so easily because they'd been monitoring Indonesian military traffic all year, knew just where everyone was. It seems somehow their men in Singapore got hold of a bunch of old communications with translations from Semarang via the Brits so they managed to crack the code. Security agencies are leaky sieves, Manxi. It's even just possible some of the stuff *they* got to know could get back to the Indonesians, together with how *they* got to know it. I suggest you should think about that. I don't think I ever mentioned ... Back in the day, when you were a hot property and Soekarno was still trying to do a deal with the Dutch, he offered to throw in your extradition to them as a sweetener. You never were a good friend, Manxi, and you never inspired real friendship. You're not going to convince me your farts smell of mouthwash and, say what you like, I never saw you as the sort of person who would get herself between a good cause and a firing squad.'

'Is that all?'

'Talking of friends ... one more thing. I think you know Amir Sjarifuddin?'

'Bung Amir? Yes. A dear man. What's happened? Have the Dutch got him? Have they hurt him?'

'Before they evacuated Yogya, your friends in the republican army took the prisoners left over from the communist uprising in Madiun and shot the lot. Amir was one of them. He was some sort of a commie right? I thought you'd like to know.'

'Thank you.' I swallowed hard and blinked back tears. I wouldn't give him the satisfaction. 'By the way, Bob, those Balinese carvings of yours. Make sure you keep them somewhere nice and warm. If you have a mantlepiece over a fire perhaps that would be a good spot or maybe even arrange them around the hearth itself so they catch the firelight. Coming from the tropics, if they get too cold, they'll split you see and you wouldn't want that.'

He was surprised at my goodwill. 'Gee thanks for the tip,

Manxi. I'll do that. So what'll it be? Do you go back and work for us – nothing too nasty just keep your eyes and ears open – or not at all?'

* * *

'The war is over. You missed it, K'tut. We all thought you had run away and deserted us. Of course, everyone said you were a spy, which was absurd. But it wasn't so bad in Bangka,' said Bung Karno, waving a Merdeka cigarette. 'They could have chosen somewhere much worse.' Soldiers – Indonesian soldiers – in neatly matching pairs stamped up and down outside the tall windows. 'There was a joke that we ended up in Bangka because they gave the pilot an envelope telling him what his destination was but marked "Not to be opened until arrival". I know that fool Sjahrir said I was happy there because my room had seven mirrors, which wasn't true, but there were other compensations. One way and another, the Dutch have arranged for me to tour the whole of our glorious Indonesia in my various exiles. It is they that have convinced me of its fundamental unity across our 20,000 islands. He may claim to be a great thinker now but during the Japanese occupation, Sjahrir just sat cosily at home and read nice books while I was out there wrestling with the real issues.' We all die a little with each success of our rivals. He flared his nostrils and tapped off ash with the gesture of an orchestral conductor bringing in the flute section, letting it fall on the carpet. Perhaps he hated those chemical, blood-red carpets as much as I did. They seemed to be made to soak up the bloodshed of palace coups. 'I thought it was clever of the Dutch to drop dummies on parachutes over Yogya so that our troops opened fire and gave their positions away. They seemed to know everything about our dispositions. I stood in the palace yard and thought how beautiful the silky parachutes looked in the sunshine – like floating jellyfish drifting in the current of the sea. Even when the parachutes were Japanese you used to think of cherry blossom. When I was a boy we all flew kites and you always imagined yourself soaring up there in the clouds with your kite. Sjahrir never had any imagination. There was no poetry in his soul.'

'Yes,' I said. 'The dummies. That would be it. That's how they knew. Though I doubt those poor air cadets they strafed at Moguwo were thinking about their kites even if they were still just young boys.'

He sipped sweet, cold tea, 'I was most embarrassed for the Indians. It was nice of Nehru to send that plane to whisk us away to the UN but a little silly to send it via Jakarta. Of course, the Dutch just sat on it.' He shuffled his own backside, looked around and sighed with the satisfaction that comes to a man from arriving home after a long trip and settling his rump firmly on a familiar chair. I felt much the same. 'But anyway, it all turned out for the best. The Dutch military victory in the second "Police Action" set the whole world and the UN against them. The turning point was when the US suddenly switched their negotiating position and threatened to cut off Marshall Aid. There was some sort of a presidential order from Washington. That was it. Why didn't they think of that before? Where did they suddenly get the idea? Then the Dutch finally knew they had to make peace. So winning the battle for Yogya lost the Dutch the war and now it's just the haggling.' He looked through the window at the peaceful garden and sighed again, tapping his fingers on the arm of the chair. He always had the same perfect manicure and compulsively clean hands. Other, lesser people with dirt under their fingernails would be doing that haggling now in The Hague. 'There's no doubt any more about the outcome – not that there ever was really. Then comes the hard part – what do we do with this freedom we've won? No one has wanted to think too much about that for fear of taking their eye off the immediate problem. And at least we kept the army intact.'

I thought about my own release from the Japanese camp and the sense of sheer emptiness that overwhelmed me when freedom, my dearest hope, became – incredibly – true. To just sit in the sun and feel the wind had been enough, all that I had been capable of. Then I heard myself say quietly, 'But Pak Amir is dead.'

He shot me a warning look like I was a fly in his soup. 'Yes he is dead. It is a pity. He was a friend from the early days. I sent Lieutenant Colonel Suharto to try to negotiate a peaceful resolution with the communist rebels but they wouldn't have it. Then, in all the confusion of the Dutch attack ... well ... but Suharto did a sterling job retaking the city of Yogya and holding it, as he did for a while, to strengthen our position at the peace talks.' He bent forward and dropped his voice. 'Now, something more interesting. Tell me about this new girl called Jane Russel with the very big breasts and her special bra gripping from underneath designed by the aircraft man. I have been reading something and I knew you would know all about it. I asked the head of the air force but he couldn't explain. He just muttered something about the attachment of the wings of B-36s. And no one else in the cabinet knew. I suppose I could set the Bandung Technical College onto it.'

I gave him the most sensational version lifted from the gossip rags, spicing them up even more with innuendo-stuffed lines about 'fittings' but forbore to mention another sterling job Suharto had done. For Bung Karno's principled refusal to join the guerrillas in the mountains had not been seen by everyone as a mark of courage. He was, after all, a city boy known to like his city comforts. While he argued that the Dutch Governor General had not run away from the Japanese so he could not do less and run away now from the Dutch, perhaps the two cases were not strictly similar. There had been an embarrassing film of Bung Karno grinning and posing chummily with the enemy, being saluted up and down by them – he trim and unruffled as always – so that it appeared as if he was a man on a relaxed holiday rather than an oppressed prisoner and there was a part of the outraged republican army that had wanted to take over and squeeze the civilians out. It had been touch and go. Fortunately, a loyal, young officer had made an impassioned speech to the vacillating Yogya garrison on the evils of military coups. That officer had been Lieutenant Colonel Suharto.

* * *

27th December 1949. It was the day everyone had dreamed of and the day no one could quite believe had finally come yet, like everything that had been so long aspired to and fought for, it carried the seed of threatened disappointment within it, for every dream fulfilled is a dream lost. Bung Karno had been right about that. And what was peace but just an absence of war, a mere minus quantity with no attributes of its own? All round the world the newspapers would run the pictures of Queen Juliana stoutly signing some document with Hatta – in fact the Dutch surrender but given some more fancy and sweeter-smelling name – and people would be puzzled and a little upset that she wasn't wearing her crown, just some silly feather in her hair. The radio had been stoking up anticipation and now the first rays of the sun began to stab through the trees on what seemed, at first, just another hot day in Jakarta. But at dawn, sniffing a major event, the food sellers had already set up their stalls around the Koenigsplein, now renamed – guess what? – Merdeka Square and great, silent crowds had settled in front of the old Governor General's Gambir Palace, now renamed Merdeka Palace. Smoke from their fires began to blow and billow across the grass and the sprawling bodies, appropriately, as if in the still aftermath of some great Napoleonic battle. The silence was extraordinary. Crowds in Indonesia are never silent but today I floated through them like a ghostly vision in my best white tule and showed my pass to the smart, young guards on the gate, themselves shivering with wordless excitement. Overhead on the portico roof, fluttered the biggest red and white flag I had ever seen. Fatmawati must have been up all night, mouth full of pins, sewing it.

Inside it was like an ants' nest when the aardvark drops by, with servants rushing around glowing with self-importance and bumping into each other on more of those hideous blood-red carpets. They were downright dangerous. Why, only the other day, I had tripped over one in the Bogor palace and accidentally whacked Bung Karno in the face, giving him a nasty nosebleed, just like poor, dead Lukman at the Oranje Hotel. Luckily, he had forgiven me at once as I tended him and sponged off the gore into my blood-soaked hankie and tucked it away in my bag. A buffet was laid out on the side tables with silver serving dishes and the Indonesian dignitaries, hungry men in best bib and tucker, were already spooning away joyfully at the fruits of victory. Over against the other wall stood a clutch of Dutch military, themselves clutching hats and sourly not eating so I dived into the sumptuous fried rice, not out of appetite but to show to which camp I belonged. Anyway, once you have known real hunger you don't lightly say no to any fuel stop.

'Hallo, K'tut.' It was Bung Tomo at my elbow, still windblown as tumbleweed, as if he had just wandered in from the mountains all fluffy. That he spoke to me at all showed how alone and out of things he must feel. And those coal-black eyes still gleamed with unquenched fire. Also not eating, a man made for fasting, flagellation and self-denial. Nevertheless, politeness required me to gesture at the food before I could return to my own.

'Come and eat.'

He shook his head, locks flying everywhere. 'Already.'

'You don't look very happy, Bung. What a face to make on the day the president returns from Yogya and the new government of a free Indonesia is finally installed! Now at least, according to the terms of your oath, you can get your hair cut.'

He blinked, not used to being joked with. I didn't care. It was a day for happiness not sulking. 'You may be right, K'tut. But do you think that if a man comes back from years at the war and is presented with a baby and told it is his, he should just smile and say it is lovely and accept it even if it is an ugly, deformed, bastard child like this our new Indonesia?' He stalked over to the food table and began to rip savagely at a stick of satay with his teeth as his boys had once attacked Dutch flags with theirs.

A mass susurration, as of bees, washed in from outside. As I looked out across the pillared terrace, the crowd that stretched to the horizon seemed to rise and suddenly part in two waves like the Red Sea in Cecil B. DeMille's epic and there, like Moses, was Bung Karno standing up in the rear of a lush convertible, hand outstretched and gliding smoothly forward – dry-shod as always – leading his people to the Promised Land – slowly, slowly. War had changed from a thing of spilled guts and the stench of death to ballyhoo and silver trumpets.

'He should have come on a tank,' says a military man, headshaking.

A great agonised howl tore from a million throats, a mass oral orgasm compounded of lust, frustration and inexpressible desire rippled across the crowd. 'Merdeka! Merdeka!' The very ground shook under our feet, fear quivered in the eyes of the Dutch delegates, Bung Tomo still tore at the grilled meat and crushed it with uncompromising teeth. Time slowed. The world shifted out of focus as Bung Karno entered the pall of smoke and dust haze and finally emerged again, the car turning so the sun was a golden halo behind him, at the gate. The guards gave up all attempts to hold back the crowd, stood back and they surged forward, flag-waving, dancing, screaming and for a second I found myself again in a tram in Glasgow, a young girl with my whole life before me, as its windows smashed and tinkled to the ground around my feet. Tears began to stream down my face. Most of the Indonesians seemed to be crying too.

Bung Karno stepped out of the car and tripped lightly up the stone steps and turned, a tiny, dapper figure dwarfed by the significance of what was happening and the massive, Doric pillars looming behind him like the shade of history. He raised both arms and, for a second, it looked for all the world as if he would break into a tap dance routine or simply ascend straight into the air, twirling up like Elijah in a picture I remembered from the Sunday school wall. Then it was just him and the people. The rest of us faded into nothing.

'Diam!' He called for silence. 'Diiiam!' and began to speak, the high, clear voice floating out over the crowd and echoing back, shimmering, from across the square. I don't remember what he said. It really didn't matter. Something about his years of wandering in the desert and how it was everybody's freedom that we were marking and how we should all be friends. At the end it was washed away with a million roared 'Merdeka's, a million flags in red and white and Bung Tomo still stood behind him in shadow and tore at the impaled, burnt flesh with sharp, gleaming teeth, stick after stick after stick, his other hand full of the greasy, little spears that he had no place left to thrust.

* * *

I came out of the Information Ministry into stark, midday sun and stopped dead in my tracks. It was weeks since the transfer of power but some of my colleagues had still not quite made it back to work from the celebrations. Yet I liked to tell myself that the people in the street were subtly changed, more upright, taller, walking with more self-respect as citizens of a free country. At the bottom of the steps, across the road, a grey truck was parked with the passenger door open and a tall European in shorts and sports shirt was reaching inside for his bag as his local driver was climbing out the other side. There was something about him – even from that odd angle – that was familiar. As he turned, I recognised him at once. It was the man Wim had called Turk Westerling. The golfer. He might be dressed as a civilian but he still walked like a soldier as he made his way to the back and flipped up the canvas hood. What the hell was he doing still in Indonesia? Why wasn't he in jail or in Holland or, better still, burning in Hell? Then his driver stepped out from behind the vehicle into the road and I recognised him too. It was Uki.

I ducked behind a kerbside food stall selling the horribly sweet and sticky, moon-shaped pancakes they also called terang bulan, my blood and the boiling oil both thundering in my ears, and watched as Westerling gave orders, counting off points on the palm of his hand with his index finger. Little Uki nodded, just stopped himself in time from saluting and they set off in opposite directions along the pavement. The stallholder intruded into my view trying to sell me a pancake, waving it in my face. It looked about as appetising as an old man's ankles. At least there would be no Westerling-type chilli sauce on it. I pushed him aside and, after a moment's hesitation over the neighbouring satay stall, followed Uki.

It was hard keeping up. I had been putting on a little weight. Sedentary city life rapidly takes the edge off any imagined fitness and Uki was setting a brisk pace in the hot sun. Shadows lay across the street like iron bars. He dodged down a side passage, crossed over and plunged into an alleyway clogged with stalls. By the time I reached the end of it he had disappeared. I moved forward cautiously, looking in the shops to right and left, people dodging around me like fish around a cruising crocodile. Many of the doors stood open, disclosing glimpses of little, domestic hells. Here, a group of five-year-olds were sharing a quick fag in a doorway. There, in another, a woman was wiping diarrhoea off the legs of a toddler with her hand. I was more than halfway down when I saw him come out of one and set off again with a package under his arm. He criss-crossed several more streets with me in tow and disappeared again into a garage. I hovered uncertainly, eyes fixed on the open double doors. Mostly, it was bicycles, not cars, being repaired in there with loud sounds of Wagnerian metal-bashing. I walked up and down, undecided. I pretended to look at some cloth on a stall, watched a man grinding ice on a toothed steel barrel that would have made a great instrument of torture for Turk Westerling. Suddenly, someone touched my elbow. I turned. Uki.

'Let's get out of here,' he hissed. 'You shouldn't be here. The others wanted to shoot you. Follow me.' He raised a placatory hand to the open garage door where another man stood in dramatically ripped overalls, looking out grimly with something hidden behind his back and we set off again to a nearby coffee stand shaded under a tarpaulin. We ordered two coffees – black, full of grains, stultified with sugar. I never understood how the Javanese could not know how to make a decent cup of Java. But those vegetable rolls there looked good.

Uki smiled. 'Fat,' he said, pointing at me. When Indonesians say you are fat, they mean you are looking well, a compliment. 'Did you really think you could follow me and not be seen? How many white women with red hair and in batik dresses are there on the streets of Jakarta these days? How are you, sister?'

'I saw you,' I puffed. 'I saw you with Westerling. What the hell's going on? Let me have a couple of those lumpiah rolls there.'

He blushed. 'You saw me?' He looked away. 'You don't understand, K'tut.'

'Damn right I don't. You know who he is? What he did?' The rolls were delicious.

Uki nodded and sipped the grainy brew, like sand with caffeine in it. 'It's not what you think. Times have changed. There are different enemies now. It's not simple like back in Surabaya. You know the government troops shot Lukman when they retook Madiun? The republicans. He was one of the prisoners taken to the jail there after the communists surrendered. They stood him against a wall and shot him in cold blood. A friend of mine saw it with his own eyes and he was lucky to hang on to his eyes.'

'Oh my god! Poor Lukman.' I saw him again in my own mind's eye back in 'simple' Surabaya, grinning, proudly wearing his own hot blood on his young face like a trophy, so very much alive. We all smiled so much more then. Now it was a lost art for me.

'We used the Japanese to defeat the Dutch but now we are free of direct Dutch rule, we Sundanese have to use them against the Javanese. The agreement is for a federal United States of Indonesia under the Dutch queen but the republicans want a single, united Indonesia under the Javanese. They will gobble up the lesser states like our own, Pasundan, one by one. Westerling has managed to bring together all the forces in Sunda into APRA, the Legion of the Just Ruler – Muslims, communists, colonial troops and Sunda nationalists – to hang on to our independence.' Their meetings must be something to see. 'They have sent an ultimatum to the republicans to respect the federal constitution. Pak Dion and Uncle Wirno have explained it all to me. And we have leaders with magical powers – much stronger than Bung Karno's. They are wise men who have seen much. Even the Dutch respect them.' His eyes glowed with passion.

I groaned and held my head. 'Independence under the Dutch? Magical powers? They're trying to play you off against each other to stay in charge. How do you think the Dutch conquered the Indies in the first place? They set one group against another. Don't you see that?' I took an outraged swig of gravelly coffee and choked. I had grounds. Perhaps another roll would clear them.

'Of course that is what the Dutch will think but they are stupid and we can use them for our own ends.' He drew himself up proudly. 'We have a plan.' He thumped me on the back until my coughing fit subsided.

'What's the plan?' I gasped. People were staring. I hoped it wasn't one of Wim's dogeared plans.

'Ooh, I can't tell you that but it's a very good plan. We have supplies and equipment and it's already here in Jakarta, ready to go. Turk says we can't lose. After all, he says he is the Just Ruler of the Joyoboyo prophecies. You know the prediction that there would come a time when carriages would move without horses, when wires were stretched round the earth and then the Japanese would come and chase away the Dutch ...'

'Yes, yes, and be replaced by the Just Ruler after one maize harvest ... Bung Karno is always going on about it too. I've heard it all a thousand times.'

'Well, there you are then. It is destined to be.' He waggled his head in self-satisfaction. Then, shyly. 'Can I ask you something, sister? Why did you never go back to Bali? You were always telling us how it was paradise, but you never went back. Perhaps you should go back now. You would be safer there.'

I sipped more coffee and choked again. 'It wasn't that I didn't want to but the Bali I knew has gone. I couldn't bear to go back and see it all smashed and broken. You know how, in the West, some couples go back to the place where they spent their honeymoon – the holiday just after they have got married. It is always a mistake. It invites comparisons. I know when I was in Bali, now so many years ago, people were already saying, "Ah you should have been here twenty years ago. *Then* it was really paradise." But now? I think it would break my heart.' It was true. But the world also has a cruel way of making us no longer want something once it is attainable. When I was a little girl I lived in the absolute certainty that no cake would ever be baked in my house when I grew up. Instead, I would sit at a table and lick bowl after bowl of delicious, uncooked cake mix, all thick and spicy, from a wooden spoon even if it gave me worms as Ma warned me it would. It never happened. As soon as it became possible, the idea was loathsome, the flavour sickly. Perhaps it was the same with the taste of freedom.

I took a rickshaw back to the house and told the driver to ride past Wim's godown. Sure enough, there was the same grey truck I had seen parked outside the ministry and crates were being manhandled onto the back. Westerling, it seemed, had taken over Wim's warehouse – lock, stock and gun barrels – so maybe some of the hundreds of explosive Balinese busts were still lodged in there somewhere, waiting to burst upon an art-hungry world. In theory, the old colonial army was supposed to be absorbed into the new national force but huge mutual distrust and lack of money meant that fragments of all sorts of war-surplus military had been left to moulder in every corner and backwater of the archipelago. By the front gate, the Ambonese guards were still in place as if they just went with the building. They must have been wondering just who it was they were working for and who they were guarding it against but out of long habit they simply saluted any Dutch uniform or face that came their way. As people who had waited for nearly four centuries for independence, maybe they weren't the pushy kind.

* * *

'Don't go to the office tomorrow. It will be dangerous for you. Uki.'

I stared down at the note, effortfully scrawled on the back of an old envelope, one of those pinky-brown ones the post office uses. Could Uki read and write? I wasn't sure. Maybe someone had had to write it for him. He had been at a Koranic school where chanting off by heart is the main activity. A small boy had slid the note under my door at dawn and pedalled away furiously on a bike far too big for him. I saw him as he skittered round the corner at the end of the street, skidding in the dust. I turned the note over. There was an address in the Menteng area left printed on the other side in a precise, official hand.

'Oh, Uki, Uki.'

I wondered whether the note had been written last night in which case 'tomorrow' meant today or whether it was still tomorrow. I looked at the clock. The gado-gado salad seller would be round soon and I had to be ready to run down the path before the neighbours snapped it all up. Either way, I padded into the bathroom and tentatively splashed chill morning water from the big jar over my feet. People swore that way it didn't come as a shock to the body. Yet it made me gasp and shudder as I spooned coldness over my head and shoulders and my heart raced and the blood roared in my ears. Through a curtain of hair and water I scanned the chipped, old floor tiles for wisdom as I tried to worry the cheap, harsh soap into foam and fought for breath against rising panic. What should I do? Which way did duty lie? If I did nothing people dear to me would be killed. If I acted, Uki was at terrible risk. I groaned. Mildew-smelling water swirled down the plughole in which, as if conjured by magic, Westerling's smirking face appeared. That decided it. Perhaps Lukman had been right, it was who you hated that ultimately defined you, not what you believed or who you loved. A *cicak* lizard slalomed around the walls and nodded vigorous agreement. I slipped a sarong over my wet body and tottered carefully back to the living room – the floor tiles were lethal when wet – and picked up the great Bakelite sledgehammer of the telephone, a perk of Information Ministry employees. Would it work today? Often it didn't but even a broken telephone was still a valuable asset, an addition to a state employee's list of excuses for not going in to the office. It had never felt heavier in my hand.

* * *

The news started trickling in as I sat at my table in the Ministry of Information. It began as a slight ruffling of feathers among the journalists as we sat in the usual fog of cigarettes and stale coffee stink and exploded into a real cat among the pigeons. At dawn, colonial troops had seized Bandung and driven the Siliwangi Division out of their own headquarters. There was still a Dutch military unit up there and some of the Siliwangi troops had sought safety in their barracks and asked for their big brother's protection against their big brother's other army. The world was still making crazy alliances. Trucks from Bandung had been stopped as they headed for the capital and were now ablaze, cutting off the road link. Maybe they contained military supplies but no one was sure. There had been sporadic firefights around Jakarta. A warehouse in the Chinese quarter had been seized and found to contain arms and ammunition, road blocks had been doubled and groups of men in stolen National Army uniforms had been discovered moving into the centre and been either captured or shot. Following a tip-off a private address in Menteng had been raided. Of course, none of this had officially happened until the editor of the day decided what version of all this was the government line and that would take hours, in which time rumours would have flashed around the city at the speed of light. I gathered up my possessions and left. The Ministry of Information was always the last place to find out what was really going on.

I knew what I must do. I retraced my steps of a few weeks ago, threading my way through empty streets and closed stalls back to the garage. People here had already smelled something on the wind, kept away or battened down the hatches as they had so often before in recent history. The garage looked deserted with the double doors firmly locked against the world. I knocked. It sounded obscenely loud, like a fart in a cathedral. An eye at a crack in the door and then the sound of a bolt being drawn. A gap opened an inch or two. Uki. I pushed my way in and Uki rebolted the door and turned. It was dark inside with just a little light filtering in from high windows at the back. He was wearing an army uniform and looked terrified and suddenly about twelve years old.

'It's all over,' I said. 'The coup has failed. You have to run for it. You can't stay here. They will come for you. Once you saved me from that terrible communist colonel who kidnapped me. Now I can help you.'

'I was supposed to shoot the cabinet today but nobody came for me like they promised.' He sounded peeved, like a little boy who had been denied an ice cream he had been led to expect. Ice cream. There was a new place round the corner that sold ice cream. It was pricey but they did a great chocolate sauce. I shook the idea away.

'There's no time for that now. I mean, it's all over. You have to ditch the uniform and run. Go west into the mountains. They are still fighting in Bandung but it's only a matter of time.' I dug in my bag and handed over a wodge of old notes. 'Here's some money, enough to get you out of the city and back to your village. The men with magic can protect you there.'

He took it reluctantly and stood looking at me, unconvinced. 'What about Turk Westerling? I can't just abandon him.'

I was exasperated. 'You can be sure he will take good care of himself. People like that always do. He's probably already on a plane to Singapore with his pockets stuffed with gold. You have to understand you are fighting for your own life. Go!'

He looked as if he was going to cry, raw fear in his eyes. 'No, not Singapore. If this fails Turk has a plan to start again in West Irian. They will found a new Dutch colony in West Irian, begin all over again in the jungle.' His mouth squared again for crying. 'I don't want to go to West Irian. They eat people there and I haven't got anything else to wear.'

I swore under my breath, looked around, grabbed the ripped overalls off a nail, ripping them more. 'Get rid of the army shirt, wear these.' He obeyed as if in a daze. It didn't look right. I seized a hunk of metal, some car part – a big end, a small end, some sort of bloody end – and shoved it into his hands as a prop. 'Carry that.' I opened the door and pushed him out into the dusty street and he wandered off slowly like a zombie, a caged bird suddenly released into the frightening wild, the money still clutched in his bewildered hand. At the corner he turned and waved sadly, like a lost child. I never saw Uki again.

Chapter Twelve

A gleaming, briliantined combo oozed smooth South American music across the floor. Fair-skinned Bataks from Sumatra, they could have passed as Italians which would not have made their choice of South American music any less bizarre. The floor itself was made of the very latest vinyl tiling and the current shift of state-approved wives, with their coal-black chignons spiked with gold hairpins, were testing it with curious feet, scuffing, pirouetting, deliberately spilling wine to see the effect. They had heard much of this American marvel but never seen it before. I thought it was gross. The waiters had let down the blinds on the unsuitable, overlarge windows to keep the Jakarta sunset from blinding the guests who clustered under the air-conditioning vents like moths round the lamps at home. That was controversial as everyone knew the president hated air-conditioning and did not even permit electric fans in the palace. People were already dazzled anyway by the lights that exceeded the 10 watt bulbs in general use in those days but they cooed and twittered loudly enough at the many other modernist marvels of Bung Karno's new Hotel Indonesia that had replaced the Hotel des Indes as the only place to be seen. Soon the old establishment would be bulldozed as an unwanted colonial memory and this flimsy, American-designed egg box would become the new icon of Indonesia. Many of the guests were busy holding their ice-filled glasses up to the sunset and looking through them with wonder as though they were looking through stained glass windows. Everyone marvelled at the perfect, translucent cubes, rare as diamonds but flowing like water tonight. On the top floor, the presidential suite had sexy, bulletproof glass but guards had been posted there to prevent the swarms of curious children from riding the lifts above the second floor. And outside, the new Welcome Monument was lit up by blazing spotlamps, a superhuman male and female Indonesian couple in bronze, leaping like dolphins and waving. Bung Karno had rampaged through central Jakarta leaving a trail of construction behind him. The woman clutched a bouquet that looked like a Molotov cocktail she was about to swing round and hurl through the plate glass windows. But it was time to forget all that. The revolution was over and life had become an everyday thing. War had dissolved into mere political pageantry. But the sense of satire lurks deep within the Indonesian soul. It might be outlawed but it could never be snuffed out and was never fooled. All the pretentious statuary of the new Jakarta had nicknames that deflated their public pomposity. Bung Karno was enormously pleased that the huge, towering pinnacle of the national monument, gushing flames at its tip, was known as 'Soekarno's last erection' – though perhaps the word 'last' aroused in him some small anxiety.

There was still a lot of talk about the hotel, even a whole year after its opening. Why was the president of a currency-poor nation squandering money on prestige projects when millions lived in destitution? Didn't people want rice not monuments? The cash was said to come from war reparations squeezed out of the Japanese so why was it not going to those who had suffered under them? Each brick was cemented with the blood of the martyrs of the revolutionary struggle! Actually, of course, there weren't that many bricks – it was far too modern a building for that – but journalese clichés die hard. Bung Karno always said we had to feed minds as well as bodies and I had quoted that and written all the other, predictable answers – waffling on about the generation of foreign exchange and modernisation, neo-colonialism and development – in a dozen press releases until I myself was irked by them and their pathetic fictions. The hotel was there as just another stage for Bung Karno since he was an addicted, hambone performer hooked on limelight and needed to star on it.

The ladies had now discovered the deodorized American toilets with their built-in cisterns and hushed flush and they were flocking for the experience of not pulling a chain but pressing a button like the one that launched the atom bomb. But Allah! It was true then that these people wiped their uncircumcised backsides with paper not washed them clean with water! They gagged in horror.

The band switched to 'Terang Bulan'. They seemed much more comfortable playing that. Perhaps it was Bung Karno's deliberate snub to Malaysia who had grabbed the corny, old song as their national anthem and outlawed its public performance except in their own service. They had tricked it out with new words full of patriotic mush but to me it would always be about sneaky crocodiles lying doggo in forgiving moonlight and just waiting to bite your legs off. Confrontation of the new, neo-colonial federation even in music. The slogan 'Crush Malaysia' was now the new '*Merdeka*', the best Bung K could do by way of a new storyline to revive interest and jack up the ratings. He had just delivered it in a speech I had written. The music suited the jerky, cocky strut that was his version of dancing.

I was covering the reception for the international press but I was deathly bored. I had lived this life too long. Over the course of more than ten years, journalism had become a weary treadmill in a hamster's cage. A sudden, American homesickness gripped me. Not to miss American luxuries when they were over the other side of the world was one thing but now here they were in the middle of my own city, tempting me, making me abruptly tired of what was suddenly pointless poverty and discomfort. For me they didn't mean novelty but nostalgia. I wandered across to the reception desk where a very dark, very handsome young clerk in a very dark, very handsome new suit was standing, nervously gripping the counter with both hands and lobbing perfect grins at the world. It is wonderful the way that each generation sloughs off the sins and stains and disappointments of the last to emerge bright, shiny and hopeful. The thought struck me that he could have been Uki's son – no, nephew. I wondered how Uki was. *Where* he was. In the west of Java, the embers of Westerling's uprising were still glowing and smoking underground but the flame was long snuffed out – like Westerling himself, smuggled back to Holland by the Dutch. Someone told me he had become a very bad opera singer there. So much for the new homeland he planned to hack out of the jungle in West Irian with his bare hands. Enough of the past.

'How much is a suite per night?'

The clerk grinned again and bowed and wrote down a figure on a piece of paper, turned it round and slid it across the counter-top back to me with both his beautifully maintained hands and the light gesture of a concert pianist. They almost put Bung Karno's to shame in that the nails of the little fingers were kept extra long and polished. Bung K's hands had long fascinated me and he would occasionally fling out some throwaway, personal revelation that took your breath away like a medicine ball to the stomach. One day we had been discussing my views on Dutch foreign policy when he suddenly began talking about a girl he knew as a schoolboy.

'*She* was Dutch. I was crazy about her, insane with love. Can you believe it? Oh, I would have made any sacrifice. Just before we had sex, when I knew it was coming, I even cut the fingernails on my left hand and filed them smooth on the brick wall of the school till they bled, so as to be ready! Women don't like sharp fingernails in certain places, do they K'tut?'

One glance at the paper told me why this soft-handed clerk didn't dare put the price into words. It was outrageous. I gasped, half at the price, but also half in memory of Bung Karno's blithe declaration.

'Breakfast is included,' he mollified. His breath smelt of peppermint. He had been stealing the after-dinner mints. 'With choice of tea or coffee.'

'With choice of tea or coffee? And free milk and sugar as well? And use of a teaspoon? Wah! Very well then,' I said, radiating stunned admiration. 'In that case, I can hesitate no longer. Reserve it for me at once. I'll send for my luggage tomorrow.'

He clapped his hands together in glee. 'And how will madam be paying. American dollars?'

'You will send the bill to my friend Bung Karno,' I instructed and waved across the floor at him. Bung Karno still looked very suave in his brushed *peci* that concealed the bald spot and jazzy, military ribbons but perhaps a little heavier in the thigh and with a suggestion of jowls – still surrounded as always by the prettiest women. But nowadays, there was an air of one of those cunningly mummified Hollywood stars who had got typecast too young and ended up endlessly reprising the same undemanding rôle in a soap opera that he had once played in a Cecil B. de Mille epic of the wide screen. Of course, neither soap opera leads nor dictators often have great endings do they? Their chief virtue is just to go on and on in a dull and comforting familiarity till they are written out of the script in an abrupt cataclysm. He was a little surprised at my uncouth gesture but smiled and flicked back an acknowledgement to the greeting. The light caught his fingernails. He was always a gentleman.

The clerk took in the acknowledgement and stood abruptly to attention. 'Yes, madam. Of course. And how long will madam be staying?'

'Indefinitely.'

I had given my life to Indonesia and now that Indonesia had become an American hotel it seemed only proper that I should live in it. After all, as midwife and godmother, I had helped a hundred million people to freedom, hadn't I? I headed back across the room to the buffet and grabbed a fresh plate. Some of the chafing dishes were starting to run low and you could never be absolutely sure they were going to refill them again.

* * *

Although everything was in theory closed for the night, the sleepy watchman saluted and waved me up with an extended, courtly arm contained within a ragged sleeve, scruples soothed by my Ministry of Information pass – which it was too dark to read anyway – and a few coins. The light of the full moon – *terang bulan* – washed the upper layers of mellow stone in golden light and trickled down the terraces though they still radiated the heat of the contesting sun. In silhouette, the ancient temple of Borobodur sprawled contentedly over the hillside as it had for more than a thousand years and looked like a souvenir drawing in Indian ink, or a fat Buddha about to let fly a sated belch or maybe a stack of giant Chelsea buns. On the lowest level, someone had repeatedly daubed '*Merdeka*' in red paint but it was already weathering and flaking away beneath the tooth of time, just as the structure's original fairground colours had been bleached like those of Greek statuary and medieval cathedrals to the classic white of antiquity. History strips things down to the bare essentials. I mounted the steps slowly – one by one – bringing my feet together at each step and squeezed through the narrow passageways, each uniquely carved with panels that marked the upward trajectory of the slim, Buddhist aspirant towards nirvana. I panted a little, having reached the age where our bodies start to take their revenge on us. Creatures of the night, indifferent to the sacredness around them, scuttled about on their mundane business. In the distance an owl hooted to Javanese a scary 'ghost bird' to me a comforting sound of enduring Nature.

The massive building had withstood indifferently fire and earthquake for more than a thousand years, the succession of religions and dynasties, the convulsions of history, the fulfilment of the Joyoboyo prophecies, the Indians who brought cloth, the Portuguese who brought custard tarts, the Dutch, the Japanese, the British and the new, political faiths they dragged along with them and still it stood unmoved and implacable, having shrugged off centuries of volcanic ash and risen again. It had even survived the vandalisation of the Christian Department of Works that had tried to bodge it back together with cheap cement and the Muslim Javanese fanatics who had sought to blow it apart with expensive explosives.

These days, I blanched a little at the endless demands to climb ever higher, drawing comfort and strength from the rootedness of the towering rock of ages, smooth beneath my hands as beneath those of the millions of pilgrims who had trod this path before me. It was as if their faith had soaked into the stonework and consolidated it into some new and immutable substance. We spiralled up from the world of desire, up through the world of forms and out into heavenly formlessness and dissolution.

I felt the need to come here beneath the forgiving stars from time to time just to reassure myself that, through so much history, so much revolution and war and blood, the unfaltering rhythm of the great heart that is unchanging Indonesia beat steadily across the millennia. It beat through my blood too. After all, I was equally a creation of many times and places yet bound by none. My father was a famous archaeologist lost in the jungle or – I forget – was it an explorer? – who determinedly pushed beyond the boundaries of the known. I slid a worn, gold case from my pocket and selected a clove cigarette, lit it and puffed until my racing heartbeat steadied and slowed. When they come to make a movie of my life, Borobodur will be an essential backdrop. Perhaps there will be a big scene where I stride across its summit with Bung Karno and we look out over the world with pointing fingers to map out the course of the free Indonesia that we have jointly sired.

I walked up to one of the Buddha figures, trapped in its latticework cloche of stone – so like the baskets put over Balinese fighting cocks when they are given an outside airing – and stretched through to touch the cold, raised hand like Adam reaching out to God in the Sistine Chapel, transient clay reaching out to permanent stone in a gesture that was purely human and – I suppose – the very opposite of the intended, Buddhist message. I stared out over the arid plain where pale oil lamps glowed in simple huts with woven walls and people lived unchallenged by such neighbouring monumentality. I liked the speculation that Borobudur had once been erected here in the centre of a vast, primordial lake, layer after layer, a giant lotus blossom reaching up from the dark, primeval mud towards heavenly enlightenment. Perhaps one day I would paint it in exactly that way. Probably it wasn't true. But then, as I often have to insist in a literalist world, why stick to an ugly truth when there is always something so much more lovely to say?

Dreaming in English

'Why do you write your novels in English when Turkish is your mother tongue?'

It is a question I hear often. Each time, I need to pause for a split second. How can I explain? I try to offer a compact, rational answer. Yet I also know deep down that my urge to write stories in a language other than my native tongue was an irrational choice, if it was a choice at all. I did not exactly decide to write in English. Rather than a logical resolution, it was an animal instinct that brought me to the shores of the English language. Perhaps I escaped into this new continent. I sent myself into perpetual exile, carving an additional zone of existence, building a new home, brick by brick, in this other land.

Being a foreigner and an outsider in the English language intimidates me sometimes. My children make fun of my accent: they find it fascinating, an odd blend of unlikely ingredients. It is a challenge to write in English, both intellectually and spiritually. Yet the joy and the pleasure I derive from the experience are so much greater than the fear. And whatever pain there is, it is certainly less than the pain of feeling like a stranger in my motherland. Somehow, that is heavier.

I started learning English at the age of ten when I became a student at a British School in Madrid, Spain. It was the flexibility of its anatomy and the versatility and openness of its vocabulary that struck me most. Soon I was scribbling secret poems and stories in English.

When I took the step of writing my novels in English first, about fourteen years ago, I was already an established author in Turkey. Immediately there was a negative reaction in my motherland. They accused me of betraying my nation, an allegation I had heard before. They claimed I was 'forsaking' my inherited language for the language of Western Imperialism. 'How can she be one of us now?' declared a critic. 'If she writes in English she is not a Turkish author any more.'

I have never understood this either/or mentality. All I know is the more they want me to fit in, the more my soul resists. I refuse to make a choice between

English and Turkish: in truth, it is the commute back and forth between the two that fascinates me to this day. As a nomad, I pay extra attention to those words that cannot be ferried from one continent to the other. I am more aware: of idioms, colloquialisms and street slang; meanings and nuances; linguistic cracks, gaps and silences. Languages shape us while we are busy thinking we are in charge of them.

I write my novels in English first. The English is translated into Turkish by professional translators (whose work I admire and respect), and I then take the new Turkish version and rewrite it with my rhythm, my energy, my vocabulary. I love using old Ottoman words, many coming from Arabic and Persian, which have been plucked out of the Turkish language by a modernist nationalist elite in the name of 'purity'. Critical of this linguistic xenophobia, I use both old and new words while writing in Turkish.

Separation can be a form of connection. Writing in English creates a cognitive distance between me and the culture I come from; paradoxically, this enables me to take a closer look at Turkey and Turkishness. *The Bastard of Istanbul* is a novel that concentrates on an Armenian and a Turkish family and the unspoken atrocities of the past. Had I written this in Turkish, it might have been a different book: more cautious, more apprehensive. But writing the story in English first freed me from the cultural and psychological constraints I internalize unconsciously in Turkish. Sometimes, absence is actually a bond and distance can help you to look closer.

I respect novelists and poets who see their mother tongue as their primary source of identity but I sincerely believe my own homeland is none other than Storyland: a vast expanse where static identity is replaced by multiple belongings and the boundary between dream and reality is fluid. This is what keeps me going despite my broken accent and enduring foreignness. I believe that if we can dream in more than one language then, yes, we can also write in more than one language.